WAR LORD

SCOURGE OF ROME

ADAM LOFTHOUSE

B

Boldwood

First published in Great Britain in 2025 by Boldwood Books Ltd.

Copyright © Adam Lofthouse, 2025

Cover Design by Colin Thomas

Cover Images: Colin Thomas

Map Design by Simon Walpole

Every effort has been made to obtain the necessary permissions with reference to copyright material, both illustrative and quoted. We apologise for any omissions in this respect and will be pleased to make the appropriate acknowledgements in any future edition.

A CIP catalogue record for this book is available from the British Library.

Paperback ISBN 978-1-83678-532-3

Large Print ISBN 978-1-83678-531-6

Hardback ISBN 978-1-83678-530-9

Trade Paperback ISBN 978-1-80656-083-7

Ebook ISBN 978-1-83678-533-0

Kindle ISBN 978-1-83678-534-7

Audio CD ISBN 978-1-83678-525-5

MP3 CD ISBN 978-1-83678-526-2

Digital audio download ISBN 978-1-83678-528-6

This book is printed on certified sustainable paper. Boldwood Books is dedicated to putting sustainability at the heart of our business. For more information please visit https://www.boldwoodbooks.com/about-us/sustainability/

Boldwood Books Ltd, 23 Bowerdean Street, London, SW6 3TN

www.boldwoodbooks.com

War Lord is for my dad. Enjoy your well-earned retirement!

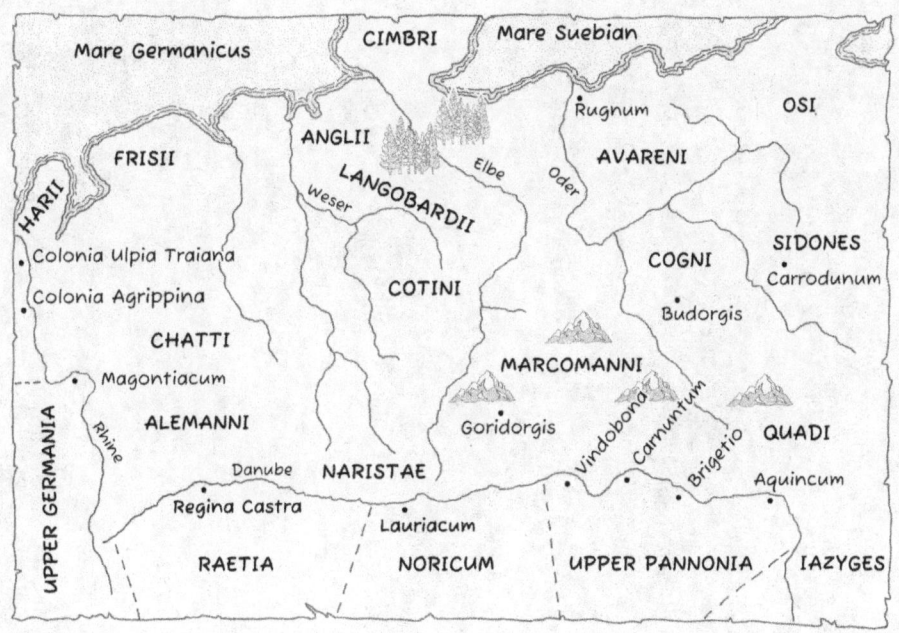

1

Now, I'll be the first to admit that I have always been a man to hold a grudge. I can't stand the thought of someone getting one over me. Just the idea that there is a whoreson out there who thinks he can pull the wool over my eyes gives me the shivers. So when someone tries it, I feel it important to make an example of them.

'Look, would you just come out? I promised my wife I'd be home by sunset. You're making me into a bad husband, and I don't think that's very fair.'

'If I come out, you'll kill me! And I want to go home to my wife too!' came a muffled reply.

With a sigh, I took a step back from the wooden door and planted my sword in the earth. There was a storm coming. The air was thick as honey, sticky heat making me irritable. Black clouds ruled the skies, the god of thunder up there, awaiting the perfect moment to unleash his fury. I wasn't certain who would be the first to blow. Me? Or the god?

'Come on now,' I said with another sigh. I leant closer to the door, lowering my voice. 'You're making me look bad in front of my men.' I looked back; ten armed warriors leaned on their shields. A couple looked to me, the others up at the clouds, probably wishing they had worn waxed cloaks despite the heat. Each had bloodstains on their skin or clothing. Thankfully, none of it was theirs.

'You are a murderer and a coward!' the muffled voice called, shrill in its fear.

I puffed out air. 'Bit harsh. We had an agreement, Filibert. You took my amber; in return, you were to give me thirty head of cattle.'

'You got your cattle!'

'No, no, my friend. What I got was thirty half-starved cows that were so weak, only fourteen survived the journey home. The carcasses of the dead would not provide enough meat to feed my two boys for a Roman week. Do you *know* how much food my boys eat? Honestly, Filibert, watching them devour plate after plate of food is something to behold. You could have seen it for yourself, if you had personally brought me the cattle, as had been our agreement. I would have given you such a feast! Instead, you sent six men half the distance and had me come to them. You broke your word, Filibert.'

'That's rich coming from you! Oath breaker! That's what men call you.'

Well, even I've got to admit, he had me there. Once upon a time, I was the great Lord Alaric Hengistson. Leader of the Ravensworn, five hundred blood-thirsty warriors at my back. I stood in my war finery under a blood-red banner, the black painted raven ruling the skies just as I ruled the earth below it. I was a lord of war. Unbeaten in battle, wits as sharp as my blade. I had been known to take the odd bribe, switch sides in the midst of battle and more often than not end the day victorious, toasting victory with the very man I had vowed to kill that morning. But I *was* victorious. And above all else, that was what was important.

But then, back in those days, I still had both my eyes. 'I'm a changed man, Filibert. You should know that! I honour my word these days. It is as unbreak-able as the iron in my hand.' I scooped up my blade and swung it at the empty air. It was about the only thing I had left from the glory days. It was not a fancy weapon. Four feet of iron, the grip black leather wrapped over the hilt. It had been my father's sword, and he had bestowed it on me the day I left home. Let's not get me started on him.

'Iron can be fickle! And so can your word! If you want me, you'll have to come in and get me.'

I sighed again. I did a lot of sighing. Leading men gives you plenty of reasons to sigh. Parenting even more. 'Right.' I took four steps back from the wooden door and rolled my shoulders. I could hear my men murmuring behind me. Doubtless bets were being placed. I could almost hear the *chink* of

Roman coins changing hands as each of the bastards laid their stake. I clenched my teeth, whispered to myself. 'You're Alaric fucking Hengistson. No man can stop you.' And then I charged.

It may well be true that no man can get the best of me. I was strong and hale, a devil with a blade. I'd always imagined that I had the Trickster sitting on my shoulder. Loki manoeuvring me through life, using me to keep himself entertained. I'd played on it, encouraged the whispers. Unfortunately, as full of cunning as I might have been, I was not *quite* as strong as I thought. I smashed into the wooden door and rebounded off the damned thing so hard the ground rose to meet me quicker than my one remaining eye could make sense of it. My sword went flying, helmet askew. Pain lanced from my shoulder, down to my knees, and back up to my thick head.

Dizzy, hurt, I staggered back to my feet, slapped the dirt off my tunic. It was new, a fine blue that shone with colour, even on a dull day. It was streaked with brown now. 'So now I'm going to be late and I've ruined my new tunic. Definitely not getting any tonight.'

My men were trying to cover their laughs, to give them some credit. But they were better killers than they were actors, and not a one of them managed to straighten their smiles before I turned on them. 'Get some wood and get a fire going. We're burning this fool out of there.'

I walked back to the door. 'You hear that, Filibert? We're going to burn this little shed with you in it! Now I am a merciful man. Come out, and I'll grant you a clean death.'

'A death's a death as far as I see it! Burn me then, you coward!'

'We'll see who the coward is,' I muttered, walking over to my fallen sword and returning it to its scabbard. My men were back double quick with some wood, and whilst one set to work getting it burning, I ran a rueful hand down the rickety wooden door that had unmanned me. 'What you got blocking this door, anyway? A sheet of marble?'

'This place is more secure than that fortress you've built yourself! I've a load of salted meat in here too. I could withstand a siege, I tell you!'

'A siege, huh? Let's see how long that meat of yours lasts once the fire gets going. What will burn to ashes first, do you think? You? Or your salted meat?'

'Piss off! Oath breaker!'

'Don't say I didn't warn you.' I turned back to my men. Six of them were laying large branches along the edge of the barn, two others scampering behind them, covering the branches in leaves. My two remaining men were holding burning torches, evil grins on their faces. 'Do it,' I said with a nod.

Now, I won't say I was feeling particularly good about myself as I moved away from the barn. I stayed close enough that I would be able to hear Filibert's screams. But far enough away that I would not smell the stench of his burning flesh. But I was still sore from my doomed charge on the door, and my pride stung like it had been mauled by a horde of bees. It had become a grudge. And I hold my grudges, hold them closer than my own family.

The flames caught. More smoke than fire to start with, but soon enough, the flames were licking up the sides of the barn, the bright yellows and reds dancing in the dreary light. I could hear the first sounds of Filibert's panic as the smoke seeped into the barn. A cough, an incoherent shout, followed by more coughs. I was just about to clap my lads on the shoulder and call it a good day's work when, all of a sudden, an earth-shattering *crack* filled the air. I jumped in shock; to my shame, I may have even yelped. Just slightly, you know. Before we could comprehend what had happened, there was a burst of light across the black clouds and the first drops of rain *chinked* off my helmet.

Of course there was. There was more sniggered laughter from my men. I imagined more bets had been placed as they gathered firewood. What would come first? The fire or the rain? I should have known the gods would interfere with my plans. They were always there, scheming. Always watching. The rain came down in an all-out assault, battering us to submission. We all did that stupid thing people do when it rains – stand slightly stooped, head cocked, as if it was making the blind bit of difference. We were soaked through in moments, and our fire reduced to sizzling smoke.

'Seems the gods are on your side today, Filibert,' I called, a sardonic smile on my bearded face. 'Alas, I am out of time. Promised the wife I'd be back, see. And I always keep my promises. I want you to remember that, Filibert! I have promised you a death. One day soon, I shall return to take it.'

'Maybe I'll get to you first!' he called back, buoyed by his changed circumstance.

'Good luck with that, maggot,' I spat. With a nod to my men, I bade them follow, and together, we trudged off into the rain.

* * *

'Honestly, Alaric, it was only made three days ago!' Saxa tutted to herself as she wrenched the mud-soaked garment off me. With a wince, I rubbed my shoulder once my wife had claimed her prize. I was no spring chicken, and a hard life lived of war and marches, all with the weight of my mail on my back, had done my body little good. Pretty much all of me hurt every day. I would wake and lay still for a moment, wondering which part of my body would be the first to protest as I made to rise. If it were not for the desperate twinges of my ever-weakening bladder, I swear some days I would rather not get up at all.

'Wasn't my fault,' I muttered, still rubbing my shoulder. Didn't matter how fierce a warrior you were, how many enemies you had slain in battle, getting on the wrong end of your wife's moods turned all men into muttering, quivering, nervous wrecks. And my wife was the daughter of kings. She could kill you with just a look.

'Are you going to tell me how it happened? I assume that poor Filibert is dead?'

'Actually, the rogue hid in a shed and we couldn't get him out. I'll get him soon, though.'

'His wife is a good person. So he sold you some thin cows. I hardly think you need to go off and kill him.'

'It's the principle, my love! You know that. And besides, those cows were a disgrace. More meat on a bird's wing than there was on all those cows put together.'

Saxa turned to me, fixed me with one of her piercing glares. I gulped. She had been a plain lady in her youth, short and stumpy, pale and unremarkable in every way. She had become my wife as part of an alliance between me and the Chauci. Over the years, though, she seemed to have gotten more beautiful at the same rate I had gotten uglier. Where I was now one eyed, with a fattening body crisscrossed with scars, Saxa had grown into her pudgy face. The baby fat had melted away, leaving sharp cheekbones and a strong jawline that gave her a striking appearance. Her eyes were bright and always seemed to be on the move. She missed nothing. And if there were crows' nests on their flanks, the imprints of smile lines on her cheeks, all they did to me was enhance the beauty that was hers. Out of the two of us, I had been the one deemed a catch on our wedding day. Even the most loyal of my men would be hard pressed to say that now. And I did not have many loyal men.

'Have you ever considered,' Saxa said in that sharp, deadly tone of hers, 'that you killing every man that agrees to trade with you does not bode well for your future business plans? Remember what you promised me? When you came home last year, broken from your little trip to the north?'

'Aye,' I said, sighing again. 'No more blood.'

'I don't know what happened on that venture of yours. But in the year you have been back, I have not heard you boasting of your victories once. In that, your silence says more than words ever could. You were broken, Alaric. Changed. Why, even after your defeat to the Romans, when you came back without your army and your eye, you maintained more character than you did in the weeks after your return from the north. No more blood. No more war. That was what you said.'

'And I meant it!'

'Oh, did you? So why did you kill that nice merchant who tried to sell us some wine from Hispania?'

'He changed the price once he knew who I was!'

'And the spice merchant from Syria?'

'Didn't like the way he was eyeing you.'

'And the Pannonian peddler? Off on an adventure in Germania? Why did he deserve to die?'

'Don't like Pannonians,' I mumbled, knowing she had the better of me.

'Have you ever stopped to consider that if you kill every man you think is trying to get one over on you, or even attempts to negotiate with you, that you are very quickly going to run out of men who will do business with you?'

'No.' I found a sudden interest in the floorboards beneath my feet.

'A merchant, that was your chosen path, remember? And your plan was, still is, a good one. We can make a good living trading the amber you're getting from the north. You just have to acknowledge that in business it won't always be on your terms! Grow up, Alaric.' Saxa stormed from the chamber, my dirty tunic in hand.

I sat down on the bed and pondered what she'd said. Truth be told, I knew she was right. But I was pig-headed, too full of myself. I was the great Lord Alaric Hengistson. In my mind, men should kneel whenever I walked by. Should be so grateful I was willing to do business with them, they should agree to every term I set. Deep down, I knew that was not the case. Seemed I wasn't quite ready to let that knowledge rise to the forefront of my mind just yet.

'Papa!' a shrill voice shrieked, snapping me from my reverie. Ludwig ran into the bedroom, an oversized helmet bouncing off his head, a mock wooden spear in his hand. 'Surrender!' he growled, lowering the spear. I held up my hands, but could not stop the smile spreading across my face.

'Come here, you little warrior.' I moved my arms, so they were held out wide, and Ludwig charged straight into them. 'Have you been behaving for your mother?'

'No,' his muffled voice said, buried in my chest.

'Of course you haven't.' I chuckled. 'Where's your brother?' Ludwig was the eldest of my two sons. At just nine years old, he stood almost as tall as me. Once his body developed and his shoulders broadened, I thought he would have the makings of a fine warrior. Not that I said that within earshot of his mother, of course.

'In the stables. He's always in the stables.' I smiled at that. Eric was seven, and more different from his brother in every possible way. Where Ludwig was tall and lanky, Eric was short and squat. And where Ludwig was a live wire, a real chatterbox who would talk the ears off even the most patient person, Eric barely spoke a word at all. Both had been that way throughout their childhoods. Ludwig had screamed the hall down as a baby; Eric had barely cried at all. It concerned me that Eric was so quiet. He could speak, and I would often notice him talking quietly with Saxa. But to me, he spoke barely a word. I'd had stables built in the spring, twenty good horses brought from the east, where the endless grass plains were natural breeding grounds for the beasts. Eric had taken to both the horses and their upkeep immediately.

'Come, let us go find him.' We left the hall, walking out into a bright, clear morning. I'd not made it home before sunset the night before. In fact, all had been asleep in the hall, barring a couple of guards on night watch. That morning, though, the previous day's storm seemed a distant memory. The air was crisp, clean, carrying on it a hint of morning dew. My hall was built on the conflux of two rivers, the Elbe and the Saale. One bled into the other, the waters shimmering different shades of green in the sunlight. We were surrounded by woodland and open country. I had found the spot many years before, whilst still building the fighting unit that would go on to become the Ravensworn, and made it my home.

It had many benefits. First, it was smack in the middle of the three surrounding tribes, and none had the right or the power to call it their own.

Second, it was far enough away from the capitals of those tribes so that their chiefs never ventured close. Third, most of the people who had ever known of its existence were dead. Obviously, many of those dead were men who had been my friends, and I would have much preferred they were still with me. My old friend Ketill, once chief of the famed Harii, who had met his end fighting on my behalf. Ruric, my once trusted second in command, who had wanted nothing more than for me to be happy and at peace. I fear he will never get his wish.

There were many more who had gone on to the Heroes Hall over the years. I wondered if they were there, then, toasting each other in death, feasting for ever more. I hoped they were. In the short time that I had been back from my... let us call it eventful trip to the tip of Jylland, I had built up something of a bustling community. Despite having skulked in shadows and shut myself away from the world for so many years after I had lost my army and my eye, I had finally integrated myself back into the community.

I had made a point of keeping in touch with the people of the Cimbri in the far north. They, too, were re-building their lives after they had almost lost everything, and they were making a fine job of it. The small celox, a Roman scouting ship I had stolen many years before, was in constant use. On the trips north, it would bring pelts and wine, oil, salted meat and anything else we could transport to the Cimbri. On the return journey, it would be laden with amber. What a precious recourse that was. The Romans adored it, using it to fashion jewellery, incense, even medicine, and I had once heard of a Roman noble having his dead body coated in the stuff at his funeral. So once the amber had made it to my hall, we would cart it up, and travel either south or west, trading with the Romans for whatever we could get our hands on.

Only snag in the plan was, as far as the Romans knew, I was dead. I had been killed by Centurion Silus all those years ago, when the bastard had massacred my army and took my eye. He had left me for dead, thinking that even if I survived my wounds, I would have a hundred scheming chiefs clamouring for my head. To be fair to the man, he had not been wrong. But I had shut myself away, told no one outside my family that I was alive. I'd have stayed like that, too, had it not been for Eadger arriving at my doorstep, pleading with me to go north and save his people.

To get around this small inconvenience, I had built up a little network of traders. These were the men that would journey to the Roman borders and negotiate on my behalf. As far as the Romans knew, they were dealing with many separate traders. But these men were all in my employ, and I made sure they were paid their fair share of the profits. To help keep them honest, I had invited them all to build their own homes in the clearing outside my hall. So where there had once stood a grand, lonely feasting hall in the middle of nowhere, there was now a small community hosting over a hundred souls on the banks of the two great rivers. But traders needed guards to keep them safe. The Romans called Germania the wild lands, and in that they were not wrong. It was not just me who was famed for breaking oaths. In our land, allegiances changed with the wind. We had long since known that if we banded together and took on the Romans, we would win with sheer weight of numbers alone. But alliances between the tribes were fickle at best. We were proud people, and that pride was sometimes the making of our own downfall.

To unite the tribes, we would need a man capable of leading. Finding one of those would prove no great hardship. There had been many before who had tried. King Agnarr had united a collection of tribes in the north and they had come to be known as the Suebi, a tribe in itself. It had lasted a fair few years, but after his death and that of his successor – I *may* have had a hand in that – the peoples had drifted their separate ways, each falling in after their own chiefs. There was one man in the south who still harboured such dreams. Balomar, king of the Marcomanni. An old friend of mine. I had made a name for myself fighting in the pits of Goridorgis, the Marcomanni's capital. It had been there I had first dreamed the idea of the Ravensworn, and Balomar had encouraged me the whole way.

But I digress. Traders needed protecting, and for that, we needed warriors. Some fifty in total had answered the call. Many would have come expecting decent coin in return for little actual work, and that was fine. In theory, guarding a merchant and his small caravan of goods was easy work for these men. Men who had killed for a living most of their adult life. Who had stood in the crush of a shield wall and locked eyes with their foe. There was no short supply of such men in Germania. And having the added bonus of getting to serve the famed Lord Alaric made recruitment much easier. My only niggling doubt was how many of these men were secretly working for someone else. How easy would it be for an old enemy of mine to send one of their men into my employ, there to feedback all that was happening in my hall?

Saxa assured me I was overstepping my own fame. Surely, she argued with me, there was no one who held a grudge against me that strongly, that they would wait all these years before striking back. To be fair, she had a point. Gods, she always had a point. But I knew I was not the only man in Germania to hold a grudge. And if the Romans got word of me being alive? If the *primus pilus* Silus of the Fourteenth legion knew I was living my best life up here in my feasting hall? You could bet your shiniest gold *aureus* he would be in the first boat over the Danube.

All these fears were a constant strain on my tired old brain. But, especially when around my boys, I tried to push them from my mind. 'There he is,' I said in a cheery tone as Ludwig and I entered the stable. Eric was there, sweat on his brow, his chubby face bright red with exertion, sweeping out an empty stall. He smiled nervously at me as I approached and engulfed him in a hug, leaning down to plant a kiss on his sweaty head. 'Hard at work, as always. You were here before the sun came up, I assume?' He gave me a nod, but didn't reply. 'You see, Ludwig, this is what it takes. Hard work and a true love for what you do.'

'Are you going away again soon, Papa?' Ludwig asked. He too picked up a broom and began sweeping, not wanting to seem lazy in front of me when his brother was grafting.

I noticed Eric look up to me sharply at that, a slight quiver in his lips. I had been away for a lot of the last year, and I have to admit a part of me was self-ishly pleased that both boys seemed anxious that I might be taken away from them again. 'I am. I'm going south in a couple of days to meet with an old friend. His name is Balomar, and he is a great and powerful king.'

'Will you go to war with him?' Ludwig asked. Excitedly, he upended his broom and wielded it like a spear. I laughed.

'No, son. There will be no fighting. I'm simply taking him some amber for his people to trade with the Romans in Pannonia. Can't do it myself, see? I'm not exactly popular down there. But he can, and he'll fetch a fine price in oils and wine and other luxuries to keep us going through the winter.'

'Mama likes figs,' Eric mumbled, almost a whisper. My smile broadened to hear his voice, regardless.

'That she does, my boy. And figs she shall have! Though they will not last the winter. Might be she needs some help polishing them all off once they get here.' I favoured the lad with a wink. 'I know.' I rose back to my full height, appraising my sons with my one remaining eye. 'Why don't we ask your mother if the two of you can come with me? Make it into a proper boys' trip, hey?'

Their screams of joy were deafening, and my smile was so wide it could have split my wrinkled, bearded face. 'Go then, find her and ask! I need to check the horses will be ready, and then I'll join you.' They scampered off, Eric puffing as he pumped his little legs as hard as he could to keep up with his lanky brother. I had no need to check on the horses, but I knew full well if I asked Saxa I would get a flat no. But even she, stern as she was, was sure to melt at the sight of their angelic faces. I chuckled to myself at the thought, and my spirits high, I picked up a discarded broom and finished sweeping.

2

The boys' charm won out on Saxa, as I knew it would. And three days later, they were sitting at the front of a wagon loaded with amber as we journeyed south.

'Could you tell us a story of the old times, Lord?' Faramund asked me as we walked.

I felt the other warriors' ears prick at Faramund's question and allowed a slow smile to spread across my face. 'The old times? Whatever do you mean?'

'Tell us a story of the Ravensworn, Papa!' Ludwig cried out. He was clad in a mail shirt our blacksmith had made for him. In truth, it was a poor bit of mail, the links too small, the gaps between too big. If actually used in battle, it would have all the defensive qualities of a woollen tunic, but Ludwig had been beside himself with excitement when presented with it. I don't have the words to describe how good it made me feel, seeing him so happy. And being made the way it was, it was still light enough for Ludwig to move freely whilst wearing it. He was still just a boy, after all.

'Surely I have told all the stories from my glory days. What is it you wish me to tell, Faramund?'

The son of a farmer from the eastern front, Faramund had lost his parents to a Roman raid when he was fourteen. Three hard winters scrounging for food and warmth, staggering around the wild woods of Germania, and he had ended up in the lands of the Chauci. My father-in-law, Dagr, had taken the lad in and put a spear in his hand. Four years later, he had forged a name for himself, and had even been part of the shield band Dagr marched north to rescue me on the tip of Jylland.

He had been all too eager to serve under me when I got back home. 'Tell us a story of your battles with the Romans!' another of the warriors chipped in. Heimirich was another young warrior. Tall and broad, straw-coloured hair that ran past his shoulders. He had a vicious-looking scar that ran left to right across his chin. He told people it was from a shield rim smashing into his face in battle, but I had it on good authority it was a knife slash from an old lover.

I made a good show of sighing, though in truth I was, as I always was, only too eager to tell a tale of the good old days. 'So I was in the south,' I started, and paused to hear the murmured excitement of the gathered men. 'In the lands of the Quadi. Balomar, my old friend and the man we are travelling to meet, had asked me to bring the Ravensworn down to his lands, as he expected an attack from the east. So I had the men set up camp in some open ground on Quadi territory, not making any effort to keep quiet.

'Trouble was, it wasn't just the Quadi that had seen our campfires. The Roman have these great watch towers, all along the Rhine and Danube, some of them even on our side. They must have seen the smoke, sent a runner back across the bridge at Carnuntum, and before we knew it, over a thousand of the bastards were marching towards us!'

That got a few gasps. If I'm honest, it was probably three hundred at best. But I was in a storytelling mood. And it did no harm to remind those young fighters who it was they served. 'What did you do?' Faramund asked.

'We met them in battle, of course! See, the Romans fight in a tight shield wall, their great rectangular shields covering their boys from chin to ankle. Their armour is thicker than ours. Those dreaded short swords are unbeatable once they close on you in battle. So you have to find other ways to beat them.'

I grinned at the expecting silence that followed. I had ten warriors with me in all, and each of them hung on my every word. 'What I did was have Ruric, my trusted old second in command, take command of the bulk of my men. He formed a shield wall and took the brunt of their assault. I tell you now, with Loki as my witness, when those cursed Romans let their spears fly, it blocked out the sun. But Ruric was as unmoveable as stone, and my men were the hardest bastards in Germania. They caught the spears on their shields and used their swords to swipe them off. And when the Romans closed with them, they sheathed their swords and got out their daggers. Anyone want to tell me why?'

'Can't swing a longsword in the press of a shield wall,' Faramund said, beaming.

'Correct. These swords of ours' – I brandished my own – 'are forged for single combat. In our lands, when one army fights another, there is very rarely any cohesion to the fight. It is a collection of individuals fighting one another. But the Romans fight as one. Shield to shield, with each centurion in charge of eighty men, given the autonomy to make his own decisions on the battlefield. It makes them unbeatable when up against a disorganised rabble such as a German army. However...'

I swear I could *feel* each man holding his breath. Ludwig almost squealed with excitement; even Eric looked as though he was about to burst. 'My men were not an untrained barbarian rabble. They were the Ravensworn. They matched the Romans' formation, going shield to shield with them, their daggers swiping at faces and ankles, causing chaos. And just when the Romans were forcing them to concede ground, just when it looked as though the day was going to be lost, out I came from the trees, a hundred men at my back. We charged their right flank and were cutting them apart before they even knew what happened.'

I smiled at the memory. Good times.

'So you won the day?' Heimirich asked.

'Of course we bloody won! Sent them scarpering back over that fancy bridge of theirs like a man with his tunic around his ankles who's just been caught giving his chief's wife a taste of his—'

I stopped talking. Stopped moving. Around me, everyone else stopped, confused. One of the warriors had the sense to halt the carts, the horses pulling them scoffing out air, stamping hooves on the hard mud. And then there was silence.

It is never silent in the forests of Germania. You are, at all times, surrounded by wildlife. Birdsong is constant, as is the rustle of the woodland creatures scurrying around the detritus-littered ground. But right then, the silence was absolute. Taking a few steps forward, I came to a junction on the track. We were walking south, but there was a path running east to west that crossed our route. We do not have roads in Germania, nothing like the paved streets that cover the empire, providing easy routes for their armies to march from one province to another. We have dirt tracks. In the summer, they are firm and on the whole a smooth enough surface for our carts. In the winter, when the rains set in, they are slush. Almost impassable.

That day, though, the dirt was firm, small dust clouds kicking up under the wheels of our carts. And on the east to west road that crossed our path – footprints. A Roman footprint is easy to distinguish. They wear leather boots or sandals with iron studs on the bottom, leaving a unique imprint on the ground. The path was littered with them. 'What's the problem, boss?' Faramund asked me. Turning back to my men, I saw the confused looks on their faces as they stared at me.

'Look,' I said, pointing to the ground. I gave up counting the different sets after I got to thirty. Clearly, a large body of men had moved through here. They were heading east. I racked my brain. We could not have been more than six miles to the east of Carnuntum, home of the Fourteenth legion. What were a group of Roman soldiers doing our side of the river? And this far north? We must have been at least fifteen miles north of the Danube. It had been a long time since a Roman unit had been confident enough to venture this far away from home.

Something caught my eye, a flash of colour dangling from a tree branch. As I approached, my fingers clasped around a small piece of red cloth, snagged on the branch and torn free. Roman soldiers wore red cloaks. They were uncommon north of the river, red being an expensive colour to dye. 'Romans?' Faramund asked me. His hand gripped his sword as he spoke, eyes darting along the path.

I did not reply at first. Something, *something*, just felt off. As much as I hated Rome and all it stood for, I could well admit that when it came to both warfare and subterfuge, they were not to be trifled with. Their armies were almost invincible, their agents, the *frumentarii*, cunning. This just felt wrong. 'Hmmm,' I mused, rubbing the red cloth between finger and thumb. 'Almost feels like we were meant to find this.'

'What do you mean?' Heimirich asked me. The young warrior took the cloth from my outstretched hand and examined it himself. These young warriors had never faced the might of Rome in battle. They had heard my stories, listened to other greybeards speak of their victories and defeats. But hearing tales is one thing. Living it another.

'I don't know.' A sudden tingle at the base of my spine had me rooted to the spot. I turned in a slow circle, eyeing the surrounding trees. My senses alive, I breathed in the pine resin that dominated the air, felt the soft kiss of the breeze on my skin. And still, I heard nothing. To me, that meant those prints on the ground were fresh. Nothing sent the forest wildlife scurrying for the shadows like a mass of armed men passing by. 'Shields!' I barked, sending my men scurrying. 'All of you, into the trees. You two, that way. You two, over there.' Two by two, I ordered the men into the surrounding trees. Drawing my sword, I returned to the cart my boys were on and stood protectively over them.

'Anything?' I called, unable to bear the tense silence a moment longer. Two by two, they came back. Some white with fear, others gripping spears in shaking fists.

'Nothing.' Faramund shook his head. 'No more footprints off the path.'

I grunted. Something still niggled in my mind, like an itch I couldn't find. 'We make for Goridorgis and we do it at a jog. Tight formation around the carts, eyes and ears on the trees. Understand?' I cast my eye over each warrior, ensuring they understood. Might just be that my boys' lives depended on their diligence. 'Good. Let's move.'

* * *

We made it to the capital of the Marcomanni without incident. I was still tense, though, as our carts trundled through the wooden gates. We do not build grand cities and towns like the Romans do. In our hearts we are a nomadic people, used to sleeping under the stars and packing our gear away the next morning, moving off to the next source of food or water. In the more recent past, though, we had begun to put down roots. Small towns sprung up, with different tribes building their own communities, having their own place to call home. That was in part due to the fact we had run out of land to roam. To the elders of our people, it seemed as though the world was shrinking. In the far east, there were alien tribes coming from the great grasslands in search of better hunting. To the west and south, the Romans. The sea remained our northern barrier, and our tribes were stuck in the middle of it all.

'My men have seen or heard nothing,' Balomar told me with a shrug. He was a bull of a man, all chest and shoulders. I could only marvel at the mail he wore snug tight over his bulging belly. I reckon I could have made armour for two from it.

'You're not worried?' I asked, gratefully taking a cup of un-watered wine from a slave.

'Not overly.' The king of the Marcomanni shrugged again. 'There are always soldiers north of the river. Besides, I have a treaty.'

He might, but I sure didn't. 'A treaty you are actively looking to break,' I said with a smirk. It was common knowledge in that part of the world that Balomar was seeking an alliance with the other tribes that bordered Rome. He wanted war. To be free from the chains that bound his people. He had a treaty, and that was true enough. But that treaty dictated that his tribe must pay a yearly allowance in amber, furs and anything else of value to Rome. In return, the feared legions would leave his people alone. It had been a treaty worth signing at the time, when the tribe's previous chief had gambled it all in battle and lost. But many years later, the people had had enough.

'The Romans know nothing.' The king waved a careless hand. 'And nor will they. Their agents do not have as many spies in my hall as they think they do.'

I smiled. We all knew that the cursed *frumentarii* had slaves in their pay. Slaves see and hear everything, but are never seen. Perfect for picking up snippets of conversation and feeding it back to their paymasters. Balomar, though, had weeded them out pretty quick. Now the slaves took the Roman coins they were slipped under the cover of darkness, but the only information they gave up was the lies Balomar whispered to them.

'How can you be certain?'

The king smiled, then. 'I put my theory into practice a month or so ago. I told one of my slaves to pass on we were going to raid across the river. Gave him the date and time. Then, at said date and time, I hid in some bushes on the northern bank of the Danube and watched their pretty little soldiers march up and down, searching for the army I had brought to steal their wives and children.'

I chuckled at that. 'Surely that burns your slave, though? The Romans will not trust him again.'

'Who cares? Besides, I threw the little traitor into one of the pits. He did not die well.'

The pits were something I knew all too well. Fighting pits dug out of the mud. Only desperate men went down there, where the light was dim and death almost certain. I had been a desperate man once. Hungry for reputation, eager to forge a name for myself. I had fought and killed until my arms were slick with blood and my boots sunk in the slush. But I had emerged. A changed man. A harder man.

I sucked air through my teeth. 'I mean, it's not exactly a sight that will encourage others to play the double agent for you, is it?'

All I got was another shrug. 'You think too much, old friend.' There was a touch of rust to Balomar's red hair and beard that had not been there on my last visit. I dreaded to think how much grey had wormed its way into my own dark locks. I could see it, woven into the black of my beard. It was bad enough that my hair seemed to be falling out at an alarming rate. I didn't think I could pull off being bald. My mother always told me I had an egg head.

'Sometimes I wonder if you don't think enough.'

Balomar's dark eyes fixed me with an evil glare. 'There are not many people who can talk to me like that in my own hall.'

'I know. But I'm one of them.' I hid my smile behind my wine cup. 'But you can't keep killing slaves and expect the others to step up.'

'Why not? They're just slaves.' One appeared then, refilling my wine cup without a word. Her eyes never left the floor. She had tanned skin and wore a thin tunic I thought had been cut intentionally low to show off her breasts. 'Roman?' I asked as she left.

'Aye. I take slaves from wherever I can. It's easier to get them from the empire than it is from other tribes.' It was the worst of insults to be taken as a slave by another tribe. Serving the people your own were at war with. Must have been unbearable. But it was a regular enough occurrence. If a warrior was killed in single combat, a tradition before battle as old as time itself among our people, then it was common for the dead warrior's family to be enslaved by his victor. I had fought in single combat before battle many times, and won them all. But never once had I insisted on taking the loser's family home, there to cook and clean for me until they died. How easy would it be for one of them to slip some poison into my wine or food? I would never sleep well, a nagging fear that my throat would be cut in the night. The whole concept had always seemed like lunacy to me.

'You teach them our tongue?'

'They pick it up easily enough,' Balomar said. 'Why all the talk of slaves, brother?'

I shrugged. 'Curious, is all. But back to the soldiers. Are you not concerned?'

With a heavy sigh, the king rose to his feet and scowled down at me. 'You're putting me off my wine. If there are Roman soldiers north of the river, then they are there for a reason. Some chief or other would have pissed them off and they've come to settle a score. Whatever it is, it does not concern me. Are we done?'

'Aye,' I said, rising myself. 'I'll let it go. How long before your men are back?' My carts, laden with amber, had gone on south once we had reached Goridorgis, one of Balomar's merchants acting as the go-between. My warriors had accompanied the man to ensure I was not being shortchanged. That left me free to roam a place I had once called home.

'They'll be back by nightfall. The journey is short, as you well know. If you were so keen to see it done you could have just sent one of your own merchants. I'm told you have enough in your pay.'

'And miss out on seeing you?' I said with an amused expression.

'Suit yourself. Now, I have some business to attend to. You make yourself at home.' With that, he was gone.

I spent an hour or so wandering the mud streets. I passed the hut I had lived in when I'd first arrived as a young man. I had left my father's farm and walked for mile after mile, not sure where my next meal was coming from. It was in Goridorgis I had made a name for myself. There I had met Ruric, and the dream of the Ravensworn had first come to light. They were good memories, all told, despite the horrors I had faced in the pits. I did not walk near them, wasn't sure I could bring myself to peer down into the gloom.

Instead, I walked out the south gate and surveyed the open country. The land was better in the south, the climate a touch warmer. Rolling hills of farmland as far as the eye could see both east and west. To the south, a thicket of trees that hid the view of the River Danube. I smiled to myself, wondering with some amusement what the Romans would make of me being so close to their border. There were still men there who would pay good coin to know I was even alive, let alone within striking distance. Pride had ever been my Achilles' heel, and we all know how it ended for him.

Perhaps I overestimated myself. It was possible enough that the Romans no longer had any interest in me. The Ravensworn could well be a distant memory for them. In truth, there couldn't have been many soldiers on the frontier who had even fought against me. There was one, though, who I knew was still in armour. Centurion Silus had been my enemy long before he had taken my eye and slaughtered my men. Summer after summer we had fought. Not many full-scale battles, but there were marches and counter-marches, each of us trying to get an edge over the other. In truth, when all was said and done, the scores came out pretty even. Until his victory had been all but complete, that is. He should have killed me then, when he had me on my knees at his mercy. But he didn't. He contented himself with taking my eye, thinking my enemies in the north would finish the job.

I wondered if that decision had given him sleepless nights in the years since. I sincerely hoped it had.

Turning my eye away from the surrounding landscape, I found the smile on my face returning as I approached a small hut based a hundred yards away from the wooden walls of the town. My boys were scampering around outside, thrusting at each other with wooden swords and making a right racket. Childhood was truly something to cherish. No cares, no responsibilities, just there for a good time. Out of the hut emerged a figure that never failed to raise my spirits.

Sedric had spent the year since we'd returned from the north in peace. He had put his mind to learning the trade of a smith, and was making a fine go of it. 'You look well,' I said as a way of greeting, reeling the big man in for a hug. As bald as the day he was born, Sedric stood a full head taller than me, with a build to rival any warrior in the land. He had a horrible scar atop his head, a keepsake from our time fighting together at the fortress of Tastris, battling for the survival of the Cimbri. He had been one of my warriors, then. One of only three who'd travelled on that Gods-cursed trip. Of the other two, Batur had perished before we had even reached our destination, a viscous sea storm knocking him overboard. Kai, the last of the three, had been wounded in battle on some unnamed beach, and had recovered only in time to be killed on another. I remembered them both every day.

'You look horrible,' he said with a wink. He was genuinely happy with his new life. The path of the warrior had not been one for him. His experiences in the north had taught him that. He was changed when we returned home; sombre. He slept little and had fitful nightmares when he did. It had been on my suggestion he come down to the lands of the Marcomanni. I knew Balomar would find a use for him around his capital. 'Come inside. I've made you something.'

Sedric did not take off his leather apron as we entered the gloom of the hut. My boys stayed outside, not even acknowledging the arrival of their father. Too lost in their games. I left them to it. In the hut was the forge Sedric worked on. The heat was extraordinary. The fire was in the centre, built up in a stone oven. Huge billows to pump air to the fire's core rested on wooden benches to one side. Above, a giant chimney broke through the roof, keeping the small chamber as clear of smoke as reasonably possible. 'Here, Lord. For you.'

I was still appraising Sedric's setup and had not seen him disappear around the fire and come back with his hands full. He held what appeared to be a Roman cuirass; the type worn by their high-ranking officers. It was an iron breastplate with leather straps that would tie under each arm. The quality of the work was not in doubt. I had seen enough of them over the years to spot a good one. I'd even sold a few I had taken from the corpses of dead officers in the past. But never had I thought to own one myself. 'By the gods, lad,' I whispered, stepping forward to get a better view.

In the centre of the breastplate, cast in gold that glowed in the fire's light, was a raven in flight. 'You made this?'

'Well, Lord, I had some help...' Sedric trailed off, suddenly self-conscious. 'But the raven on the front was my idea. See, we cast it in iron to start with, then smelted the gold and poured it on after.'

'My friend,' I said, genuine tears welling behind my one remaining eye. 'This is the finest gift anyone has ever given me. Thank you.' I could have made a show of refusing, claiming to not be worthy and so on. But my old friend had already gone to the trouble of making it, and I expected there had been many frustrating practice attempts before he got it right.

'Let's get it outside, Lord. You can try it on.'

We came out squinting into the bright sunlight. My boys were rolling in the mud, clearly bored by the wooden swords. Hastily, I took off my mail and threw it to the ground, and Sedric helped tie the straps of the cuirass under my arms. It fit like a glove. 'How do I look?'

'Like a lord of war,' Sedric said, unable to keep the smile from his voice.

Smiling to myself, I spun around, so I was facing south, and was about to ask my sons what they thought, when my one eye caught sight of the black smoke drifting atop the pine trees.

'What's that?' Sedric asked, moving up alongside me.

I judged the position of the sun, the hours the merchant and my warriors had been away. 'Nothing good,' I muttered. 'But I'm going to go and find out. I'm going to get the king. Will you stay and watch my boys?'

Sedric would not go into battle again, and I would not let him suffer the indignity of being asked. The man had fought for me, bled for me, killed for me. He hadn't slept well since. 'I will guard them with my life, Lord,' he said, and I knew that to be the truth. Without another thought, I turned and sprinted back into Goridorgis. My men were in those trees. And if my hunch was right, so were Roman soldiers.

3

Pine resin in my nostrils, blood hammering in my ears. We ran like the wind. Well, Balomar's hearth warriors did. The king and I huffed and puffed at the rear, each of us silently promising to lay off the wine and put more hours in on the training square. Deep down, we both knew it to be a lie.

But as a horde we burst into the trees, senses alive, swords gleaming in our hands. It wasn't hard to find my men. The cacophony of battle is anything but subtle. My boys were doing me proud. They fought in a circle, shields tight, protecting the cart and merchant between them. Around them, red cloaks billowing, short swords stabbing, were Roman soldiers. Balomar's men screamed a war cry as they covered the last ten paces, launching themselves onto the Romans' backs.

I was a moment or two behind them, and my first kill was a thrust to a throat, my blade biting on bone before I pulled it free with a spray of scarlet that was hot on my skin. Ducking under a lunge from a spear, I used my left hand to heave the weapon before me, skewering the man on the other end when he came within reach. Balomar had claimed his first kill with his great war axe. My old friend Ruric had fought with one, and that man had been an artist on the battlefield. What Balomar lacked in finesse he made up for in brute strength, and he smashed the axe down, cleaving it through helmet and skull and near on cracking the head in half. The axe stuck in the corpse, and he had to drop it, catching a sword blow with his bare hand, using his other to punch its bearer in the face. Balomar was a king born to lead men into battle. Wrenching the Roman sword from a limp hand, he tossed it in the air to change the grip, then swiped it across an exposed throat, his next blow taking a man in the thigh.

Snaking a path through to my men, I rolled left to dodge a shield thrust at my face, but my one eye caught the insignia on the front just before I twisted away. A Capricorn. I knew then who these men were. None other than my old enemies, the Fourteenth legion. Made sense; they were the closest available unit Rome had to put in the field in that part of the world. But still my belly twinged with both excitement and fear at coming up against my old foe once more.

'How we doing?' I called to Faramund, who was still fighting despite looking like a three-day-old corpse.

'There must be a hundred of the bastards! They came out of nowhere!'

I wanted to ask if the trade had been done, wanted to see what was under the leather cover of the cart. But it didn't seem like the time. Instead, I picked up a discarded Roman shield and forced my way between my men.

'We are Ravensworn!' I bellowed, my voice all gravel. I knew my men would be tired, bleeding, adrenaline wearing thin. They would have been fighting a while by then, even though Balomar and I had got to them as quick as we could. I turned back briefly, seeing the merchant standing over a fire that flamed little but smoked a lot. Smiling at that, for the man had had the foresight of alerting us to their peril, I made a mental note to double his pay, or at the very least bother to learn his name, before I turned back to the fray.

The ground was littered with the dead. Miraculously, none of them mine. Balomar had lost two hearth warriors in the initial charge, but the king himself was still fighting like the devil, wielding his little Roman sword at anyone foolish enough to get close. 'And Ravensworn don't lose!' My men gave a hearty cheer to that. I knew they would, and when the Romans came for us again, we fought with renewed vigour. Nothing inspired a man on the battlefield like fighting shoulder to shoulder with your brothers. I took a blow on my shield and pushed the board straight back, snapping it into a nose and watching with glee as the blood spurted from the wound. My enemy still recoiling, I sprang forward and buried my sword in his chest.

A flash of light to my left and instinctively I ducked, the whoosh of a blade scything the air above me. I rose with a roar. The Roman had overstretched and his sword was high and wide. I leaped inside his reach and slashed my blade across his face. I'd stabbed him twice before he hit the ground, never to rise again. 'Ravensworn!' I howled to the treetops, lost in the joy of battle. But that battle was ebbing. Our enemy might have had the numbers, but they had lost their nerve. They darted for the trees, for the shadows, wherever they thought we could not get them. A horn sounded, not one of ours, and the last of them broke off and ran, leaving their dead and wounded behind.

'That's good work, lads,' I panted, leaning on my stolen shields. 'Extra round of ale for you all tonight, I reckon.' I turned to the merchant, still huddled over his smoking fire. The man was pale as snow, a tremor in his fingers. 'My men would all be dead if it were not for you. What's your name?'

'Erik, Lord,' the merchant stuttered out. 'Was always told to light a fire if we had trouble close to Goridorgis.'

'Well, Erik, my men owe you their lives. That was quick thinking. Tonight you shall have a reward; for now, I give you my gratitude.' I shook the man's hand, pleased to see some colour returning to his face as he accepted the thanks of my warriors. I walked among the dead, my feet carrying me to Balomar. He was puffing like a blown horse, walking like a lame one. Cuts crisscrossed his face, a horrid-looking wound on his left shoulder. 'I've had worse,' he assured me as I approached.

'Rome must think you've gone soft, if they're willing to attack a merchant caravan this close to your home.' I said it in part to jest him, though I thought there more than a little truth to it. Rome feared Balomar, respected him. I had never known of his people being attacked unprovoked in his own lands.

'You always were a fool,' the king hissed. 'Go study the bodies,' he said.

'The bodies?' I repeated, perplexed.

'Gods, brother. I know you've only got one eye left, but would you just go and use it!'

Muttering to myself, I walked over to the nearest corpse in Roman armour and kicked him over, so he lay on his back. 'Yep. Looks like a dead bloke to me!' I said, offering Balomar one of my finest grins.

The king rolled his eyes. 'Look at the man's face. Tell me what you see.'

'I see a fucking great big hole where his eye was.'

'Don't test my patience, Alaric!'

With a sigh, I squatted down and gave the corpse a good once over. I was tired, thirsty, and I took a little time to catch on to what my old friend was saying. 'Gods below,' I cursed, rising back up. 'They're not Roman!'

I moved to the next corpse, and then the next. Mind racing, heart hammering. 'Who are they?'

'That, old friend, is what we are going to have to find out.' The bodies may well have been in Roman armour. They may well have been fighting with Roman weapons. But they were undeniably German. For a start, each was a hulking brute, the mail shirts they wore just about reaching their waists. Then there was the hair, a mixture of red, brown and jet black. But each man wore it long, reaching their shoulders or below, clearly visible under their helmets. And every single one of them sported a beard.

Romans were much more particular about their appearance than us. For the most part, they wore their hair short, and almost always they were cleanly shaven. Long hair and beards attracted lice, and nothing spread quicker through an army than those little bastards. Not even the plague. And then there was their build. Short and slim, for the most part. Something about the spoilt way they were raised, I supposed. Not like us in Germania, where you had to be a big brute just to stand a chance of reaching adulthood.

'They're kitted out in gear from the Fourteenth,' I said.

'That one eye of yours never misses, does it?' Balomar mocked me, coming to stand next to me, kicking a corpse for himself. He moved over to another body, rolled it over and studied. 'This one's different,' he said.

'Different how?'

Balomar hawked and spat, a bloody gruel flying from his mouth. 'Skin is darker, eyes look smaller, more like slits. He's not local.' Rising back to his feet, the king ordered two of his men to strip the body.

'Why you doing that?' I asked, removing my helmet and pawing at my matted hair. Gods, I needed a drink.

'Curious,' Balomar mused. Once the body was stripped, the king studied the corpse once more, rolling it over when something caught his eye. 'Wotan's beard,' he whistled. 'Would you look at that?'

I moved over, my thirst forgotten as my own curiosity took over. On the dead man's back was one of the most remarkable things I had ever seen. He had been branded with a horse, the mark burned into his skin. 'Fuck me,' I breathed. 'That couldn't have been pleasant.' It ran from the shoulder all the way down the man's back, stopping at the waist. 'Who was he, do you reckon?'

Balomar said nothing for a moment, a hand rubbing at his bloodied beard. 'I don't know. But there are no tribes in our parts that do this to their bodies.' He walked over to the stripped kit the dead man had been wearing, prodding it with a toe. 'Wonder how they managed to get their hands on that?'

'Only one way of finding out, I suppose.' I wiped my sword clean on a stolen Roman cloak, sheathed it, then turned to my old friend. 'Looks like I'm going south.'

* * *

'Will you stop breathing so loud!' I hissed, gently lifting my oar from the water. It was the night after the battle in the woods. We had spent the remainder of the previous day digging graves, making a point of stripping the dead men's armour first. Two more of the enemy dead had sported matching brands with the one Balomar had found. These men too had slitted eyes and sun-darkened skin. We had questions stacking up as fast as we had enemies. I was hoping to get an answer to one or two before someone else tried to kill me. My new cuirass had got through the battle unscathed, much to my delight, though I had elected to leave it back in Goridorgis for my jaunt south.

'How they going to hear me breathing from all the way up there?' Faramund hissed back at me.

'Just try to control yourself,' I said. It had been my idea to row a small boat across the Danube, rather than risking crossing the bridge. Truth was, I was trying not to pant just as much as Faramund was. My shoulders were on fire, my back frozen rigid. Even my legs ached, though I think they were pains in sympathy for my upper body. I was not a young man, not as fit and strong as I once was. Halfway across the river, where the currents got stronger and beds of weeds and algae grew thicker, I had begun to deeply regret my decision.

It was the dead of night, and we were in the hands of Nott, the Dreamweaver. She was the goddess of rest, of dreams, and I had often wondered since my encounter with the Allfather in the distant north whether it had really happened, or if she had just been playing games with me. I had been a man of the Gods once. I had worshipped the Allfather as the father of the gods, and had often styled myself on his son, Loki. But, as far as I could see, the gods had betrayed me, or at least become bored, and I had drifted from their attention.

But I felt her presence there on the river, and perhaps the Sly One had even paused to take another look at me, as I attempted to sneak into an empire that long thought me dead. We were beneath the wall of Carnuntum, a horror of red brick and chiselled stone. Gods, how I hated those walls, annoying things that had long defied me. The Romans were as good at knocking them down as they were at building them. Alas, those skills of engineering that could bring a city to its knees were far beyond us barbarians from the wilderness. So if I could not knock this wall down, I could at least sneak through it.

'What's the plan, Lord?' Faramund whispered once he had got his breath back.

'There's a door, see it?' I pointed through the inky dark. A small wooden door, almost level with the water line. At low tide, the door would lead out to the mud flats on the riverbank and the people of the town would be free to pass through and access the river. The poorer citizens would wash their clothes; the more affluent would use it as access to their river barges. The door was always manned, and usually by someone far less scrupulous than a legionary.

'Aye, I see it. But how do we get through?'

I rummaged through the coin pouch tied to my belt, producing two silver coins. 'With these.' Us Germans had very little use for coins, or any precious metal, for that matter. Furs and cattle, wine and grain were our currency. Coin didn't keep you warm in winter, didn't keep food on the table for your children. We would sell our amber to the Romans, but more often than not, we would not ask for coin in return. Rome had forbidden her merchants from selling or trading iron to us. A sensible precaution, as much as I resented it. Rome would rather we did not have access to metals we could turn into weapons to use against them. There was a reason swords and helmets and mail were so sparse north of the Danube. Most warriors went to war armed with just a spear. Almost none had mail. A good chief or king would ensure his hearth warriors were armed and armoured to the teeth. The rest of his army was made up of farmers.

Back in my heyday, though, I had seen the value in silver. Men didn't need it, but they wanted it. I was a ring giver, distributing my silver among my men as I saw fit. One unit did a better job than another, they got more silver. Simple. It kept the men hungry, eager to please. I still had a couple of chests full of the stuff from back in the day, though not a soul apart from my wife knew it. The chests were buried in the woods, and whenever I needed to access it, I would take a stroll on the pretence I needed some time alone. If the men serving me knew, I'd never be able to leave my hall without fear of it being long gone by the time I returned.

'You just pay?' Faramund asked, dumbfounded.

I rolled my one remaining eye. 'We bribe someone, you fool. The town employs guards at every gate and door in and out of the city. They aren't soldiers, and they certainly aren't competent. Just watch and learn, pup.' We gently rowed the boat so we were level with the door. I knocked twice, gently, not wanting to alert more people than was necessary. I heard the scuffle of boots on stone the other side, and with a snap and a squeak, the door was unlocked and pulled back.

'Who's there?' a voice said. I saw a greybeard with squinting eyes under a flat peak peering out.

'Two coins for you if you let us in, friend,' I said in Latin, a language I'd had no need to speak in many a year.

'Two? Piss off, lowlife,' the gruff voice said, and the man made to shut the door.

'Wait!' I hissed. 'Four then,' I offered.

'What's happening?' Faramund asked. He spoke no Latin, so could not follow the conversation.

'Inflation. That's what's bloody happening,' I grumbled, hand back in my pouch to fetch two more coins. I planted them into a waiting hand and watched with barely disguised disgust as the guard tested each coin by trying to bend them with his teeth. 'Satisfied?'

'Aye, they're good. Come in. Can't promise I'll still be here when you want to leave, mind. My shift finishes in an hour.'

'Then I'll just have to pay the next guy, won't I?' I cut back at the guard, clambering out of the boat and into Carnuntum.

When we were both in and the door closed behind us, I told Faramund to cover his face with his hood, and we were off into the darkened alleys of the city.

'That was easy,' the young warrior said when we were alone.

I chuckled. 'Welcome to the most corrupt empire that ever existed. The right coins in the right palms get you pretty much anywhere you want to go.'

'So why we going to the effort of sneaking in when it's dark?'

'Because I'm not stupid,' I snapped back. 'The less people who see us the better.'

'Where we going, anyway?' Faramund looked nervously left and right. I smiled, looking at him. The wonder in his eyes at the paved roads, the stone buildings. All neatly ordered in rows, the streets as straight as an arrow.

'This place is what the Romans call a backwater, by the way. You should see some of the cities they have the other side of the Rhine. As for us, we're headed for a tavern.'

'What's at the tavern?'

'Ale? Wine? But it is not *what* is at the tavern, but *who*.'

'Are you going to be this cryptic all night?'

'I preferred it when you never questioned me and called me Lord. Just keep your mouth shut, your head down and follow me.' We walked briskly through Carnuntum. Thankfully, the streets were quiet at that time of night. Down the main thoroughfare trundled a line of merchant carts. In some cities, I knew the local governments had banned the use of carts on the roads at night, due to the racket their wooden wheels made on the cobbled roads. Them being there worked to our advantage, as the constant noise of the carts, horses and merchants masked our footsteps as we passed houses, closed shops and bakeries, where the smell of freshly baked bread wafted out from the closed doors. 'They bake through the night, ready to sell it with the dawn,' I explained to Faramund, who sniffed the air in wonder.

After no time at all, we arrived at our destination. The Flying Eagle was the preferred tavern for the officers of the Fourteenth legion. It was on the eastern edge of Carnuntum, so closest to the fortress that flanked the town. There it was anything but quiet. Soldiers lined the street outside, the tavern doors tied open to allow for easier access to the men who stumbled in and out, most laden with jugs of ale or wine. There was singing and shouting and laughter, two men coming to fists as one bumped into the other, sending a wine cup spiralling to the floor. They were quickly pulled apart.

'Surely we're not going in there?' Faramund hissed to me. 'We'll be killed!'

'No shit.' We stood at the edge of a shadowed alley, hoods pulled low, all but invisible unless you knew where to look for us. 'We wait here and watch.'

'Watch for what?'

'For the man we are here to see.'

'An old friend of yours?'

I sucked air through my teeth. 'Not exactly. But what happened in the woods, that is an issue for Rome as much as it is for us. It means someone within the empire is selling Roman kit north of the river. And I'd bet you anything you'd care to wager that these bastards will do anything to find the man who did it. Trust me, the last thing they want is an excuse for the tribes to unite against them. And if a bunch of Germans are rampaging the borderland, killing their own cousins in Roman kit, that is exactly what will happen.'

'Is that not what your friend Balomar wants, though?'

I nodded, trying to hide my sigh. Explaining politics to Faramund was akin to trying to teach a dog siege warfare. 'Aye. But he needs it on his terms, where he is in control. We don't know who these men are, what tribe they're from, who they're working for. We need to find out. Easiest way to do that is to find the man who is giving them the gear, then go from there.'

'And this man we are waiting for, he will know?'

'He'll know where to look, at least.' I stopped speaking, my ears pricking. From somewhere within the multitude of men to my front, I heard a familiar voice. I'm ashamed to say it was a voice that still brings a chill to my spine. Centurion Silus, *primus pilus* of the Fourteenth legion, barrelled his way out of the tavern. A full head taller than any man around him, he wore just a plain blue tunic, arms bulging on his flanks.

'Disperse! Away now! Any man that leaves here after me will be parading with their century come the dawn tomorrow!' Good-natured groans and jeers followed, the big centurion smiling and shaking the hands of the men who passed him. Soon, he was all but alone on the street. He and two of his comrades helped the tavern staff bring in the tables and chairs left strewn on the roadside, and then with their goodbyes said, they were off into the night.

'Is that our guy?' Faramund asked.

'Aye. It is,' I said, unable to keep the trepidation from my voice. 'His name is Silus, and he is the senior centurion of the Fourteenth legion. Those other men who just left, they're all officers in his legion.'

'Loki's shining cock!' Faramund cursed. 'All those bastards were officers from the fucking Fourteenth? And we're just lounging over the road from them! We'd have been screwed if they saw us.'

'What's up?' I smiled at him through the gloom. 'You said you were up for a bit of fun?'

Faramund muttered something about me having funny ideas about what the word 'fun' constituted, but I wasn't really listening. My feet were following the giant soldier as he made his way through the town.

'He's going the wrong way if he wants to get back to the barracks, isn't he?' Faramund asked quietly as we followed at a discreet distance.

'He isn't going back to barracks. Silus has a house here in Carnuntum that he shares with his wife and son.'

'I didn't think Roman soldiers were allowed to marry?'

'They're not. But when you're a legend such as he, it seems the cream are happy to turn a blind eye to certain facts.'

'Cream?'

I sighed. 'Cream of the crop! The high ups! Gods, man, you don't get out much, do you—'

I stopped speaking very quickly. We had turned a corner, me more focused on trying to shut Faramund up than watching our quarry. When your quarry was a man such as Silus, that could be a costly mistake. The blade at my throat assured me it had been.

'Who are you? And why are you following me? Speak quickly, or I'll spill your lifeblood over those cobbles at your feet.'

'Well, that's rude,' I said, turning my head slowly to the right, so my would-be murderer got a look at my face. 'I know it's been a while, but I wouldn't have expected you to forget your greatest enemy so quickly.'

I smiled at the stunned face that stared back at me. 'Impossible,' Silus breathed.

'Improbable, I'll grant you. But you must have known I'd be back at some point. You reckon that tavern back there will open back up for an hour? You and I need to have a little chat.'

4

My ale was warm and weak, but a brazier at my back kept the night's chill from my bones, though the company to my front did nothing to warm my heart.

'Why are you here?' Silus asked me. Beside him sat his long-time friend and optio, Vitulus. The man was short and wiry, a complete contrast to the huge and powerfully built Silus. Both men fixed me with stares that offered nothing but hatred. I couldn't blame them for that. The feeling was mutual.

'My men were attacked yesterday,' I began. 'By a mob of Germans dressed in this.' From beneath my cloak, I pulled out a folded red Roman cloak and laid it on the table before me. 'They wore your cloaks, your armour, your helmets. Even fought with those pissy little swords you're all so fond of. I want to know how they came about it.'

Silus puffed out his cheeks. He raised a paw-like hand to his two-day stubble and massaged his cheeks. 'You think we gave it to them?'

'How else would they have got it?' I countered. Faramund sat to my left, nursing a cup of ale. His gaze flickered nervously from me to the two Romans sitting opposite us. He had no Latin and must have been anxious to know what we were saying, but I had no time to translate for him.

Silus and Vitulus shared a look before the centurion responded. 'We certainly would not have given kit over to the enemy. You know as well as I do what the repercussions could be if we did. But...'

There was something he knew, or something he had heard. I could see the man deliberating, clearly not keen to share what information he had with me. 'But?' I prodded.

'Someone could have given it to them.'

'Careful, sir,' Vitulus hissed at his superior.

'Someone?' I nudged again.

'We have had reports of gear going missing from one of our *fabricae*,' Silus admitted.

'Which one?' I asked. Arms factories were kept under lock and key by the Roman state. Unsurprisingly, they were not keen on people, Roman or not, getting their hands on military kit.

'Ratiaria, though there are two others less than a day's journey away. It's possible the stock goes missing being transported from one to the other.'

I nodded, thinking. It had always been something of a mystery to me just why the Romans decided to build weapon factories so close to the border. Surely even they could see there would be more opportunity for things like this to happen? It made sense in one way. Weapons and armour could be made and shipped in a relatively short time period, reaching the legions stationed along the Danube in a matter of weeks. But if it were me, I would have deduced that the risk outweighed the reward. Though in my opinion, there were no Romans that thought with such clarity.

'Has anyone been sent to investigate?' I asked.

Silus merely shrugged. 'I am a soldier, not an officer of the state. If there was something to investigate, the local governor would be the man to order it done. I imagine the *frumentarii* would be the people to actually do it.'

Perhaps the *frumentarii* were the ones slipping the gear over the border, I thought, though I kept that to myself. 'I need to know who is being given this equipment. We stripped three of the corpses; all had an image of a horse branded on their torsos. Whoever these men are, they aren't local to me, and they certainly haven't come from your turf. I need to know where. We *both* need to know. Can you get me an in?'

'To the *fabrica*? Piss off, Alaric! I do not have that kind of influence. Even if I did, why would I let a barbarian into one of our weapons factories? Even you must be able to see the madness in that!'

I conceded his point. 'You understand what will happen in my country if these attacks keep happening? People talk, Centurion. How long before these unprovoked attacks get tongues wagging? How long before my people decide to join forces and put right their wrongs?'

Silus sucked air through his teeth, clearly uncomfortable. He knew as well as I that Rome would struggle to hold back a united German army. We could put north of fifty thousand men in the field, and that was just the tribes that bordered Rome. The empire had unrivalled resources, but how long would it take them to move men from the east, from Africa, from Britannia, to help their comrades? I could see Silus weighing this all up in his mind. 'Horses branded onto their backs?' I nodded. 'So it is in both our interests to get to the bottom of this,' he said eventually.

'Aye,' I agreed.

'So we shall do it together.'

'What?' I exclaimed.

Vitulus spat ale down his tunic. 'Together?'

Faramund looked thoroughly confused, looking from me to the Romans. 'Together,' Silus said with a nod. 'I'll get you an in to the *fabrica* at Ratiaria. I know a man there. You will have to pose as a slave. Your friend there, he speak any Latin?' I shook my head. 'Then send him home. He'll be no use to you. I'll give you one of my men. They'll go in with you, also posing as a slave. In a couple of weeks, I'll dream up a reason to need to visit, and we can discuss what you have found. Do we have an agreement?'

I pondered it. I didn't like it, but I saw the logic. Silus would not want it to be common knowledge that there was a Roman giving Germani war kit. It would bring unwanted eyes to him and the province as a whole. Could be there was more at play than I knew. Relations between the army and the state changed with the wind in the empire. But I figured I was getting what I wanted, even if I didn't like the method. 'Fine. When do we go?'

Silus refilled our ale cups, sat back on his stool. 'Give me six days. I need a bit of time to get it organised, and I will need to speak to my superiors.'

'Wouldn't want them thinking you'd gone rogue, hey?' I said through a smirk. 'Always been the good little soldier, haven't you?'

He ignored the dig. 'How is it you're still alive, anyway?' He changed the subject. I caught him studying the mass of scar tissue where my left eye had been. 'I thought you were as good as dead when I took that eye. There must have been a queue of chiefs waiting to take their slice of flesh from your back.'

'I can look after myself,' I said with a wink. Not really a wink if you've only got one eye, I suppose. To Silus, it must have just appeared as a blink. 'I laid low for a while. Not got many warriors following me like back in the day. But I do all right. Had quite the victory in the north last year, though I'd assume word of that never reached this far south.'

'Can't say it did. Couldn't count on both my hands the amount of times I've been asked by *frumentarii* agents about you over the years. Seems like everyone is always after news of you.'

I won't lie. That brought a huge grin to my face. 'Course they have been. I'm Alaric Hengistson, scourge of Rome. Good to know you maggots haven't forgotten who I am.'

Silus sniffed. 'Far as I can see, without five hundred men at your back, you're just one tired old man. Don't put too much stock in your own fame. There lies the path to hubris.'

'Coming from you?' I said with a smirk. 'Anyway, nice to know you've been worried about me. Must have been getting awfully peaceful around here.'

That brought a smile from both Silus and Vitulus. 'I swear, Alaric, you've got more lives than a cat. Never thought I'd be sitting in a tavern sharing a jug of ale with you, that's for sure.'

'The world is a funny old place at times, I'll grant you. I am surprised they haven't pensioned you off yet. Looks as though it must be getting snug under your mail.' I pointed to Silus's belly, which was, to be fair, a great deal bigger than mine.

'Ha!' The centurion cackled a laugh. 'I guess you're right there! Too much easy living. I'm a year or so away from my golden ticket out of here. Not that I plan on going far.'

'Born in Pannonia, die in Pannonia? Am I right?'

'Sounds about right to me. Vitulus and I have our eyes set on a plot of land just east of here. Think we can set up our own little colony.'

'A whole town of people that want me dead. Think of that,' I said, still grinning. 'I'll be sure to come and visit.'

'Bring your sword if you do,' Vitulus cut in. 'Let's be clear – this is strictly business. Right now we both have the same aim. Never happened before, sure as hell won't happen again.'

'Agreed.' I drained my cup and slammed it down on the table. 'And I think it is time my friend and I were on our way. Six days?' I said to Silus.

'Aye. Come across the bridge. I'll make sure the lads know to expect you.

And Alaric,' the centurion said, rising to his feet. 'No fucking funny business, you hear me? The man I send in with you will be there to keep an eye on you just as much as any potential traitor. First sign that you're up to no good, he'll kill you.'

'Not if I kill him first,' I said, rising and leaving, a thoroughly confused Faramund following in my wake.

* * *

'This is the worst day of my life,' Habitus said as Ratiaria came into view. It was a walled city, small compared with Carnuntum, the red-tiled roofs looking glum on the cloud-filled day.

'Worst day of your life so far,' I said with a grin. 'I reckon tomorrow, and the day after and after and so on, will be much worse. Life as a slave is pretty shit. Not sure if you knew?'

'How long are we going to be here?'

'As long as it takes.' I shrugged. 'Couple of months, maybe?'

'Months!' Habitus winced and spat on the dirt. 'Bollocks to this.' Habitus was the legionary Silus had appointed to accompany me into the *fabrica* at Ratiaria. He was short and slim, lithe muscle on his shoulders and arms visible beneath his tunic. He was an easterner by birth, and Silus had selected the Syrian for his foreign looks. His dark skin and thick black hair he wore down to his shoulders certainly gave him a different look to the bulk of the men of the Fourteenth, who were, like their senior centurion, born and bred in Pannonia.

'So what did you do to piss Silus off so much you got sent on this little jaunt?' My own spirits were high. I was up to mischief, my favourite pastime. I had used the six days I had as wisely as I could. My men had been sent back north from Goridorgis, my two boys with them. I'd asked them to pass on a message to Saxa for me, and promised I would be home as soon as I could. My wife, may the gods bless her, was well used to my coming and going by that point, and she knew I was at my happiest when out in the world, seeing what mayhem I could create.

She would also understand the need for my little mission. A band of native warriors rampaging around Germania dressed as Romans was something that would end up affecting our lives in one way or another. Best to nip it in the bud, as they say. I had also spent time with Balomar, the two of us scheming up contingency plans for every eventuality we could think of, as well as coming up with methods to stay in touch. It was, I thought, time well spent.

'Can't say for sure.' Habitus rubbed his beard as he spoke. 'Thought I'd been on my best behaviour for the last few months.'

I cocked an eyebrow. 'So you're saying you normally aren't?'

The Syrian allowed himself a smile. 'I nearly shot Vitulus with an arrow a while back. I was out training in the yard, saw a few of my tent mates lugging wooden crates in at the optio's order. Thought I'd loose one just over their heads. You know, just a bit of banter.'

I smiled, just picturing it. 'What happened?'

'Wind picked up just as I loosed. The arrow veered off to the right, skimmed the top of Vitulus's head. The bastard had me on latrines for a week.'

Chuckling, I thought of the wiry optio, wondering how he would have taken it. 'Didn't think there were many archers in the legions? They have their own units, don't they?'

Habitus nodded. 'Aye, they do. But my father taught me the bow from a young age. I've never gone more than a week without practising. Always take it to battle with me, too.'

'They let you do that?'

'Aye. Silus always asks me to take out a chief or two when we're up against your mob. Nothing sucks the courage out of an army more than seeing their commander spurting blood before anyone has had a chance to swing a sword.'

I thought that sounded true enough. 'I'm slightly hurt you've never tried to shoot me.'

'I did, a couple of times,' Habitus conceded.

'Perhaps you're not quite the shot you think you are then,' I said with another grin.

We walked between eight legionaries. A tent party sent from the Fourteenth commanded by a young tribune. Rufus Julianus was the son of some senator or other from Rome, his father a personal friend of the emperor. This little expedition through friendly territory was his first independent command, and the pup had been jumping at shadows the whole three-day journey from Carnuntum. Even then, the walls of his destination in sight, I could see the hairless youth scanning the river to our left, seemingly certain a barbarian horde was going to appear from behind the nearest bush. I could make out the Carpathians in the distance, the snow-peaked tops of the mountains appearing through the clouds. I had a sudden longing for home, even though those mountains were as much part of Rome as the road I walked on. Like Habitus, I hoped this would not take as long as I feared it would.

'Don't make much of him,' I said quietly, nodding to the tribune. 'If this is the next generation of commanders, then I reckon your empire will be done for in about ten years.'

Habitus scoffed. 'They're all like this to start with. Besides, men like him only serve the bare minimum. Three years or so on the frontier, then he'll be back to Rome in some cushy little civilian post, making the lives of us ordinary folk miserable.'

'Ahh, the glory of Rome,' I said a little too loudly, the surrounding soldiers turning to glare at me with disdain. They didn't know who either of us were, Silus picking soldiers from a different cohort so Habitus would not be recognised. All they had been told was we were two runaway slaves who needed returning to Ratiaria. Our hands had been in irons the entire journey, even our ankles locked up whilst we slept. It had been humiliating at first, but I had quickly learnt to accept it. A means to an end, nothing more.

I sensed the young tribune relax as we approached the walls, him calling up to the soldiers at the gate. We were admitted without pause, into a clean and clear street that seemed to run right through the city. There was much to admire about Rome and her empire. I have never shied away from that. Ratiaria was another example. It was pleasant, the neat little shops that lined the road adding to the character. We passed barbers and bakeries, tanners and a *fullonica*, the fullers outside swapping the full vats of urine for empty ones. There were also plenty of things to not admire about the empire, using urine to wash your clothes definitely being one of them. Give me river water any day.

We passed through the city, thankfully attracting little attention. After we had been walking a while, we came to another wall and gate, and I thought for a moment we had missed our destination and had arrived at the eastern wall of the city. But it seemed Rome did not mess about when it came to the security of their weapons factories. Three guards came down to meet us, one in the crested helmet of a centurion. There seemed to be some confusion, as the centurion repeated there had been no runaway slaves from the factory. Eventually, the man had to give in to Julianus and his superior rank, and we were shown into a small yard, the tang of smelting iron heavy on the air.

Our escort left us without a word, presumably to check in to some comfortable inn for the night before their journey home the following day. Habitus and I were left unattended in the yard. 'There's no way there are weapons getting out of here without anyone noticing,' he said through a sniff, eyes roaming the yard. High thick walls behind us, and twenty soldiers in view along the battlements and the yard floor. It was like stepping foot into a legionary base.

I was thinking the same thing. 'Agreed. But there lies the issue. It cannot be some great secret. Someone here with influence is up to something, and all their underlings are in on it.'

'How the fuck are we meant to get to the bottom of it when we're supposed to be slaves? Not like we'll be able to snoop around.'

'We'll think of something,' I said absently, my one eye still roaming the yard's contents. On the far side was a line of carts, the iron they contained all but spilling over the top. I wondered what Sedric would make of the place, and once more marvelled at the skill the man had shown in forging the *cuirass* he had gifted me with such little resource around him. On the left were bundles and bundles of leather hides, waiting to be fitted to the front of shields. For the shields themselves, I could see the piles of wood stacked up next to the hides. The whole thing was alien to me. I had an invested interest in the use of weapons, but when it came to their making, I had taken very little interest.

As I have said before, in my country, weapons and armour were things only the wealthy could own. Rome was forbidden from trading iron with us, and as a people we were no great miners. I was snapped from my chain of thought by the centurion, who had appeared at the gate, marching to us. 'Names,' he said with no preamble.

'Alaric.'

'Habitus.' We had spoken about using fake names, in the end deciding it was pointless. No man there would know the two of us, and it would have been another pretence to keep up throughout our stay.

'I am Centurion Apollonius of the Sixth Flavia Felix. I am in command here. I was not made aware of the impending arrival of the two of you. I'm told you were picked up in Carnuntum as runaway slaves, is that correct?' We both nodded. 'Well, I don't know where you ran from, but it certainly wasn't here. The two of you worked in a *fabrica* before?' We both shook our heads. Apollonius sighed. 'Then you are nothing more than two mouths to feed. I shall write to my superiors and see if we can get you moved to somewhere more suitable. Until then, you do as you're instructed. I'm not a monster. All I ask is you tend to your duties as best you can, and I'll see you well fed and looked after in return. Clear?'

For what it's worth, I took what Apollonius said at face value. He had the face of an honest man, his iron-grey hair cut short, flat to his head from years spent under a helmet. His eyes were a light green, opaque and watery. He carried his years more there than he did on his body, which the man had clearly taken care of. I guessed him to be towards the end of his service, sent to the *fabrica* from his legion as a sort of reward for what he had done. Must have been easier running the day to day of a factory in a peaceful city than living in a campaign tent. The land to the north of the Danube from Ratiaria was Roman, they having conquered Dacia some fifty years previous. But all that meant for the men of the Sixth was they were asked to cover more ground, the men of their legion spread thin across the vast province. And I knew very well it was far from peaceful.

Dacia gave the empire vast quantities of iron, as well as the more valuable gold. Though where gold was used for nothing more than making pretty trinkets for senators to buy their wives, iron was for the army first, and civilian use second. It made more sense to me then, looking at the carts laden with lumps of the grey metal, just why they would put *fabricae* so close to the German front. They could have it from the mine to the factory in less than a week. And Rome always had need of iron.

Apollonius bade us follow him through the yard and into the factory itself. It was impressive, to say the least. The first thing to strike me was the heat. It hit me like a shield boss as we ducked in through the small door. Immediately, breathing became more challenging, the air so thick you could almost reach out and grasp it. Two forges were set against the wall to our left, the clay they were moulded from scolded a dark red. Four men in heavy leather aprons and gloves stood around them, talking to each other quietly as they peered into the flames, the glistening blades thrust into them.

'Blades are forged here, though the two of you will not be going anywhere near our forges.'

'Why not?' I couldn't help myself asking.

'Because forging blades is skilled work, and the two of you will not be here long enough to master it.' Apollonius kept walking; we passed rows of tables where men stood in lines, making spear shafts from planks of wood, and finally, we reached the far end of the *fabrica*, where the air was less like that of a furnace, and more like that of a public latrine. 'Here is where you will work. Hektor, over here.'

A short, bald slave scurried over from a workbench, eyes never leaving his feet as he walked. 'This is Hektor. He is in charge of the production of hides for our shields. You two will work under him for the duration of your stay. Hektor, this is Alaric and Habitus. They will not be with us long, but show them the basics of what you do. I'm certain they can be of some use.'

Without another word, Apollonius turned on his heels and left us. And so begun our stay as slaves in one of the weapon factories of Rome.

5

'You need to get all these hides through the factory to your station. Once that is done, I will show you how to cut them,' Hektor said in a matter-of-fact tone, before turning and scurrying back inside.

Habitus and I shared a look. There must have been three hundred hides, stacked up in carts to the right of the gate we had entered in the day before. We had both slept woefully, each allocated a stinking cot that was more lice than straw the evening before. I scratched at myself. I felt as though someone was lighting small fires in my hair, my beard, and worse, my groin. Habitus had bags under his eyes so big he could have carried his breakfast in them. If there had been any breakfast, anyway. So far, we hadn't even been given the courtesy of having a morning piss.

With a sigh, I set off, scooping up as many hides as I could off the cart, loading it onto a small flatbed trolley I would then have to pull through the factory. I'd thought to ask why the carts could not just be unloaded inside the factory rather than the yard, but had held my tongue. The guards atop the gate watched us with lazy smiles on their faces. To them, a couple of new slaves in the *fabrica* was a kind of sport. I'd overheard bets being placed the night before as I lay fidgeting on my pallet as to which of the two of us would last the longest. Oddly, I had been pleased when shorter odds had been placed on me.

Habitus followed my lead and soon we had just one cart left to unload.

Once that was done, we both stood panting, throats as dry as old parchment, bladders bulging.

'You can piss in there.' Hektor pointed to a couple of huge clay amphora that stood by a shallow pool in the corner next to our workstations. I'd seen the soldiers piss in the pots the night before, and even as I watched, another slave walked over and emptied his bladder before we could get to them.

'Why in there?' I asked. Habitus winced at me. I think he already knew the answer.

Hektor just smiled. 'You'll see.'

We did as we were told, and then pleasingly were offered a small breakfast of figs, hard bread, and a cup of greasy water. I took mine with the gratitude one might on seeing a lavish feast laid out in their honour. I was starving. Once we had eaten and my request for seconds had been turned down, we followed Hektor to our workstations, and as the slave fussed over his preparations, I took a moment to take it all in.

The forges were a patchwork of orange, the four men in their leather aprons crowded around them. Thick black smoke curled into a chimney built into the roof, mercifully clearing the majority of it so we did not suffocate. At the workstation between us and them, mail shirts, already made, were being washed and polished so they gleamed even within the dreary light of the factory. They were not made there, but in another *fabrica* south in Naissus. It interested me that different factories specialised in different things.

And then there were the wood workers. The men who took lengths of oak and made them into spear shafts. The process seemed brutal. Sanding and rubbing down, oiling and then repeating the process. The smiths could make swords in half the time it took these men to make the spears. This, too, fascinated me. Coming from a land where only the rich had swords and spears were more common than ploughs.

'Are you listening to what I am saying?' Hektor slapped me around the side of the head, and suddenly I was concentrating again. 'I said, here are your stencils.' He picked up a wooden block, carved so it resembled the shape of a rectangular legionary shield. 'You place the stencil in the middle of your hide.' He did just so, the hide laid out on the wooden worktop. He took a small knife and began cutting into the hide around the stencil. 'And just like that, we have a hide for a shield.'

Again, I was impressed. It was all so clinical, so efficient. The local tanners would have got hold of the leather first, cutting and shaping it so it was ready for dispatch. That was then sold to the *fabrica,* and it was then their job to make of it what they needed.

'You will spend your mornings cutting the hides into shape. Discarded edges go in the bin over there.' He pointed to a large wooden crate in between the workbenches assigned to Habitus and me. 'The slaves on the benches opposite you will take your discarded leather and use it for their work. And the finished hides go over by the pool. After lunch, I shall show you what happens to them next. Any questions?'

We both shook our heads.

'Then get to it. There are knives on your workstations.'

We set to work. It was exhausting. The hides were heavy, and soon I was feeling a twinge in my lower back from bending to scoop them up one by one, and then stooping over the workbench to cut around the stencils. That too was hard work. The hides were tough. They were, after all, to be used for the front of shields, and would be a legionary's first defence in battle. The irony of it all was not lost on me. There I was, the famed scourge of Rome, helping to make shields for the very men I might well be facing on the battlefield in the near future.

As I worked, I counted the men working around me. There were thirty-four of us in total, all leather working to some degree. Habitus and I were cutting the hides for the front of shields. Four men opposite us seemed to be making neck ties for helmets, using the scraps of leather we discarded. To my right was a clutch of men making leather sandals, three cobblers overseeing them as they moulded the soles. The distinction between the slaves and freedmen was clear. Although we all wore nothing but grubby tunics, and though we all sweated and grafted the day away, it was obvious to see those who were giving orders and those receiving them.

Past the cobblers was another row of workbenches, six slaves doing what we seemed to do, cutting around stencils and piling up the hides as they went. Though I noticed a team of four slaves working alongside them. These were stitching together the hides around three sides, and another two were waxing the finished products. These then were the covers for the shields. Legionaries would always cover their shields on a march. It protected them from the weather, stopped the wood rotting or going so soft the shield became useless in battle. Again, it startled me.

The *fabrica* had not seemed a big building as we had approached, but the scale of the work going on inside was huge. And this was just what I could see clearly. There must have been close to three hundred men inside, all hard at work on something that would contribute to the great mincing machine that was the Roman army. This was what made them so invincible in the field. I could only imagine having such resources at my disposal.

Back in the day, when five hundred armed and armoured men had marched under my banner, keeping them in full battle gear had been a night-mare. For a while, I'd had a retired smith from within the empire tag along with us. I'd paid him a fortune in silver, and he was worth every coin. He soon had four other men trained in the dark arts of forging iron and mending mail and making us everything from blades to cooking utensils. Without him, I'd have been dead in the first major war we fought. How else would I have replaced all the broken kit in time for the next battle?

I set back to work with renewed vigour. *This* was how wars were won. Before the battle had even started. This was how Rome came to rule the world. Infrastructure, cooperation, and a lot of money. One day, I assured myself, the money would run out, and all this would crumble. It was a dream, and one I clung to.

It was perhaps an hour before lunch; I had a stack of hides cut and ready to go over by the bath when one of the slaves working on the sandals to my right hissed in my direction. 'You,' he whispered in my mother tongue. 'What are you doing here?'

He was a grizzly old man, more hair on his arms than his head. His beard, though, white as winter snow, was still thick, and he had taken the time to run a comb through it that morning. 'I am a slave,' I said with a shrug, keeping my eye on my work. It would do me no good to draw unnecessary attention to myself. Looking past the man, I saw three more with their heads turned in my direction. One was unmistakenly from the tribes, his long, fair hair tied in a topknot. He had rounded shoulders and thick arms, and he glowered at me. The other two were different. Somewhere between myself and Habitus. Their skin was tanned, their eyes slits as they stared at me. I wondered where they could be from. Perhaps Habitus would know?

'You are no slave,' the man said, grinning at me to show the yellow stumps where there had once been teeth.

'What do you know of me?' I scoffed, but I could feel my heart beat harder. Discovered, already?

'There are not many one-eyed men in Germania.'

'We are not in Germania, brother.'

'No. But we were once.' The man stopped, peered cautiously around, and crept over to my workstation. 'Never thought I would see the mighty Alaric Hengistson brought so low. You have no business being here.'

Slowly, I eased the knife out from the hide I had been cutting. Turning to him, letting the greybeard see the blade, I spoke with all the authority I could muster. 'You will not utter that name in here. And my business is my own.'

The man chuckled. 'There are more than three hundred slaves in here, *Lord* Alaric.' I heard the mocking tone in the word 'lord', but decided to ignore it. 'Many from north of the river. I am not the only one to have recognised you. I'd watch your back if I were you. As I said, you shouldn't be here.'

I cursed. What a fool I had been. There had been me, thinking it hubris to assume I would be recognised among the slaves of the empire. But how could I not be? How many greybeards were there like this one? Clearly, the man had been a warrior. There were livid white scars under the hairs of his arms, which still held more muscle tone than most. How many more had recognised me as Habitus and I were paraded through the day before?

'Might be I'm here for a reason,' I said. I rubbed absently at my missing eye, trying to keep my tone casual. I didn't bother covering the grievous wound in those days, and had learnt to find some amusement in the disgusted expressions on people's faces as they stared at the pink, scarred flesh. 'You know anything about some weapons going missing from here?'

The man laughed. 'Gods, you really do live up to your reputation, don't you? You haven't even asked my name.'

I suppressed a tut of irritation. 'Sorry, friend. What is your name? I feel you have a story to tell.'

'That I do. Name's Edwin, and I am not your friend. I'd keep your questions to yourself if I were you.'

'Why would you not be? We are kinsmen, you and I.' Pausing for a moment, gambling that the man knew something I wanted to know, I pressed on. 'Why would I want to keep my questions to myself? Seems a reasonable thing to ask.'

'In that we are. I was Chauci,' Edwin said. 'Until I was taken captive one night, during a raid led by the Fourteenth legion. Guess you'd know all about that. As to your questions' – the man cocked his head over his shoulder, locking eyes with his three friends – 'let's just say you're playing with fire. You're just going to end up getting burned.'

My blood froze. I barely registered what Edwin had said about fire. He was Chauci, taken on a raid by Rome. I didn't need him to tell me how many years ago it had been. He was speaking of the night my mother had died. The night my lifelong war with the Fourteenth had begun. The knife fell absently from my hand.

* * *

I wake to screams, to the clash of iron and the tang of burning in my nostrils. I wake into a nightmare.

Stumbling from my small room, hastily putting on trousers and a tunic, I am still wiping sleep from my eyes when my father grips my shoulder. 'Rome has come, Alaric,' he says in a hushed voice, though there is no one to overhear us in the tumult. He is holding his sword, my father. His hand fits the worn black leather of the grip like a glove. 'Stay here with your mother. Get a spear from by the door. There's a good lad. I will not be long. I promise.' With that, he is gone.

My mother cowers, her head under the bedsheets. She shakes in the grip of fear. 'All is going to be well, Mother,' I say to her, lowering myself onto the bed, feeling the warmth where my father's body has just departed.

'This is all my fault,' she says through rasping sobs. 'They are here for me. Because of him.'

'Because of who?'

'Your father.'

'No.' I shake my head firmly. My father was a warrior once, had the scars to prove it. But he is a farmer now, and proud of the peaceful way he puts food on the table. 'No, Mother. Father has done nothing wrong.'

She shakes her head with such force I fear her neck will snap. 'No. No, you do not understand. He has gone too far this time. He has got too powerful. Even Fridumar fears him now.'

Fridumar, chief of the Chauci. A fattening coward who rarely leaves the great hall better men built for him. 'Fridumar fears everyone,' I say in jest, trying to shake loose this fear that has hold of my mother.

'He will not defend us. He will leave us to our fate.'

'Fridumar will, Mother. His warriors will right now be fighting to defend our people.' My heart races now. I do not know if my mother has lost her wits. Is this the rambling of a madwoman? I do not know what to do.

'He will fight for his people. He will not fight for us. We will be abandoned, Alaric. He hates me and fears the man you will become.'

I am lost in her words. My mind raging like a summer sea, I stagger from her room and move to our front door. It lies open, my father leaving it swinging in the night air as he left to fight. I pick up a spear and venture out into the night. Our home is north of the Chauci capital. The wind skims in off the sea. To the south, all I see is fire. Rome has come. Death follows.

I stagger into the shadows, shivering from the night's chill, palms sweaty on the shaft of the spear. I pass the tarn he taught me to swim in. He is a harsh man at times, my father. And it had been a freezing day when he had thrown me into the water and watched dispassionately as I struggled back to the surface. But it is his lessons that drive my feet forwards, towards the danger and not away from it. I hear him before I see him. His retreat is a fighting one. He parries a sword thrust and jabs his own back. A man falls away to the night. Then he steps four paces back and dodges a shield barged at his face. He stoops low, sword slicing through a calf.

'Father!' I call, and I'm running to him, towards the danger.

'Get back!' he calls to me without looking. 'Stay with your mother!'

I know that to be fruitless. To retreat is to die. Perhaps to stay here is too. But I would rather die as a man, fighting shoulder to shoulder with my father, than cowering in our home. A sword comes for me from the shadows and instinct alone saves me. I throw back my head and hear the rush as the sword cuts the air beside me. Those same instincts stop me in my tracks, and my retreat becomes an advance as I lower my stance and thrust my right arm forward, my spear lodging in something with a wet thud.

I pull on the weapon but it is stuck, and eventually I let go, heeding my father's calls to retreat. Together, we stumble back to our home. Our precious little home, where we lived a quiet life offending no one. Soldiers come from the night bearing flaming torches. I stop counting when I reach thirty. We are done for. They grab us and throw us to the dirt. Face down we lay, waiting for the death blow to come. But it does not. I will spend the rest of my life wishing it had, if only to spare me from what follows.

My mother is dragged from our home. Her clothes have been torn off, and she comes without complaint, silent, eyes boring into mine as she is dragged past. 'All will be well, Alaric,' she says.

But how can it be? How can anything be the same again after they have torn my world apart? 'Just keep your eyes on me,' my father says, his own fixed to mine. And I do as he says, and try to block out the screams that come from my mother.

6

I woke in a cold sweat, white-knuckled fists gripping my blanket. 'I thought I'd had a troubled past,' Habitus said and whistled. 'But oh boy, you, my friend, take the prize.'

'What was I saying?' I said, trying and failing to unclench my fists. I could still picture the flames, my mother lying face down in the dirt. Roman soldiers all around her, all waiting their turn...

'A lot of things. Don't think they need repeating. I finished your shift for you, by the way. You were out of it all afternoon.'

'I was?' I tried to recall the day before, but it was all a blur, and my head pounded like it had taken a blow from Donar's hammer.

'You were muttering with one of the other slaves. Then you were on the ground, shaking and sweating. Never seen anything like it.'

There is no greater insult to me than that sympathetic look men give you when they think you are weak. I despise it. I am the man who toppled kings, who broke shield walls and led the most fearsome fighting unit in all of Germania. I am not weak. But there I was, lying in a puddle of my own sweat, shaking hands refusing to unlock. A vision of my mother's last moments on this middle earth fixed in my mind. 'You going to get through this?' Habitus asked, but I paid him no heed.

Staggering from the corner of the chamber that slept a hundred or more of us slaves, I stumbled through the throng of sleeping bodies. Some were awake,

I noticed, and I saw the stares fixed at me as I passed. Remembering Edwin's words the day before, I wondered how many of those men recognised me. The thought had my heart hammering. I exited our sleeping chamber, down a narrow corridor, thankfully seeing no guards. I walked through the *fabrica* until I came to the door that led out to the rear yard. I'd not been out there as of yet, but I had seen other slaves using it.

Outside, the dawn air was mercifully cool, and I sucked in great lungfuls of it, trying to calm my frayed nerves. Three deep breaths, and I felt the trembling in my hands begin to cease. I walked a few steps, and after a moment was able to laugh softly at myself. What a fool of an old man I was becoming. I wondered what would the great Lord Alaric have made of this trembling wreck of a man? It wasn't the first time it had happened to me. Our ship beaching in the far north the year before, me in my battle gear, ready to leap into the melee. I had experienced a similar thing, and only Sedric being next to me had stopped the thing from gripping me completely.

Perhaps I was finally losing my edge? I walked shakily to the river. There was clear access, no gates, no guards. I fell to my knees and splashed cool water on my face. It was calm, there, in the dawn. The river swirled lazily, and if I closed my eye, I could picture my hall, the great river to the front. My boys running riot through our small community, Saxa calling after them, exasperated by the mud on their clean tunics.

It brought a smile to my face and calm to my mind. When I opened my eye, Alaric was back. Two ravens landed on the riverside, not ten paces from where I knelt. I felt the gods around me then. There were the Allfather's birds, Huginn and Muninn. 'Come to check in on me?' I said softly, my eye fixed on them. One of the ravens stared intently at me, as if daring me to move closer. I did not. The other hopped towards me and tilted its head, as if studying me. I remembered passing out on a beach in the far north, waking to a fire built up at my side, a mysterious figure in a hat beside me.

I remembered the waterskin by my side when I awoke again in the sunlight. I'd passed it off as a dream. Once I had thought the gods were with me. When I had five hundred men at my back, a blood-red banner streaming the air above me, I had thought myself invincible. So cunning, even Loki favoured me. That had all ended the day I lost my eye. But the sight of those two ravens invigorated me. They stayed a moment longer before flying away; I watched them until they passed out of sight.

When they were gone, I paid more attention to my surroundings. It surprised me there were no gates to the river. Anyone could gain access. There had been no soldier guarding the door as I left the factory. It stiffened my resolve that the weapons must have come from Ratiaria. How easy would it be to smuggle them out here? How easy for the tribesmen to row a boat down the river and pick them up? You wouldn't even need to be there when they did it, as long as you had dropped them off beforehand.

It was then I noticed the gleam of metal in the mud banks at the river's edge. Leaning forward, I scooped up what appeared to be a brass fitting for a helmet, and there was some leather and a small copper ring I recognised as being part of a sword scabbard. I could have howled in triumph. I knew exactly what was happening. Now I just had to prove it.

With renewed purpose, I turned and walked back inside. I did not see the men on the far side of the river, watching me intently.

* * *

My first hint of proof came later that very day. Habitus and I had been forced through our routine from the day before. We dragged in the hides from the front yard and spent our morning cutting them up. I had tried to string up a conversation with Edwin again, but the man had resolutely ignored me all morning. It was at lunch, in the meagre canteen set aside for us slaves, that I overheard a conversation.

'It's not enough time,' one slave hissed across the table.

'It has to be tonight.' It was Edwin that spoke, leaning across the table and speaking in a hushed tone. 'We need to act before we are discovered.'

'Do we know who the duty guards are?' Edwin was speaking to the Germani slave who had stood behind him when the two of us had spoken on the factory floor. The two others, with the sun-darkened skin and slit eyes, sat with them, all huddled across the table. There was something about the two of them that bothered me, but I couldn't put my finger on what. My nerves still frayed from my episode the day before, and I tried to put it from my mind.

'It's Elector's tent party. You know how lazy they are. Plus, there is a wagon train of armour coming in. If we take a few off, they won't be noticed. Once the inventory is taken, it will be harder to get our hands on them.'

I kept my eye fixed on my plate of food, but my ears were burning. Edwin's head spun around and I could feel his eyes burning into me, but I did not move. Hektor had spoken to us all about a change in our routine planned for the following day. Inventories were done when big deliveries of equipment ready to be moved on were taken in. The name Elector also interested me. He was the optio assisting Apollonius in the command of the *fabrica*. I had suspected from the start that there must be some involvement from the soldiers garrisoning the place. But it seemed I had been wrong. For one, these men were aware that Elector was lax in his duties, therefore making their task easier. Secondly, the slaves were speaking in my native tongue, not Latin. Their accents, though, were interesting. Edwin spoke like me, his dialect an exact match. Even without him telling me he was Chauci I would have guessed it. His companions, though, spoke with a gravelly undertone I had not heard before. If I didn't know any better, I would have guessed our tongue was not their own.

That afternoon, we were relieved of our normal duties to take stock of the latest delivery of armour. It heartened me to see the amount of replacement kit the Romans needed to keep their armies on our borders equipped. It meant my cousins among the tribes were doing a decent job. Between us, Habitus and I counted five hundred replacement helmets and moved them from the front yard to the rear, stacked up in crates, awaiting a transport ship to take them west along the river. I kept my eye on the slaves I had seen talking in the canteen. I didn't know their names, but they certainly knew me. I'd seen their stares in my direction when they thought I wasn't looking. Once more, their sun-darkened complexion and slitted eyes caught my attention. Was it similar to the corpses Balomar had stripped after our battle in the woods? I'll admit I still wasn't feeling quite myself, and didn't trust my judgement. But I felt a nagging need to see if the men had a brand on their backs. But how to do that? Wasn't like I could just walk up to them and lift their tunics. I'd never been that way inclined.

It was not until after our evening meal I got to speak to Habitus out of earshot of anyone else. 'They're doing it tonight,' I said to him as we washed dishes in the kitchen. Each night, the guards picked two slaves to clear up after the evening meal. That night was our turn.

'How can you be sure?' Habitus asked. He sounded tired. I knew he did not believe we were going to discover anything of significance. He was waiting in hope for Silus to walk through the door and tell him it was time to go back to the Fourteenth. I thought that was a week off, at least. Apollonius had not followed up on his threats to have us moved on to somewhere else. I guessed the centurion had been convinced that two extra pairs of hands about the place was no bad thing. If there was one thing Rome did not have a shortage of, it was slaves.

'I told you! I heard exactly what was said. And us being here is perfect. No one is going to miss us when they do the evening roll call. The soldiers know we are here. All we have to do is sneak out to the backyard, and we'll find out exactly what's going on.'

The Syrian sighed, wet hands rubbing his beard. 'Fine. But what are we going to do exactly if we get caught? We need a story.'

In the corner of the kitchen were two sacks of waste from dinner. 'We take them with us. Anyone asks us, soldier or slave, we just say we're taking the rubbish out.'

'I don't like this, Alaric. We've only been here two days! I think we need to keep our heads down.'

'Gods, man! You were the one asking me how long we're going to be stuck here! The sooner we find out what is going on, the sooner we are out.'

'And what do we do if you're right?' he asked me. 'Who do we tell? I've no way of getting in touch with Silus until he arrives.'

'We don't have to tell anyone. Just us knowing will be enough. Silus will deal with it once we tell him.'

'Will he?' Habitus asked in a small voice. He let the plate in his hands fall back to the sink. I've seen plenty of men fall into despair before. I could see it happening again before my eye.

'Wotan's eye! He's *your* commander, not mine! What do you think?'

Habitus took a breath before answering. 'I think he'll do what is best for Rome. But what is best for Rome might not be best for us.'

I let that sink in. I'd gone into this fully prepared for the old bastard to try to stitch me up, and I'd made provisions in case he did. Hearing those words from Habitus, though, filled me with dread. 'He won't leave you in here to rot,' I said. 'You're one of his. As for me, you let me worry about me.'

'Oh, trust me, Alaric. I'm *not* worrying about you. You know how many mates of mine are dead because of you?'

I shrugged. 'They're dead because they signed up to the army. Not because of me. And trust me, I've lost plenty of good people to your lot, people who were nowhere near a battlefield.'

'Like your mother,' he said, fixing me with a look. 'How is there a connection between Silus and your mother?'

'What makes you say that?' I said, dumbfounded. Me, who prided himself on possessing wits quicker than his sword hand, and I'm wicked with a blade.

'You kept saying the same thing over and over last night,' Habitus said, hesitant. 'I just need to know if I can trust you. I mean... Gods, I know I can't *trust* you. But trust you in this little endeavour of ours. Alaric?'

I slumped down to the ground, knees up to my chest. Habitus was in front of me, hands on my shoulders, saying something, but I couldn't hear him. My breath came in ragged gasps, and my heart thudded so hard in my chest I thought it would break from its cage. My hands tingled then went numb, then too my feet. I was gripped, unable to shake myself free. My body was in a weapons factory, my mind in the distant past. At the one battle I could never win.

* * *

All is fire. Thick smoke forces its way up my nostrils; dirt covers my face. A soldier kneels on my back, holding my arms out wide. My father is opposite me. He is wounded; blood runs in rivets down his bearded face.

'Alaric, just look at me. Everything is going to be fine.' But there are tears in his eyes, and pain, so much pain in his voice. 'Just look at me, son. We're going to get through this. All of us.'

I cannot speak. I am fifteen years old, and terror grips me. My father was a warrior once, and proud of it. But it was for my mother he swapped the sword for the plough, and he had done his best in the last ten years to make a success of being a farmer. Our home is small and cold in the winter. Our land unsuited for the growing of food. My father built a barn to store the grain he was planning to grow. No one told him, though, to raise it off the ground so the rats cannot get in. Even now as I lie here, tears flowing from my eyes, rats feast on the food that is meant to last us through the hard months.

'Don't move!' the soldier atop me growls. He punches me on the back of the head, and I eat dirt. A dog growls in the distance, and I hear the pad of paws on the ground as the beast runs for us. He is Fenrir, our hound, named for the Allfather's legendary

beast. *My Fenrir is no wolf of the gods, though, just a normal hound. 'Shut that thing up!' a Roman officer in a crested helmet shouts, and two spears fly through the night, and my hound barks no more.*

'No,' I sob. Why is this happening? Why would they do this to us? I think of my mother's words, the crazed words of a woman who knew her time had come. Still, I could make no sense of them.

'Centurion Silus!' a voice barks. 'Over here. Take these two around the back of that old barn and finish them off. Once this lot are done with the woman, we're out of here.'

'Yes, sir!' I hear the man respond, and I see the salute he throws from the corner of my eye. 'Vitulus, you're with me.'

We are hauled to our feet. My father still speaks to me, tells me to comply, tells me all will be well, but I am not listening. I catch a glimpse of my mother, the greatest woman I have ever known, in the firelight as we are dragged away. She is face down in the dirt, silhouetted in flames, and ten soldiers stand around her whilst another grunts away between her thighs. I cannot describe the pain, the anguish. I don't know whether I want to fight these bastards until I am downed, or just meekly accept my fate. How can I go on after this?

'Stand there,' the man named Silus says. I am spun around, my back to the barn, and I see him for the first time. He is young, a button nose beneath storm-cloud eyes, indecision written over his bearded face. The man with him is shorter, slighter in build. He sports a beard so thin it would be mocked in our lands. I read the doubt on their faces, and my eyes turn to the swords in their hands. Could we rush them? I look at my father, and he gives me a shake of the head. He is beaten. He will take his death and reunite with my mother on the other side. It is his only hope now.

'That is your wife?' Silus says to my father. He speaks slowly, but my father has a little Latin, and what he knows he has taught me.

'It is,' my father says, and his voice catches. Before he can stop himself, he is crying once more. Shaming himself in front of the enemy. But he has no shame left. Not now.

'I am very sorry,' Silus says. 'Not all of us are monsters. You know of your mother's links to the Suebi?'

I do not understand any of this, but my father nods, wiping tears from his beard. 'I do. I know you are here because you fear them.'

'Aye,' Silus says. 'I did not know we would be doing this, though.' He shakes his head.

I wonder where the men of the Chauci are. Our capital is just a short run away to the south. Surely our chief has seen the flames? Surely he is coming? I choose to believe he and his warriors are right then fighting their way to us, or dying in the process. Surely they would not have abandoned us? I think again of what my mother said to me. She must be wrong. She has to be.

Silus turns from us, looks out to the woodland beyond the barn. 'I want the two of you to run into those trees, and don't stop running. I will tell my superior I threw your bodies in the tarn.' He gestures to the body of water. 'Do you understand?'

My father nods, more tears spilling. 'We do. We do. Come, Alaric, we must go now. Come.'

I am too staggered to speak. My whole life, I have been raised to believe a Roman soldier would follow an order to the letter. There is an old joke that ripples among the tribes. If a Roman soldier is ordered to fart, he will do so, or shit himself trying. 'Alaric, come!' My father has hold of my hand, and he drags me away, past the two soldiers. My eyes fix to Silus as we pass him, and he stares back at me, his eyes full of sympathy and shame.

He thinks me weak. I vow to myself I will meet this man again. And it will be the last time he gives me pity.

7

I was still in the kitchen when I came back to. Habitus threw a bucket of water over my head in the end. He hovered over me, his dark eyes squinted as he looked me over. 'Mate, you've got some issues.'

'Tell me something I don't know,' I said through a ragged breath. 'How long was I out?'

'Not long. You still want to do this?'

I nodded, unable to speak. Habitus held out a hand and pulled me to my feet, where I stood shivering. He passed me a cup of water and I necked it. 'Don't suppose there's any wine in here, is there?'

'I don't think they supply that for slaves,' Habitus said. 'Come then, let's get this done.'

We left the kitchen. The corridor outside was empty, and we heard nothing as we walked through, sacks of waste in hand. We passed the sleeping quarters assigned to the slaves, and I stopped to peer in, Habitus hissing at me. But I needed to check something. I saw the two empty bunks in the corner where Habitus and I would usually be. The rest were occupied by sleeping men, exhausted from another day's hard graft. It was then I noticed what I had been looking for. A clutch of empty bunks, right in the middle of where a large group of Germani slaves slept. I did not need to check who those bunks belonged to. Five were empty, and I was certain we would find those men in the rear yard.

Carrying on, we were just ten paces from our destination when we heard voices. 'I've got a pass for the races tomorrow. Putting my coin on the Whites! Got a good feeling this time.'

'Gods, Marcus, you said that last month!'

'I know! But I've had a tip. Two of the horses they're running are being prepared for the Circus Maximus in Rome! If the Whites think they're good enough to run there, surely they're going to crush it up here!'

The second voice sighed. 'Please tell me that little whore from the brothel hasn't given you another tip.'

'Fulvia has contacts! Believe me, brother, this one's a cert.'

The voices muffled as the soldiers walked out of earshot. 'They don't seem very alert,' I whispered to Habitus.

'I'll take that as a win for us. Also need to work out how I can put some money on that race. If there's horses being prepped for the Circus running, I could make a fortune! No one bets on the Whites; they're shit. Bet the odds are brilliant.'

I rolled my eye. Chariot racing was one of the more popular pastimes for the citizens in Rome. I'd snuck into a circus on the Rhine frontier once and watched in disgust as perfectly good horses were slaughtered for no reason other than entertainment. It sickened me. Gladiators hacking each other to pieces I could understand; at least those men knew what they were doing. We carried on down the corridor until we reached the entrance to the rear yard.

Dumping my sack by the open door, I peered out into the darkness. I'd no idea what time it was, but it must have been late. The night was black as pitch, rolling clouds obscuring the moon. But even if I could not see, I still had my ears. 'Over there,' I whispered to Habitus, pointing towards the river. There was a chink of moving metal, the scuffle of footsteps. I tried to picture the scene in my mind. A small group of men, lugging weapons and armour to a collection spot by the river. Would they wait for it to be collected? Or leave it there for their collaborators to pick up?

I soon had my answer. Just as Habitus and I had crept out into the yard, we heard footsteps moving towards us. We ducked left, hunching behind an empty cart. 'Is that all of it?' a voice said in the Germani tongue, but in that alien accent I couldn't place.

'Think so. Can't see anything else here,' said a second voice. I knew it then to be Edwin. I could picture the greybeard saying it, half hunched as he squinted in the darkness. 'Told you we should have brought a torch. I can't tell if we have enough.'

'And alert the guards to what we are doing? We might as well have announced it at lunch! Come, let's be gone from here before one of those lazy soldiers thinks to get some air.'

Footsteps came our way, and Habitus and I crouched lower behind the cart. Habitus kicked up some dust as he moved and it rose lazily up to my face and tickled my nose. I breathed in deep, sure I was about to sneeze. 'Don't you dare!' Habitus hissed at me, but it was too late.

I held it in as much as I could, the only noise escaping me a soft coughing sound as I buried my face in my hands. 'You hear that?' a voice in the darkness said. Edwin.

'Aye,' came the reply, and the footsteps came crunching our way.

'Now we're for it,' Habitus whispered, his head swivelling left and right as he sought a way out.

'No running now,' I said, rolling my shoulders. 'You take the smaller one, he's Edwin. I'll take the big bastard.'

Two pale faces loomed in the moonlight around the side of the cart. We didn't give them the chance to shout out. I leaped at the bigger of the two men, the one with the alien accent. The one I suspected might have a horse brand burned onto his torso. We crashed down onto the dirt, dust spiralling around us. I had no weapon, but neither did he, and I gave him no chance to use his superior strength. I rolled on top of him, my legs pinning his arms to the ground, his legs flailing but doing me no damage. My fingers found his face, my thumbs his eyes, and I pressed down hard as I could, all my bodyweight crashing down onto his most vulnerable part.

There was a loud pop, and something hot and sticky sprayed my face. His legs stopped thrashing. I rolled off, gagging at the stench of whatever it was that soaked my beard. Using the back of my hand to wipe clear my eye, I spotted Habitus hunched over, panting, Edwin prone on the ground beside him.

Quick as thought, I turned back to the man I had killed and rolled him over. Lifting his tunic, I could just make out the marking on his back. Sure enough, he had been branded with the image of a horse. 'Knew it,' I muttered to myself. Habitus staggered over and joined me.

'You well?' he asked, nose scrunched up. 'What's that smell?'

'His eyeballs,' I said through a ragged breath.

'Nice. I just hit him with a brick.' Habitus jerked a thumb behind him. 'Much cleaner.'

'Good for you. Come, I need to wash this off me. Let's see what they were up to.'

We walked over to the river, the sounds of it guiding my feet. Distracted, eye on the water, I only knew I'd reached the weapons dump when I tripped over it. 'Wotan's eye,' I breathed as I stumbled back to my feet. Before me, in a great heap, seemed enough weapons and armour to arm a small army.

'How many times do you think they've done this?' Habitus asked. He stooped and picked up a helmet, replacing it in his hands with a sword, then a bow. He let out a low whistle as he pulled the string. 'This is decent. How is no one noticing this is all gone?'

I splashed river water over my face and scrubbed my hands, then rubbed my beard. I had been part of the team that had helped take inventory of the factories' finished stock. 'They're manipulating the count,' I said after a time. 'Think on it. When we were counting earlier, a slave with a tablet was recording the numbers we called to him. Those slaves must be in on this. Say they want to take fifty swords; all that slave has to do is lower the final count by fifty, and then no one knows they're missing.'

Habitus grunted, seemingly in agreement. 'I just can't believe that not one of the soldiers has noticed this happening. How lax in their duties do they have to be?'

I laughed at that. 'Is Roman incompetence so hard for you to comprehend?'

'I suppose not,' Habitus said with a sigh, letting the spear drop back to the pile. 'Just disappointing. We need Silus to come, and fast.'

'We've only been here a few days. I don't think your mate is going to come any time soon.'

'Then what do we do? I know a bit more about how this works than you. If we take this to Apollonius, he will do all he can to suppress it. He can't be far from retirement, right? He isn't going to want a mark on his record, or anything getting in the way of him getting his pension.'

I nodded. Made sense to me. Men were ruled by fear, whether they liked to admit it or not. Imagine fighting for twenty-five years, only to be robbed of your pension at the last by a group of plucky slaves that thought they could pull one off under your nose. You wouldn't stand for it. 'We keep our heads down, we know the slaves responsible. When Silus gets here, we tell all, and then we both get to go home.'

If only life were so simple. At that moment, two things happened. A light appeared on the river, the strokes of oars beating the water reaching my ears a moment later. And there was a scuffle of noise at our rear, two torches appearing at the doorway of the *fabrica*. 'Who's there?' a voice called in Latin, and hobnailed feet ran across the yard floor. 'Look, there's someone on the ground! Blood!'

'Shit,' I muttered, ducking behind the pile of weapons. Habitus did the same, and we shared a grim look in the darkness. Enemies to our front and rear, nowhere to hide. I'd probably faced worse odds in my time, but right then I couldn't remember. 'We need to move,' I said to Habitus.

'No shit. But where to?'

'Swim across the river,' I said, readying myself to leap into the water.

'I can't fucking swim! I'm from Syria!'

'Course you can't,' I sighed. A voice inside my head was screaming at me to abandon this man I had only known a few days. He was a Roman, after all, no friend to me. But there in that yard we were brothers, both fighting for the same cause. And you can call me an oath breaker all you want, but I do not abandon my brothers. 'Grab a sword!' I said, snatching one up and throwing away the scabbard.

'Who are we fighting here?' Habitus called. My first inclination was to take out the guards running at us. But those men were colleagues to Habitus, and he was looking out to the approaching ship with his teeth bared. We really were in a pickle. 'Why don't you grab a bow and shoot some arrows at that boat! I'll deal with the guards.'

With that, I was off. All the uncertainties, all the visions and panic that had been gripping my heart, melted away. Strip me down to my core and I am a warrior, and the battlefield is my home. I charged through the night, like a Draugr from one of my father's stories. The great undead, old warriors who refused to sleep quietly in their graves. My father used to tell me they would walk the earth when the moon was up, and to meet one was to meet death itself.

This time the memory of my father made me grin. I'd had a troubled child-hood, but it hadn't all been bad. It had taught me the value of strength, the flaws of weakness. I stalked through the shadows and was on to the Roman soldiers before they even knew I was there. I took the first one with a hack to the neck, warm blood plastering my face. Wrenching the blade free, I spun just in time to bat away a thrown torch that would have blinded me. Two steps forwards and I slashed the short sword, meeting my opponent's with a screech of iron, sparks lighting up the night. 'We need backup! Sound the alarm!' my assailant called, and I growled, hacking once more, wanting to finish the man quickly.

Habitus was loosing arrows behind me; I could hear the *thrum* of the bow and a shout of triumph as one hit home. I was still slashing in the darkness, half blinded by the light of the thrown torch. I tried blinking rapidly to clear my vision, my one remaining eye having to work twice as hard, but to no avail. The Roman ducked and slashed at my legs and there was a moment of white-hot pain on my left calf before he danced back into the shadows.

I was panting, stooped. No longer young, that was true, but still the fearsome warrior whose mere name spread fear across my homeland. Perhaps I should have learnt my lesson the year before; fighting my way across the northern tip of Jylland had very nearly been the end of me. But there I was, still living like it was the glory days. Pain lancing up my calf, I fought a fighting retreat for ten steps before the legionary backed off, content to wait for backup to finish me off. Reaching Habitus and the pile of weapons, I scooped up a Roman shield, the rectangular board heavy and unfamiliar in my hand. But I needed a shield. Breathing heavily, I turned to see how Habitus was faring.

'You know, you've been nothing but a disappointment this whole trip!' Habitus snapped at me, loosing an arrow as he spoke.

'What?' I panted out.

'All the stories I've heard about the great Lord Alaric, chief of the most fearsome fighting unit in the north. We used to shit ourselves when we heard we would be facing you. And look at the state of you! As if the panic attacks and nightmares weren't enough, a brief skirmish and you're shattered! Get a grip, man!'

'Only fair...' I said through a ragged breath, 'that I give these whoresons a chance.'

Habitus flashed me a grin. 'Looks like this lot don't fancy it,' he said, gesturing to the ship that was now rowing away back west. 'The guards dead?'

'One is. However, I fear we may have caused a bit of a commotion.'

There were more torches coming out of the doorway into the yard. Quite a lot of torches. In resignation, I threw my sword and shield to the ground, lowered myself to my knees. I hated submitting, but I could see when I was beaten. 'Now might be a good time to introduce yourself,' I said to Habitus.

Habitus called out his name and rank, standing with his arms held high and wide. He did not drop the bow, though.

'What in the gods' names is going on here?' Apollonius rasped in a throaty growl; the man had clearly been woken up.

Habitus called out again, repeating his name and rank. 'We have been sent here to investigate how your stock is making its way over the river and being used by enemy tribesmen. Tonight we found some of your slaves out here. They were piling weapons by the river. Their bodies are over there by the cart. We then found a ship making its way to pick it up.'

'Sent here?' I could see Apollonius in the torchlight. The man was red with fury. He snatched one of his men's torches and hovered it over the soldier I had killed. 'Sent here by who?'

'Sent by me, brother,' a voice said in the darkness. Torches whirled in the moonlight, and Centurion Silus's face lit up. 'I think it is time you and I had a little chat.'

* * *

I was cast in irons, thrown into the kitchens I had begun the evening in. A soldier threw me to the ground, stamping on the back of my head for good measure. 'Stay here,' he barked at me, before turning to leave.

'Gladly,' I mumbled, my mouth full of dust. I shuffled to a sitting position, sighing as I stretched my legs. My calf ached, but after a brief inspection I could see the wound was shallow enough, the blood already clotting. 'What a fucking night,' I said to myself, wishing I could free a hand to brush the lank hair from my face. It annoyed me, being taken away from the action. I wanted to hear what was being said. The fact that Habitus was still outside, standing next to his centurion, whilst I had been thrown into the only room with no other exit was not lost on me. I assumed there was a guard just the other side of the closed door.

I had a horrible premonition that this whole charade was going to be blamed on me. Cursing myself for being stupid enough to kill a Roman soldier on his own turf, I wriggled so my back was against the wall. My finger caught on something sharp on the ground behind me, and I flinched in pain. Probing with sore fingers, I found the edges of a needle. A smile touched the corners of my mouth. How many needles did the slaves sewing together the covers for the shields go through? They must be littered all over the place. Carefully picking it up, I shuffled my wrists around so I could get at the lock. Working blind wasn't easy, but I'd broken from chains before.

Counting time in my head, I reckoned a quarter of a Roman hour had gone by when the lock on the left wrist pinged open. I brought my hands round to my front and rubbed at my wrists. 'Not getting any younger.' I winced at the pain of moving the joints. It took half the time to remove the other, and then I was on my feet, unsteady still from the kick to the back of the head, half a plan forming in my tired mind.

I had always been paranoid. For many years I led a band of cut-throats and thieves. Paranoia kept me alive. But as I stood in that kitchen, bone tired, my mind ran through the likely scenarios facing me if I waited for a guard to come and retrieve me. Even if Habitus spoke up for me, even if Silus did, unlikely as that was, would any of that mean a bronze coin when I had killed one of their soldiers? Apollonius was not likely to shake my hand and thank me for my services. Silus certainly wouldn't. They had been using me as much as I had been using them. I knew full well what the deal was when I agreed to it.

'Think, think,' I muttered to myself. They were not entirely stupid, those Romans. Eating knives were kept in a locked cupboard, and a soldier had stayed with us whilst we cleaned them earlier on, locking them away when we were done and leaving us to the dishes. I tried using the pin to unlock the cupboard, but I have never been one for locksmithing and the bastard thing defeated me. The only thing I could find worthy of a weapon was a rolling pin left by the sink. 'Needs must.'

I had just been debating whether to wait for a guard to walk in and then attack them or force my way out when the door opened and two helmeted soldiers barged in. 'Shit! Get him!' one of them called, and both barrelled towards me. The kitchen was narrow; with the worktop and sink running along the wall, it was barely wide enough for them to come at me together. The first soldier pushed the second out the way, then caught himself on the foot of the second and sprawled forwards, his helmet colliding with the floor with a mighty bang. The second staggered back to his feet, but not quick enough. I leapt over his stricken comrade and smashed the rolling pin into his face. He went down. I hit him twice more for good measure, then turned and did the same to his friend.

Satisfied with my work, blood up, determined to go down fighting if this was to be the end, I pushed open the door and sprang into the corridor. Just in time for something to strike me on the back of the head with a wet thud. I was out cold by the time the ground rose up to meet me.

* * *

I hold my father's sword in a sweat-slick grip. The evening is unseasonably cold, a brisk wind blowing south off the sea. The first signs of autumn show in the red and gold leaves on the trees as I emerge from the forest. The day, though, had been glorious, and my father and I had used it to lay my mother's body to rest. My father has never been one for words, and I am too young to know which are the right ones, so we had stood in sombre silence, each of us lost in the past.

He had drunk himself to sleep as the sun slunk away in the west, my father. Lost in his cups, he had sobbed and sniffed, muttering unintelligible words and avoiding my gaze. I had stayed deathly sober. No one from our tribe had come to the burial. No one had come at all since the attack. The Romans had burned my father's rat-infested barn, but mercifully left our home untouched. Although everything that made that building a home is now gone.

To my front is the hall that Fridumar rules us from. Standing outside, I can hear the merriment from within. Men shout and laugh. Smoke from the hearth snakes its way into the clear purple sky. How can there be so much happiness in this world when I feel as though mine has ended? It baffles me. I am too numb to feel rage. Too shocked to feel anything. Clumsily, I stick the sword in my belt beneath my cloak and step out of the shadows.

'Don't see you down here much.' The door guard sniffs at me as I approach. No mention is made of the great fire at our farm, nor of my mother. In truth, I did not expect there to be.

'I'm meeting my father here,' I say in a shaky voice. My voice is breaking, so my mother kept telling me. For days on end I feel like I have been constantly clearing my throat. I sound like I've been eating gravel.

'Not seen Hengist down here for' – the door guard puffed out his cheeks – 'I don't even know how long. He's not in here.'

'Well, he will be soon,' I say too quickly.

'All right, lad, in you go,' the man says, nodding his head towards the door. I am just about past him when he speaks again. 'And I was sorry to hear about your mother. I know there's bad blood between your father and our chief, but there's some of us who think we should have done more to help you.'

So they do know. Somehow this shocks me. It really shouldn't. My father's barn burned for a night and a day. It's impossible that no one saw.

'Good to hear someone around here has a heart,' I all but spit at the guard, then walk through the threshold and into the lion's den. Inside, it takes me a moment for my eyes to adjust, the flickering light of the hearth flames causing me to squint. It is like a festival in the hall. Women dance their way between tables; men sit and cheer, taking huge gulps of ale so it runs in their beards. Jokes are called, the rebukes louder.

No one notices me. Just a boy, skin covered in ash from the flames, fingers brown with dirt from the digging. Just a boy. A boy with nothing left to lose. I walk through the throng, my eyes downcast. I might as well be a ghost. No one sees me. I am perhaps a spear's throw from the dais when I stop. Fridumar is drinking deep, one of his household warriors regaling him with some old story of war. A tale from their younger days, no doubt, when they rode horses and sailed ships, plundered and killed at will. We are a sea-faring people by nature, our harbour filled with sleek vessels that are the terror of Rome and their lands in Gaul.

Our chief, though, has not been to sea in a long time. Nor has he raised the sword that leans on the wall at his back against a soul, perhaps in my lifetime. He is an old man, past fifty winters. His glory days so far in the past, most men in the hall have not been alive long enough to see them. He is a huge man. Not muscled like my father, not tall like the warriors that ring the dais. Too much easy living has been his downfall, though his decline has been a slow one. I intend to hurry it up.

Still no one sees the dirty boy as he climbs the stairs. My senses are alive now. I smell the wood smoke and the sweat, the leather and the ale. It all hangs in the air like pine resin on a summer's day. My stomach clenches in fear. I will soon be reunited with my mother. Outside, the thought had kept me going. Now it roots me to the spot.

'Alaric?' a voice says from the dais, and Dagr, son of Fridumar, smirks at me as he emerges from behind his father's great girth. 'Thought I smelt something burning,' he jests at me, playfully knocking the arm of a warrior as he speaks, hoping to garner a laugh. He gets one. 'I'd ask what it is your mother demands this time, though from what we hear she's not speaking much.' He laughs at his own joke. This time no one laughs with him.

'Why are you here, young man?' Fridumar asks. He at least speaks with a degree of respect. 'I am very sorry about your mother, lad. She was a fine woman. Has your father sent you? I have been meaning to send a man to check on him. He is one of our own, at least.'

The implication of his words is not lost on me. My father is one of theirs. My mother was not. Was that why they sat and did nothing as foreign invaders raped her to death? My rage is back. It burns hotter than the fire that took my father's barn. 'I am here of my own accord,' I manage to utter out. 'Seems to me there is a debt to be paid.'

It is only then I realise that no one else in this stinking hall mourns. No one else has had their world turned upside down like I have. I lock eyes with Fridumar again; his dart from his son back to me. Is that guilt I see there? Could the chief of the Chauci have been complicit in her death? Not one of his warriors came to our aid, and that speaks louder than words of sorrow ever could.

Dagr laughs at my words, with all the bravado of a youth who knows he stands to inherit the chiefdom of the Chauci. Here, in his father's hall, he is untouchable. Or so he thinks.

8

Dawn was breaking when I came to. I was back in the rear yard, dumped on the dirt by the pile of looted weapons. Depressingly, the first thing my blurry eye could make out was a scaffold being erected.

'For what it's worth, I did try to persuade him not to,' Habitus said to me. The Syrian handed me a skin of water, helping me sit up.

'They're going to fucking hang me, aren't they?'

'Silus and Apollonius have come to an agreement. The missing weapons are going to be blamed on you. That way Apollonius can save face. The slaves actually responsible are going to mine in Dacia, apart from the two we killed, of course. I pointed out one of their friends to Apollonius. He grassed the rest up quickly enough when told his life would be spared if he did. Still, I expect they'll all be dead within a year.'

'Well, that's comforting,' I grumbled, rubbing the sore spot on the back of my head. I was dismayed to feel my scalp beneath my thinning hair. Must have looked like a full moon from the back.

'There's more,' Habitus said, looking around to make sure we were out of earshot of anyone else before he continued. 'The Fourteenth are marching over the river tomorrow. Seems these tribesmen in our stolen kit have caused a bit of a stir. The Quadi are rising up; word is the Marcomanni are too.'

I shook my head. 'Balomar, the Marcomanni chief, knows as much as I do about these tribesmen in Roman kit. He knows they're not your men. He won't fight.'

Habitus shrugged. 'Politics is politics. He'll fight if he has to.'

Groaning, I rose unsteadily to my feet. Gods, my head hurt. Maybe being hung wouldn't be so bad. At least the pain would be gone.

'Alaric Hengistson!' a voice called. 'In the name of Rome and her empire, I sentence you to death for your crimes.'

Silus and Apollonius walked towards me, each dressed in their full battle finery. 'Morning,' I said, giving both men a lopsided grin. I made a show of stretching, twisting as I did, glancing across to the far side of the river. Was there a rustle in the bushes? Gods, I hoped there was someone there. Two ravens swooped down and landed on the riverside. I wondered if they were the same two from the other day. I smiled. The gods had not forgotten me. 'And how are you fine gentlemen today?'

'Did you hear me, dog? You're going to die,' Apollonius spat. Silus just smiled. For him, this had been a long time coming. He could have killed me once, when he had my back pressed up against an old and rotting barn. If he had known then the man I would have become, he would not have let my father and me run off into the night. I would have been a fool to not at least consider this had been his plan all along. But I had Loki on my shoulder, and my own plans in my head.

I waved a careless hand. 'You know how many Romans have told me I was about to die? And I know, I know, before you start, fighting is pointless, accept your fate, blah blah blah.' I was strutting now, the lancing pain in my head forgotten. 'But honestly, don't you know who I am? Has he not told you?' I pointed to Silus.

'You are some barbarian from across the water who was once someone to fear. Now you are a slave in my custody about to meet his gods.' Apollonius's voice was iron, but I was pleased to see a touch of doubt creep into his gaze.

I took three steps back towards the river, feeling very grateful I wasn't wearing mail. 'Habitus. How many times did you say you've tried to shoot me with an arrow?'

The Syrian grunted. 'A few.'

'But you've never hit me?'

'Evidently.'

'A reassuring thought,' I said, and gave the Roman curs one of my best grins. One that was all teeth and didn't quite reach my eyes. 'Let us hope that streak continues.' And with that, I turned and leapt head first into the Danube.

I was an old man, even back then, and recovering as I was from a knock to the head, I wasn't exactly in prime shape. I could hear the shouting even as my head hit the water, and immediately I felt the river's current try to drag me down to its murky depths. I sent a prayer of thanks to my father then, for throwing me in that tarn by his piss-poor farm when I was a lad. There are not many people, in my land or within the empire, that are proficient swimmers. I, however, am one of them.

Even as I emerged and raised my arm for my first stroke, I heard Silus shouting for javelins, Apollonius haranguing his men to get me out, and on the other side of the river, a small clutch of warriors tramping out of the under-growth. I have said already how I used my time with Balomar before returning south to meet with Silus. The king and I made plans, one of which was arranging for some of his warriors to be over the river from the *fabrica* just in case I had need of them.

And by Wotan and his great bushy beard, I had need of them then. My one eye saw the figures emerge to my front. One threw a rope into the river for me to latch on to; the others raised their hunting bows and shot in flat arcs across the river. It is a wide river, the Danube. Seems wider when you're trying to swim across, the splash of thrown javelins hitting the water all around you. I could see the end of the rope, fifteen strokes away, and I pumped my arms, trying to block out everything else, all the fear, the adrenalin, and just make it to the rope.

I was panting like a dog when I got there. Snatching hold of the end, keeping my head down as two warriors dragged me to shore. Clambering up the far bank, breathless, I turned, another huge grin reaching my face to see the line of Romans on the other side, shaking their fists in impotent anger.

'Good job, lads,' I said through ragged breaths. 'You been over here the whole time?'

'Aye, Lord,' one warrior said. 'Our king ordered us not to leave in case you needed assistance.'

I nodded, breath thick on the air. 'Smart man, your king. Come, let us be gone from here.'

* * *

'So you learned nothing. And now I have to go to war,' Balomar spat at me over a spitting fire.

'I wouldn't say *nothing*, as such. I learned that it is not someone within the empire feeding weapons north of the river. Whoever is doing it is a man with connections within the tribes.'

'But you don't know who.'

'...No. But I saw the same branding on one of them, identical to the men we stripped in the forest. That is the key to all this, I think.'

'And how long before those Roman dogs work out it was my men pulling your fat arse out the river?'

Fat arse? I wasn't having that. 'I know you're a great king now, Balomar. But you and I have been friends a long time. I still remember when we first met, fighting in the pits your people are so fond of.' Balomar smiled at that, the memory shining in his eyes.

'I remember.'

'You remember what you said to me, when we drank ale in your smithies hut?'

'I said there were people ready to rise up against our king. People ready to take the fight to Rome.'

Balomar had been a blacksmith once. Forging iron during the day, using the weapons he had crafted to put men down in the pits in his free time. He had been a fearsome fighter, undefeated until I had bested him in a bout to first blood. More luck than anything else, and I'd be the first to admit that. But it was his fearlessness, his determination to see his people freed from the yoke of Rome that had won him his throne. 'So take the fight to Rome,' I said.

The king sighed. 'I will. But it needs to be on my terms. You know my aims.'

'You wish to lead a united Germani army against the empire, I know. Perhaps this coming battle will be the first step.'

The army of the Marcomanni were camped a few miles east of Goridorgis. Balomar had been summoned to a meeting of the southern kings, who had all been attacked by soldiers dressed in Roman uniforms. Only Balomar was adamant that those soldiers were not actually Roman – the others remained unconvinced. 'I'm telling you now, old friend, this will not go well.'

'Areogaesus will fight?' I asked. He was the king of the Quadi, the other large tribe on Germania's southern border.

'Aye, the old bastard is the one leading the charge. He's convinced it was a Roman patrol that set ablaze his crops and killed twenty of his farmers.'

'You manage to see any of the corpses?'

Balomar shook his head. 'There weren't any, from the "Romans" anyway. But it must be the same people. Something is going on here, and we've no clue.' The king slapped his thigh. 'I really thought you were going to come up trumps in that factory. What was it like, anyway?'

'The factory?' I puffed out a breath. 'Impressive. Their efficiency is infuriating. They can produce weapons in a fraction of the time that we can, of better quality too. Makes you wonder how they'll ever be beaten.'

'They have to be beaten!' Balomar thumped a hand on the turf.

'So go and beat them,' I said, giving my old friend one of my famous grins. 'We fight, we win, and then we find out who it is playing games with our lives.'

The king fell asleep soon after, snoring loudly as the fire between us died out. I stayed awake a while, listening to the quiet clamour any body of armed men always makes. I heard the chatter, the hiss of smoke on flames, and tried to switch off my roaming mind that flew through my past, searching for clues as to who would be bold enough to play a deadly game with the infamous Alaric Hengistson.

* * *

The sun must have risen somewhere, though it stayed hidden behind a wall of thick black cloud. All around me, men readied for war. Sedric had emerged with the dawn, bringing with him the moulded cuirass he had made for me. I strapped it on, once more marvelling at the genius of his work.

'I've one more gift for you, Lord,' he said through a sheepish grin.

'What is it?'

He said nothing, but pointed at the air behind me. I turned to see a red banner streaming in the breeze, a black raven flying through the claret. 'When you go to war, Lord, that banner goes with you.' I'll admit there was a tear behind my eye as I watched the banner ripple. I had not seen that banner for many years, until Sedric and I had set off on our doomed venture the year before. It flew in the midst of all the banners of the great southern tribes. There were bears and wolves, spears and swords painted onto different colours. But to my eye, the raven was the finest of them all.

A cheer ran out among the gathered men as more recognised it. Many were too young to have seen my war band in their pomp. But they would have heard the stories from their fathers. Now they got the chance to be in one. 'You get yourself somewhere safe, old friend,' I said to Sedric, gripping his shoulder and giving him a squeeze. The young man nodded. He had seen his fill of war and decided he had no part in it. I envied him his clarity of thought.

When he was gone, I found myself momentarily lost. None of my own band were with the host the southern kings had formed to take on Rome. They were still at my hall, protecting Saxa and my boys. I would much rather they were there than with me. But for a moment I was a captain without a ship. The kings and the chiefs had their household captains shouting orders, telling each group where to stand in the great line for battle. I had no one to order around, nothing to do.

The kings had gathered their host just west of a huge forest of pine. It made sense to me. The forest would guard our left flank, where over on the right the sloping valley we massed on gave way to a rocky outcrop, sporadic bushes and trees, making it unsuitable for moving men in war. That would form our right flank. We were positioned at the top of the valley, facing south. The Romans, whom we knew were aware of our position, would have to march uphill to face us. And they would have to come. No Roman commander could ignore such a blatant threat to their borders. Leave us unchecked and we could be across the Alps and into Italy within a month. Their fat emperor might even have to leave, then.

So we would wait for them to come at us, use the terrain and our numbers to our advantage. We were not blind to their numbers, either. The Fourteenth legion marched for us, supported by units from the Tenth and three units of auxiliaries. Some eight thousand men all told. It was shaping up to be one hell of a fight. A fight the Ravensworn would have revelled in. I thought about the ghosts from my past as I walked. Ruric would have been fretting, pulling his long beard and over considering every minute detail. Adalhard would have been strutting in front of his men, his long hair bare, sword sharp. Baldo would have probably tried to charge the enemy all on his own, his band of fanatics at his back. I smiled at the memories, another tear forming behind my eye.

Ketill and his Harii would have stood with me. My old friend would not have let me go to battle without him. His tribe had been fearsome in war.

Warriors painted in black, they were famed for attacking in the dark. All but
wiped from the world now, thanks to me. With a heavy sigh, I sat myself down
on a felled tree at the edge of the forest, my eye roaming the great host of
warriors before me. My mind lost in the past. War is a young man's game,
always has been. I thought back to the previous year, the battles I had fought
outside the crumbling fortress of Tastris. I remembered the blind panic I had
felt as I'd leapt from my ship on the first day, the exhaustion I had felt on the
last.

I was too old for war. A fact I had known for quite some time, but one I had
not fully been at peace with until then. Trading had brought me some happiness; spending more time with Saxa and my sons definitely had. It was a shock
to me, to realise I was not relishing the coming encounter. War was what I did.
War was what had made me the man I was. The man I had been, at least. A
horn sounded from somewhere, and a cheer rose up from the Germani war
host. The enemy was in sight.

As always before a battle, I felt the familiar twinge in my bladder, something that only got worse with age. I rose and walked a few steps further into
the forest before going about my business. It was only as I was about to turn
back around that the skin on the back of my neck began to prickle. Something
was... off. I stood stock still, tilting my head slightly as I listened to the sounds
of the forest. And then it hit me. Just like before, when I had been marching
south with my men, it was the silence that prickled me. Something had scared
the wildlife off, brought a stillness to the landscape.

Very slowly, I cast my eye from left to right. I saw nothing to disturb me,
nothing out of place. Until, when my head was turned to the right, I made out
the glint of an eye, staring right back.

'Fuck,' I muttered, before turning and legging it like a *nithing* that I
despised so much. I had made it ten paces when the first spear whistled
past my head. The forest was suddenly anything but silent. I heard the
scrape of bared iron, the shouts of men and the whinnies of horses. I felt the
earth beneath me tremor under the weight of the charging beasts. I ran and
half squatted, lowering my head as I tried in vain to make myself a smaller
target.

'Help!' I screamed, waving a frantic hand in the air as I emerged onto the
battle plain. Heads swivelled. I made out one warrior, clearly halfway through
a joke to three of his comrades. He turned towards me, the grin on his lips

dropping as he took in the horde of mounted men behind me. Rome had already come.

I've no notion of how the bastards got two thousand cavalry around our flank and hid them in that forest. The man who planned it was a genius. A now dead genius, I sincerely hope. But as our eyes had been fixed on the south, our sharpened spear tips pointing to where we thought the attack would come from, someone had been busy. The Romans had clearly been waiting for the infantry to arrive before showing themselves. But thanks to little old me, they'd had to show their hand.

I made it fifteen or so paces out of the trees before they were on me. I'd like to say at this point that I turned to face my hunters and fought them off with my trusted old sword as my comrades flooded to support me. Unfortunately, none of it would be true. I half turned to take a glance at how fucked I was, and I tripped on a rock. Sent sprawling on my face, I just had time to think of what an inglorious death it was going to be. I'd not even drawn my sword. Would I still make it to the Heroes Hall?

Flat on my face, the wind driven out of me, I bounced around like a ship's cargo in a summer storm as the mounted men thundered past me. A spear cut the turf an inch to my right, another just above my head. I stayed as still as I could. Sometimes that's the best form of courage. So I told myself, anyway. Once the ground had ceased its shaking, I risked a glance up. The Germani tribes had closed ranks and were in a fighting circle, their spear tips pointing out, so they looked like a giant hedgehog. Stumbling to my feet, I swayed slightly, then scooped up the spear that had been aimed at my head. The tip wasn't damaged.

Looking up, I took in the banner that flew between the dragoons all cavalry ride under. A slow grin spread across my face. A black circle in a field of red. These men were old enemies of mine. The Batavi. I'd fought them a few times over the years, most noticeably when my men had led them into a trap and dug pits in the ground to catch them in. Sadly, the Germani tribes were not as prepared. They rode with couched lances, the wicked blades snatching in and out as they galloped around the men of the tribes, taking lives at will.

I picked up the pace. They may not have been my men huddled in that circle, but they were the men of my people. And I was damned if I was going to lose to Rome and their German slaves. Timing is everything when darting through cavalry, and I waited for a small opening before charging through it.

They were looking in, not out, and I made it to the friendly shields without being stabbed in the back. Forcing my way in, I found myself next to Adalhard, Balomar's war lord. 'Lovely day for it,' I said to him, giving him one of my famous grins.

'Oh, look, lads,' Adalhard said, his eyes shooting me daggers. 'If it isn't the famous Alaric Hengistson, come to save us.' Despite the undercurrent of sarcasm lacing his words, the men around us did turn to look at me. I even thought I caught renewed hope in some of them.

'Where is your king?'

'In the centre, with the other lords. Just us fodder left on the outer ring.'

I grinned at that. 'You sound beaten already, Adalhard. I would have expected a man with your reputation to have more backbone.' I knew Adalhard well, as a man and a warrior. I knew his worth. What I needed then was for him to remember it.

The warrior growled at me. I could see the curls of his blond hair under his helmet, the stubble on his cheeks. His dark eyes pierced me. 'If you've got a plan, Alaric, best tell me now.'

Around us, the battle raged on. Blood spurted down my front as a warrior on the outside of our circle was speared through the chest. Another warrior leapt at his killer in retaliation, snatching hold of the harness the rider clung to. The horse, though, did not stop, and the warrior was helplessly carried along, crying out in panic, right until the moment a sword cut silenced him forever. Men were shouting, grunting, waving impotent fists at horsemen staying just out of reach. I took it all in, suddenly feeling something like my old self. I thought back on all the battles I had fought, some with longer odds than I currently faced. A plan slotted together in my mind.

'Right, here's what we're going to do.'

9

'Wait for it! Wait for it!'

We stood hunched behind our shields. The front rank of our men was armed with swords and shields. The men in the second rank had spears gripped in both hands. With their shields held high above our heads, the third rank could not hold a weapon, but I didn't need them to.

We had ridden the wave of defeat, and were still left standing to see it recede back into the sea of flesh and iron that faced us. Like rocks in the storm, we were immovable, and now we had our foundation, we could go on the attack. 'We move on my command! Remember, keep those shields touching.'

It was a plan I had used once or twice with the Ravensworn over the years. The front men held a tight shield wall, presenting the enemy with nothing but the tops of their helmets and their booted feet. The men behind them would then lunge their spears in the small gaps between shields, taking the enemy in the face or shin. I had added a third rank for this battle, men with shields held high, due to the fact our enemy was mounted and therefore coming for us from a position of height.

The trick to it would be to make sure as we advanced, the men did not separate. We were formed in a circle, so naturally as each man stepped forwards he would get a little further away from his comrades. But it was only one side of the circle that would be moving. The rest had been told to hold their positions. It had taken an age for everything to be communicated. Not for the first time, I envied the Romans and their efficiency. We had no orders that could be relayed by trumpet, no highly trained officers capable of making decisions without waiting to be told. Balomar had been right all those years ago. We needed a king, a man who could rule all. A man with the ultimate command. What we had was a coalition of chiefs and kings, each man thinking they were better than the other. They were divided by old grievances, constantly weary of letting another garner too much power. It was exhausting, and no way to lead an army.

The Batavi continued their encircling gallop. It was a tactic Rome had used before, and I thought I knew how to beat it. I was watching them intently, noticing when each unit passed. There were four wings in all, each around five hundred men. Between them, small gaps between the rearmost rider of one and the lead riders of the other. I was waiting for the standard to come back around; the black circle in a red field. Once that was in front of me, I knew I was facing the lead commander. Take him down, and the rest of his men might just lose heart.

And then, in a flash of light, I saw it. 'Move!' I growled at the men. No one had questioned when I had taken command, not even Adalhard. The feared warrior was at my left shoulder, and someone had brought over the raven banner, so it fluttered in the air above my head. Just felt right, going into battle under it. I knew there would be men of the Batavi who had seen it before. Grey-bearded veterans who had fought me in my glory days. They would see that banner, and they would know fear.

We moved quickly, scurrying like ants, tightly packed, a wall of shields that bristled with spears. The rear ranks of one cavalry wing saw us and lances smashed off shields, spears were thrown over our heads, howls of pain behind me. I ignored it all, eye fixed on the small gap between the two enemy forces. 'Get in that gap!'

The ground reverberated with the thud of hooves. I could feel the tension in the men around me, smell the fear. 'Remember your jobs!' I called, wanting to keep it as simple as I could. Simplicity is the key to war. Elaborate plans nearly always fail. Stick your sword in your enemy, and you win. Or a spear, in this case. Our wedge forced ourselves into the gap, forming a separate circle. As the column of riders galloped away behind us, we were left with a narrow front of horsemen before us. They rode in a column, making it as easy for the majority of their men to attack our original circle as possible. But now we were in front of them, not trapped to their side, and our line was fifteen men wide, theirs restricted to just four horses.

I saw the moment their commander realised he was fucked. A short man, clean shaven, olive skinned and bulbous nosed. A Roman patrician through and through. He was not some green pup like the fool Rufus Julianus who had escorted Habitus and me to Ratiaria. This was a man in his middle forties, a career soldier, who knew he had just made the biggest mistake of his life. I intended to make him pay for it.

'Spears!' I yelled over the cacophony, and in an instant, twenty spears fizzed past me. Flying in a low arc, they smashed into the legs of the foremost horses, sending the beasts crashing to the ground. That's the thing with cavalry. Take away their mobility, they quickly become a hinderance. As the horses bowed under the pressure of the spears, their riders thrown to an inglorious death, we charged. Sword drawn, I was on them in moments. I smashed my borrowed shield into the Roman commander's face, then buried my blade in his chest. Wrenching it free, blood up, I blocked a lance thrust with my shield, then hacked at a horse's leg, snatching the life of the rider as the beast stumbled.

'Ravensworn!' I called my old battle cry, whether they were my men fighting with me or not. But the surrounding men joined in, and 'Ravensworn! Ravensworn!' was the chant of the Germani as we ripped through the panicked cavalry wing. I don't know how long we fought for, but by the time we were through, the ground was nothing but churned mud that my boots struggled to grip. Dead horses scattered the field; riders were finished off by marauding warriors. Just as I had thought, the rest of the Batavi had retreated at the sight of their commander and his wing being struck down. Their banner was in our hands.

I took an offered waterskin and drank greedily. War really was a young man's game. First engagement of the day and I was done in. Horns sounded again. I recognised them as our own. Cursing, I realised the sound meant that the Roman infantry had come into view. We had won nothing yet. 'Re-group! Re-group on the kings!' a voice was calling, running around the battlefield, Balomar's standard waving in the air above him.

Huffing and puffing, I staggered on aching ankles back to the mass of Germani warriors. 'Wotan's cock, Alaric!' Balomar greeted me. 'Did we actually win? You look like you've had seven shades of shit knocked out of you!'

I gave the king a grin. 'Too old for this shit,' I said, still sucking from the waterskin like its contents were poured from the fountain of youth. 'Hell of a way to start the day though, hey?'

Balomar laughed and slapped me on the back. 'Good to see you've still got the Sly One on your side, old friend. We may need another of your little schemes before the day is done.'

He was interrupted by a young chief stomping up to him in a rage. The man had balls of spittle on the corners of his mouth, his face red with rage. I wondered if he had been a difficult birth; it looked as though someone had needed to reach into his mother and pull him out by his head. His forehead was so big I suspected he could remember tomorrow. 'Why are my men fighting on the left wing? I was promised a place of honour!' The spittle flew as he raged his accusations at Balomar.

The king and I shared a look, before he turned to the newcomer, took a deep breath in and raised himself to his full height. 'Frederick, you have what, ninety men? You are the chief of some pointless tribe who call marshland their home. I am the king of one of the most powerful tribes in all Germania. You're lucky you were invited at all.'

'I've more right to be here than him!' Frederick pointed at me. I could feel the tension rise in the men around us. Anyone who knew of me knew I was not to be trifled with. I was on young Frederick quick as a flash, my blade pressed against his throat.

'Say that one more time, you insolent pup,' I snarled in his face. 'I'll cut you a new fucking smile.'

'You get away from my chief, you old fraud!' a warrior with an axe in hand shouted at me as he bounded over.

'He's a legend! Go near him, I'll cut you to bits!' Another warrior challenged the axe man, standing in his path.

Essentially, all hell broke loose. German turned on German and anyone would think we had gone to war with each other. It is as I have said before. We were our own worst enemies. I still had my blade to Frederick's throat, and he was screaming insults at me even as I watched our army go to shit around us. Adalhard appeared at Balomar's side and he had the king's household warriors form a ring around him, shields up. Other chiefs appeared from the throng, some trying to calm everyone down, others bearing their blades, getting a few things of their own off their chests.

I sighed to myself, wondering at the point of it all. We had just won the first engagement of the day. And it had all been for nothing.

And that's the state our army was in when the Fourteenth legion arrived.

* * *

'Battering rams?' Balomar asked, raising an eyebrow.

'Just get your men ready for battle, Lord King. You hold the line, I'll do the scheming.' I winked at my old friend, then remembered I only had one eye and to him I might just have been blinking. I laughed to myself as I walked away, Balomar staring at me as if I were mad. Which, in truth, I always had been.

The lords of Germania had the men formed up once more. We were not pressed into a circle this time, but formed in a giant shield wall, our length matching the Romans. It pleased me to see our ranks were deeper than theirs. In battle, numbers weren't everything, but it was a reassuring feeling. I stood on the far left of our line with Frederick and his small number of men. The young chief had not been happy when I appeared next to him in the front rank, but he was smart enough to keep his mouth shut. He must have also noticed, same as I did, that his men stood a little straighter when I walked among them.

'Who here has a spear?' I said. A chorus of 'aye's' rose up. 'Then you men to the front. The Romans will throw theirs when they're thirty or so paces off. Shields up when they do. If your shield gets hit, get the javelin off it as quick as you can. You don't want it weighing you down. Our spears are our first defence. Use them to keep the bastards six feet away from you. Remember, they fight with those little pig-sticking swords. To use them, they have to be right up in your face. Keep them at arm's reach for as long as possible. Clear?'

Men grunted their assent. There was that quiet tension that spreads across a battlefield moments before a fight. No one spoke. Just the sounds of armour chinking as men rolled their shoulders. The smell of leather, of rotten bowels and fresh urine. Carrion birds circled overhead, their knack for finding food leading them to the slaughter. It had always amazed me how quick they would arrive. Almost as if they had scouts out meal-spotting for them. Well, they would have their feast later. But first, I would have mine.

The Fourteenth legion was a hundred paces off. I could make out Silus in the centre of their ranks, marching under the eagle. That eagle would not stay with the front ranks, I knew. Its bearer would hold his ground and let his fellow soldiers flood past him when they got within fifty paces. No legion would risk losing their eagle. It was the highest dishonour a Roman soldier could suffer. Seventy paces, and I heard the trumpet call that signified for the front ranks of the Romans to ready their *pila*. That was their spears, or javelins, and each of them held two in their right hand. In unison, each soldier moved one to their left hand, so it was held inside their shield, and readied the one in their right to throw. The gaps between the ranks opened up as they did it, ensuring no one got hit in the eye.

Gods, they were impressive.

'Shields at the ready!' I called, and other experienced warriors called the same down our line. I felt men step back, heard the collective intake of breath as they decided if they had the balls to stand their ground. 'Steady now!' I called, sensing a pivotal moment. 'The waiting is the worst part. Once they're in front of us, we'll be able to fight back. Deep breaths, lads. And hold those fucking shields up!'

I could hear the enemy now. Men calling to one another, centurions barking out orders. I scanned their front rank, my eye catching Silus in their centre once more. The bastard who had tried to have me killed. Once again, I cursed myself for a fool. What a stupid idea it had been to trust him. Habitus was easy to pick out alongside his centurion, his bow in hand. Even as I spotted him, the bow twanged and an instant later, an arrow swooshed past my head. I grinned. He really wasn't as good a shot as he thought he was.

And then, the grin was wiped right off my face. At thirty paces off, the Roman advance halted. They were on the uneven terrain left by the cavalry, walking steadily uphill. They would be tired, their nerves jangling just the same as ours. We never saw any of that, of course, just the grim efficiency of the Roman mincing machine. Another trill of a trumpet and the men of the Fourteenth bent back their right arms and loosed their javelins.

It was a warm summer's day, bright and clear. But for a moment the sky darkened, as if a sudden storm was upon us. It was not rain that hammered home from the heavens, though, but iron. 'Shields up!' I called along with a hundred others, and we raised them high, hunching beneath and praying to the Allfather it was not our time to take our place in his hall. Mine was struck twice, the second striking clean through the shield, the wicked point of the javelin scraping along my arm. I gritted my teeth and forced myself to not cry out in pain. Blood trickled down my arm, and my hand went numb on the grip of the shield. But I held it in place. 'One more volley!' I called, forcing myself to stand still.

Men fell in droves around me. Frederick, chief of the men I stood between, fell with a javelin to the head. To be fair, anyone with a forehead that size was a walking target. His shield probably hadn't been wide enough to cover it. His men, to give them credit, seemed not to lose heart as their chief fell lifeless to the mud. They closed ranks and pushed his body away without a word. Through the pain in my arm, I grunted, impressed. Never mind Frederick; those were my men now.

As a trumpet sounded once more, the sky darkened again, and with a sickening crunch another wave of javelins smashed into our shields, more men falling, more holes in our ranks. My own shield remained mercifully unhit, and I lowered it quick, using my sword to swipe the javelins from the board. Planting my sword in the earth, I moved my shield to my right hand, flexed my left a few times. The cut on my arm wasn't too deep, but it was long, running from wrist to elbow. Blood dripped to the ground at my feet. I briefly considered if I should find a way of strapping my shield to my arm, but then rejected it. I was Alaric Hengistson, and I'd survived worse than that.

The Fourteenth were closing their ranks back up, their shields presenting us with an unbroken line. They would not charge us. They had too much discipline for that. They would simply stroll up to us and start killing. Unless we could stop them. I glanced left, seeking the men Adalhard had sent into the forest. There was no sign of them yet. How long could it take to find a couple of felled trees? I did not want to abandon the men on the left flank. Left leaderless, they could well capitulate in moments. If our left flank fell, it would not take long for the Romans to get their cavalry around our wing, and then it would be over.

'Shields together!' I snapped, nodding in satisfaction as shields slapped together. 'Spears to the front ranks!' I had no spear of my own, sword already in hand, but I wasn't worried about my own capabilities. My blood was pumping, a second rush of adrenalin coursing through me. I needed to set an example for these men from their small tribe. Their chief lay dead in the mud and they needed someone to look up to. I was going to make sure they all saw me.

One final trill of a Roman trumpet and with a cry of 'the fighting Four-teenth!', the Romans quickly closed the last of the gap, bringing their shields to smash into ours. Our men did well, spears held out level, and for a moment or two we kept them at bay. The thing with a shield wall is there's nowhere to move. With a spear blocking your path you can't sliver around it, as when you do, you lower your shield and it leaves you vulnerable. Our spears scratched and nibbled on their shields, not doing any real damage, but simply being there gave our enemy pause. I took the moment I was given. Sliding out from our own shield wall, I ducked low and sprang across the small gap, covering it in three paces. Still low, I lashed out with my sword, feeling the blade bite on an ankle.

A legionary screamed and dropped down. I'd slit his throat before his shield hit the ground. Lithe as a cat, I was back upright, leaping into the gap and lunging left then right with my blade, my shield held before me, absorbing hits from the soldier in the Roman second rank. 'On me!' I yelled, feeling rather than seeing my brother warriors behind me leaping into the fray. I was hacking and slashing, snarling and growling. I was the man I was born to be. A lord of war. The Romans recoiled before me, men taking steps back when they should have been pushing forwards. A centurion smashed a soldier on the back with his vine stick, and an optio in a feather-crested helmet used his staff to push another man onto my sword.

My gilded cuirass was coated in blood. It ran in rivets through the intricate carvings Sedric had spent day after day perfecting. The golden raven dripped with gore; my sword was slick with it. The battlefield was a maelstrom of noise, as men thumped boots on the churned earth, bellowed at each other and iron screeched on iron. I grinned like a mad man. This was my home.

Somewhere behind me a warrior carrying the raven banner stepped out of our line, and I swear you could hear the cries of glee from our men in the Allfather's hall. Our left wing pushed forward, forcing the Roman line back two paces, then five. Legionaries strained on their shields, the men behind them pushing into their backs. I sensed the Batavi trying to force their mounts into the action, but there was no room for them to get around us, the forest giving us protection. So they sat on their horses, impotent, furious. What would those men have given to have a run at me? The man who had killed their commander. The thought just widened my grin.

I've no notion of how long we had been fighting. Could have been half a day, could have just been moments. I was lost to the joy of it, to the stabbing and hacking, the wails of the wounded and the cries of the victors. 'Alaric! Alaric!' a voice called my name, and with reluctance I stepped away from the battle and let a warrior take my place.

'What is it? We're winning here!' Adalhard it was, standing in front of me, sheeted in blood, panting like a dog.

'The men have the trees. And our centre is folding! We need you.'

'Balomar has the centre!' I spat at the man, not understanding. Balomar had the largest and best trained unit of us all. If he was failing, the repercussions for all of us could be dire.

'They're flooding their centre, pushing us back. He says he needs you.'

Cursing, I wrenched myself away from the battle and made for the centre, asking Adalhard to take my place on the left. He was an experienced war leader and known among the tribes. They would follow him. I called to the men emerging from the forest, three felled trees held between them. And I was off, ready to do what I was put on this earth for. Causing mayhem.

'Make way there!' I waved and pushed, pulled and threw men out of my path. The tree bearers behind me were sheeted with sweat, labouring as they were under the warm sun. We were thirty paces from the front when I let them stop and lower their burdens.

'I'm assuming there's a plan here?' Balomar asked me. He was wounded, a deep cut in his right shoulder. Two men fussed over him as he tried and failed to brush them off.

'Always a plan,' I said, flashing him my best grin. 'Why don't you get your little love bite there seen to and let me handle it.'

Balomar looked from me to the tree bearers behind me. 'You always were the sly one,' he said with a sigh. He was pale beneath his red beard, a slight tremor in his fingers. He had lost a lot of blood from the wound. I could see the indecision in his eyes. He was the king and kings led from the front. On the other hand, he was weak, wounded, and knew he was in no fit state to fight. I watched the facts tumble through his mind. Eventually, he gave me a nod and limped off to get patched up.

'Right then.' I turned to the sweating men behind me. 'Here's the plan.'

Once I had explained it, I left the men where they were and pushed myself through the ranks of the Marcomanni. Their king had left the field; their war chief was still on the left flank, plugging the hole I had left, but there was no let up from the men. Balomar was one of the few men powerful enough in our lands to employ full-time warriors. Most of the men who swelled our ranks were farmers or labourers, men who earned their living in peace. It was only in times of war they took up the spear. But Balomar had spread his warriors across his front line, and boosted by these hardened killers, the part-time fighters were more than holding their own.

I got to the second rank before I put my plan into action. 'On my word, I need all of you to duck!' I called over the raging cacophony. Some men turned to question me; others shouted in confusion. Most, though, too preoccupied with staying alive, stayed hunched behind their shields, eyes fixed firmly forwards. 'That you, Alaric?' a Latin voice called. Through a gap in the shields I made out Habitus, his bow and arrow now replaced by a sword.

'Salve!' I called to him. 'Good to see you're still alive! I'd make yourself scarce if you want to remain that way!' I looked for Silus, but couldn't make him out. The Romans regularly rotated their lines in battle. I had been hearing the trumpet blares throughout the day, seen the efficiency in which they went about it. It was another simple yet genius tactic they employed, keeping their men fresh on a long day of fighting. I was waiting for it to happen again.

For what felt an age I stood there, nerves on edge, watching the heaving match – for that in truth is what a pitched battle always was – in front of me. My tree bearers were ready behind me, and the moment I heard the trumpets call I was a man of action.

'Now!' I bellowed as loud as I could, and the line of warriors in front of me dropped to the ground. The Romans, distracted for just a moment as their line broke up as one rank retreated and another advanced, were too slow to react. My tree bearers shot forwards, their burdens held in a long line from left to right. They gave themselves a ten-pace run-up then launched the tree trunks at the Romans.

The bastards never stood a chance. The trunks smashed into the Roman line with a snapping crunch loud enough to rouse the gods. Men fell in droves, crushed under their weight, heavy armour weighing them down, suffocating them. 'Let's take them!' I called, throwing away my shield and taking my sword in a two-handed grip. I leaped back into the fray, cleaving two men down with one savage swipe of my blade. The warriors of the Marcomanni streamed in behind me, each man shouting themselves hoarse as they threw themselves at the disorientated Romans.

Spears flew over my head as we sought to capitalise on the distraction I had caused. Roman trumpets blared as their general desperately tried to repair the damage the Marcomanni and I were causing their centre. I pushed forwards, killing three more men in as many thudding heartbeats. We needed to push through them, to break their army in two and force them to retreat. We would not win an outright victory, I knew that, but if we could beat them to a standstill, hold them to a grudging draw, that would be a victory in itself.

'Keep pushing!' I bellowed into the maelstrom of noise. Men were screaming; the clash of iron on iron rang in the air. The stench of shit and blood burned my nostrils, but still I pushed on. My breathing was ragged, heart in my throat, blood thick in my ears, I blocked a thrust spear with my sword then sent the blade crashing down onto a helmet. I could see the command post of the Fourteenth legion, just three more ranks of legionaries blocking our way. Cut through them, and we would win the day.

It was then I sensed the change. The remaining three ranks of soldiers backed away, a man in a crested helmet in their front rank blowing his whistle to signal every step. Was it Silus himself? Too much was going on for me to be sure. 'They're not going to fight us!' I shouted through a savage, blood-drenched grin. 'We've got 'em, boys!'

A tap at my shoulder. Turning, I saw a beardless youth at my side, pointing with a quivering finger off to our left. We had pushed so far forwards we must have been fifty paces ahead of our right and left flank. Each were still engaged with the Romans, the ferocious, merciless crush of the shield walls still heaving and spitting at each other. But we had been fools, I realised with the sudden clarity of one who has inadvertently signed their own death warrant. Because streaming through the gaps left between the centre and the left flank came the Batavi for their revenge.

The ground shook once more as they charged, lances gleaming in the sunlight. 'Back! Back!' I tried to call out, but my throat was in bits, and all that came out was a ragged gasp as I heaved in air and tried to get my aching legs pumping. I could hear the jeers of the Romans as we turned, the taunts of those who know their work for the day is done. I stumbled over dead bodies, slipped on blood-slicked grass, on open bowels sprawled on the ground.

With every painful step I heard the thud of hooves on the ground, felt the tremble in the earth. Balomar was ahead of me, wounded shoulder forgotten. He had men formed up in a line three deep, a wall of wooden shields bristling with bright spear tips. He shouted wordless encouragement, his good arm waving frantically as he urged us on. I kept my eye fixed on him, refusing to turn and see my impending death get closer. I could hear men dying behind me now, hear the wet thud of lances finding targets.

Twenty paces. All that lay between me and salvation. I couldn't breathe, chest in agony, throat a ruin, eye blurring with sweat and blood. Feeling as old as time, all I could do was picture Saxa and my boys, their image driving me on, fuelling my need to survive. Ten paces and I could practically smell the rank breath of the horses. Men were falling behind me, the ones who lacked the desperate need to live. I'd seen it many times before, men falling for no other reason than they had lost the will to go on. That would never be me.

Five paces and disaster struck. I tried to leap a strewn body and did not have the strength in my knees and ankles to make it. Tripping on the body, I faceplanted the earth, my sword flying from my grip. Face buried in the mud, Sedric's beautiful cuirass weighing me down like an anchor, I jumped up and down on the earth as the Batavi streamed past me, throwing themselves onto Marcomannic shields. All I could do was lay still and send a prayer up to the Sly One and trust he still had my back.

For what felt an age I lay there, heart pounding so hard I felt certain it would give up and burst. So lost I was in my own desperate struggle, I did not realise the ground had ceased its shaking. Hands on my shoulders pulled me up, and blinking to clear my blurred vision, I made out the grinning face of Balomar, his grey-streaked beard spotted with blood. 'Still with us then?' he said to me, reaching out with his good arm and clamping my shoulder.

'What happened?' I asked groggily. My hands were shaking, and my legs were like anvils.

'They've decided they've had enough by the look of it.' I turned and looked back over the battlefield. Gods, what a sight. The dead lay in lines, their positions telling the story of the day. At the rear, closest to us, were the bodies ran through with the javelins the Romans had peppered us with. In front of them were the first of the dead we had lost in the crush of shields.

Beyond that, the field was carpeted in dead. 'The Romans will send an emissary to ask permission to take their dead,' I said. 'I would suggest you let them do it.'

The sun was sinking on the western horizon. We had been fighting all day. Little wonder I felt so broken.

'Of course,' Balomar said. 'I shall gather the other chiefs and feast in cele-
bration. We have won a great victory today, old friend.'

I said nothing, my eye roaming over the countless dead. A victory, yes. But
a victory at such a dreadful cost. 'You feast. I'm going home,' I said, and
scooping up my fallen sword, I trudged off, away from the field of death. The
birds would feast well that night.

* * *

*Dagr takes three steps towards me, the ghost of a smile dancing on his lips. 'So why
have you come? If not on an errand for your father?'*

*I look past Dagr, the worthless cur that he is. Five years my senior, though he is
no more a man than me. He swaggers down the steps, eyes roaming the people
thronged in his father's hall. They are his people, or so he thinks. And in front of them
he can do no wrong.*

'As I said,' I say in a low voice, 'there is a debt to be paid.'

*Dagr scoffs. 'Debt? What debt? You are owed nothing in this hall, boy,' he spits at
me, then throws his head back and laughs again. He thinks me small, weak. He
thinks himself a prince among men. That no one will touch him in his father's hall.*

*But rage burns within me. Rage. Sorrow. Guilt. A powerful concoction. His head
is still up as I bring the sword out from beneath my cloak. He does not see it. Still he
cackles, lost in his mirth. The warriors at his back do though, and they shout a
warning and reach for their own blades even as mine cuts the air between us. I swipe
for his neck, for the bulging jugular on this upstart little prick, this worm of a man
who thinks he can make jokes on my mother's passing and walk away.*

*I am not trained with the sword, and my swing is driven by pure emotion. I nick
his neck. A dribble of blood runs bright on Dagr's pale skin, but the cut will be
forgotten tomorrow. Dagr falls back though, hand clasped to his neck, and I barge
past him, ducking under one warrior and twirling past another.*

*And then I am on him. Fridumar, the fat, greying chief who sweats on his throne.
The man who did nothing as my world was torn to shreds. The man we all swore
fealty to, who in turn promised to protect us from any foe. In my mind, he is as much
to blame as Rome. I hack into him. Messy strikes that coat me in blood. I chop, I
swipe, I wrench the blade free and do it all again until there is no air in my lungs, and
my arms feel like they are strapped to anvils. They may soon be.*

I turn when I am done, look down at the hall from the height of the dais. It looks different from up here. Smaller. I am greeted with the stunned faces of hundreds of silent people. No one speaks; no one breathes. 'I gave him a better death than Rome gave my mother,' I say into the silence, then let the sword drop to the floorboards with a clang.

No one speaks as I leave. No one tries to stop me.

* * *

It was still dark when I awoke. I had left Balomar to his victory feast and trudged off north and west, reaching Sedric's hut outside Goridorgis just as the last light of the sun faded to blackness. My body was a wreck. Everything from the neck down screamed at me as I groggily rose and left the hut, emptying my bladder into the night. My feet were cramping, my calves on fire. Back stiffer than a shield, shoulders bunched and frozen solid. I was an old man. Back in my heyday, I could have fought all day, slept a few hours, then rose and done it all again.

I should have paid more attention to the lessons my body gave me on my trip north the year before. I was no longer that man. Why could I not just be happy as a merchant? Saxa had been right. I'd got myself a cushy little number, selling on the amber Isvilt and Eadger sent me from the north. So why did I feel the need for war?

Sedric was awake when I stumbled back inside, and he soon had a small fire going, a pot of porridge steaming on top. 'Are you well, Lord?' he asked as he stirred, eyeing me as I grunted and winced as I sat down on a stool.

'Oh, fine. Just some minor issues with my feet, legs, back and shoulders. Apart from that, I'm in my prime.' I flashed him a grin, and we both chuckled. 'Could have done with a strong arm like yours at my side yesterday.'

It was Sedric's turn to wince. He had seen his fill of war in the north, and had no plans to go back for another taste. 'Kai was who you needed.'

Kai had been Sedric's companion, and the two young warriors had entered my service at similar times, both requesting to be trained by me. Both men – well, boys they were then – had been exiled from their tribes, and were roaming the country as landless men. I had formed an army from such men once, a fighting force so formidable I had been the most feared man in Germania. I had been all too happy to take the two youngers in, and teach them what I knew. Kai had been a warrior born. Strong despite his slight build, lightning quick with a blade and utterly fearless in battle. We had burned his body on a beach in the north.

'Even Batur would have done,' I said, then winced in regret. Batur had been another young orphan who sought my patronage. He'd had dreams of glory, but it had been clear the way of the warrior was not for him. He had given it his best though, right until he had perished at sea in a storm. Another one sent to the Allfather's hall, awaiting my arrival. It had always weighed heavy on me that he had died not knowing how much respect I'd had for him. I'd always taken men for granted, spent their lives like Roman coins to get where I wanted. It was only after I had lost everything that I came to terms with what a monster I had become.

Youth is wasted on the young, as they say.

'He would have fought like a demon for you, Lord,' Sedric said loyally.

'I know. A jest in bad taste, forgive me. I'm heading home today. I don't think Balomar will be back for a day or two. He and his men will be too busy drinking the country's supplies of ale, I reckon. Why don't you come with me? Get some air in your lungs and some miles in your legs. Could do you good.'

The younger man smiled. 'Aye, would be good to see your boys again too. I'm in. We'll break our fast, then I'll head into town and get us food for the road.'

We ate in content silence, me wolfing down the plain porridge as if I hadn't eaten for a month. Part of me missed the rich food from the *fabrica*, the sauces and the different meats on offer every day. How easy it would be to allow myself to be sucked in to the soft ways of the Romans. The thought made me smile, though I didn't share it with Sedric. Once we had eaten, he left to secure provisions, and I went through some stretches on the grass outside his hut, hoping to breathe new life into my broken body.

Once Sedric returned we were off, making good progress as the sun shone bright on us. 'So you're no closer to finding out who's behind this?' he asked me as we walked. We had been trudging in companionable silence for a while, the sun passing its zenith overhead.

'None. If I'd have had a bit more time at the weapons factory I might have found out more. There were Germanic slaves there in on it, though it all got a bit messy real quick.'

'I heard you swam across the river?'

'I did. Well, there was a rope. It's not as impressive as it sounds. Anyway, I spent all that time there for nothing.' We lapsed back into silence. Me brooding on the situation. My body was still broken from the battle the day before. The stretching had helped a little, though the relief had been temporary. As the afternoon wore on, the aches I had awoken with came back. Worse, if anything. Whoever it was behind all this had wanted that battle to happen. But why?

My head hurt worse than my legs the more I dwelled on it. Who gained? What had they achieved so far? A cynical part of me thought Balomar could well have had a hand in it. All that had happened so far was the tribes had united and fought Rome. Wasn't that Balomar's dream? Though he and his men had been attacked by these would-be Romans, and Balomar himself had fought to see them off. Would he put his own life in danger to see his ambitions rise? I didn't think so, but I couldn't completely rule it out.

Who else had benefited? No one from within the empire that I could think of. Rome had stable leadership in Pannonia and Dacia, no young upstart commanders holding lofty ranks and seeking opportunities to prove themselves. My mind took me back to the previous year, to that worm of a king, Wilhelm, who had sought to make himself rich off a people worse off than him. Mass sacrifice, immense loss of life, and very nearly the destruction of his entire tribe had been the result. That, and he'd ended up being killed by me. His corpse paraded in front of his own hall.

Why did men do this to themselves? Why could they not be happy with what they had? The thought made me laugh as I related it to my own internal struggles. I knew too well why men did this. I was still chuckling to myself when my home came into view. I soon stopped.

'Something's wrong,' I said quietly, coming to a halt and half crouching, hand going to my sword hilt.

'What?' Sedric whispered. He had a sword hanging on his waist, though I knew he would only use it if he absolutely had to.

'Listen,' I said. And we did, silent as rocks under the canopy of the trees.

'Where are all the people?' Sedric said after a moment. 'Surely it is never this quiet?'

He had hit the nail on the head. Any settlement, even one as small as mine, was never silent during the day. There were children shouting and playing, blacksmiths hammering iron, cooks chattering over their fires. Stable hands exercising horses, merchants haggling their wares. I could go on. People were people. And they were never silent.

'Something's happened,' I said in an icy whisper, my blood freezing. Rooted to the spot, terrified at what I would find if I entered my home, I felt the tremor in my hands as I crouched there.

'I'll go,' Sedric said to me, placing a calming hand on my shoulder. It had been Sedric who was with me when I first experienced the grip of panic that refused to let go, when we were fighting far away in the north. He who had dragged me out of the water as I sunk like a corpse in my armour. And he now who gave me a reassuring nod before setting off into the deathly silence. I chided myself for the coward I had become. Should have been the other way around. Me, the experienced warrior, taking the lead and letting the younger man take his time. But there we were. Not for the first time, I cursed the cruelty of old age. How wicked it was to watch your body and mind wither, leaving you with nothing but the memories of the man you used to be.

I don't know how long Sedric was gone. Felt like a lifetime. When he came back, his face gave away nothing. 'There's no one there,' he said with a small shrug.

Was that a good thing or not? I had no idea. My knees shook as I stumbled on, determined now to see what Sedric had seen. The gate had been forced open, that was my first observation. Axes had cut the hinges, and the gate had flattened itself to the mud. There were no other signs of a struggle. No bodies littering the ground, no patches of blood drying in the sunlight. It was reassuring, but only a little.

I tried to put myself into my men's minds. What would they have done? What had I trained them to do? Through a curse I realised I'd given them very little training of any sort. Each of them came to me experienced in war, and I had spent little time drilling them the way I had with the Ravensworn in my pomp. So, what would they have done? Perhaps the more pertinent question was: what would Saxa have done?

The mud track that formed our main thoroughfare was deserted, but I could make out the footprints left by Roman military sandals. Whoever the men were who had been causing havoc in our lands, they had been here. Still I saw no signs of a struggle. Amphora were tipped over, oils and wine spilling out to stain the ground. Huts had been ransacked, their doors ripped off, straw pallets, cooking utensils and other belongings thrown out onto the street. But still no blood, no bodies.

Sedric jogged off and ducked into my hall. The doors there were still intact, but hanging wide open. He came out moments later and gave me a shrug. I didn't care what damage had been done to the building, as long as the corpses of my family were not within. The stables had been cleared, but by the attackers, or my men? Eric would not have run away and left his precious horses behind, no matter how strongly Saxa dragged him. The thought gave me small hope. But hope is forever a dangerous thing.

I had made it to the river before the fear gripping my gut finally released at the sight of a familiar ship rounding the bend, and two excited boys jumping and waving at me from the prow. It was the small celox I had taken north with me the year before. And my two boys were the ones jumping, the excitement in their voices clear, even if their words were not.

11

'They came to kill us, Father!'

'Mother said lots of bad words!'

'Faramund said we can use spears if we're ever attacked again!'

'Eric was scared! I wasn't though! I was ready to fight!'

My worries dissipated like morning dew as I grinned at Ludwig and Eric, jumping up and grabbing me even as they took turns to tell me what had happened. Saxa had disembarked after them, still looking flustered, and she kept her distance as the boys continued to squeal in delight.

'Sounds like you two have had an adventure!' I said, lowering myself and engulfing both in a hug. I kissed their cheeks, not allowing thoughts of what could have happened to sneak into my mind. Happiness is a precious thing. Embrace the moments it flourishes; let everything else wash away.

'Have you been fighting, Father? You've got cuts all over your face!'

'Yes. I've had an adventure of my own. I'll tell you about it later. Right now I need a moment with your mother. Why don't you help Faramund and the others get our home straightened back out. Can you do that?'

With more excited squeals, they ran off and left me with a beaming grin fixed beneath my beard. That soon faded when left face to face with my wife.

'Where in the gods' names have you been?' she snapped at me, even slapping my cheek so hard I had to check she had not dislodged a tooth. 'Why did you choose to go and play at being a spy when you knew full well there was a dangerous enemy loose close to home?' She hit me again, though I gratuitously noticed the second hit was softer than the first.

'I was trying to find out what was going on!' I said in my defence, in a shamefully high-pitched tone.

'And did you?'

'No.'

'So the tribes think it is Rome, and Rome thinks it is the tribes. I'm assuming there was some sort of battle?'

'Big one.'

'And you got yourself right in the thick of it?'

'I dipped in and out.'

'When are you going to grow up, Alaric?'

I gave her my brightest grin. 'Come on, you wouldn't have me any other way and you know it.'

She scowled, though I thought I saw the hint of a smile dancing in her eyes. 'Are you well?' She looked me up and down, as if seeing the cuts and bruises for the first time.

'Been better,' I said through a wince. 'Truth is, I've come to realise I'm too old for this shit.'

'Pretty sure that's what you said when you came home from the north last year. Speaking of the north.' She turned and gestured to the ship, sitting pretty in the shallows.

My grin returned as I saw two figures clamber down the ladder and onto dry land. Eadger, the former carpenter-turned-warrior, who had stood at my side as we fought tooth and nail for his tribe's survival. And Hilde, the warrior woman of the Cimbri. Leader in battle, formidable out of it. The two of them had come to be among my closest friends.

There was a joyous reunion, full of hugs and jokes and merriment. Sadly, it did not last long. 'So what happened?' I asked the three of them. Sedric had ambled over and gotten his share of hugs and welcomes, and he joined us as we moved away from the celox, where the people of my settlement were still disembarking.

'Eadger and Hilde got here yesterday morning,' Saxa started. 'Another load of amber for the merchant company you're trying so hard to avoid building,' she said with a pointed look at me. 'Not long after Faramund took the warriors out for a march, just to get some exercise in their legs. They were back almost as soon as they left, said they'd seen a Roman army on the road coming right for us.'

'And they didn't stand and fight?' I said with disgust.

'They said there were over fifty of them, and you left just a handful of warriors to protect us!'

'Well, in my defence I've only got a handful of warriors.'

'Then perhaps it is time you got some more! Anyway, we dumped the amber off the celox, then loaded everyone on and sailed upriver. We waited a day before coming back, just to be sure it was safe.'

'Did you see them?' I turned to Eadger and Hilde.

Eadger hadn't changed a bit since our last encounter. His hair was cut short. He had taken a wound to the head in the final battle for Tastris, the capital of the Cimbri, and ever since had kept his hair closely cropped as he said it cut down on the itchiness. Hilde was as fearsome as ever, though the bone armour she had been wearing when we first met was now replaced with mail, a gift from me after we had fought together the previous year.

'Aye, we saw them. There were a lot of the bastards, too many for your men to see off. It was the right decision, getting out of here,' Eadger said with authority.

'So what's the plan?' Hilde asked me. 'You got more men you can call on?'

I blew air out my cheeks. 'No, not really. Balomar might lend me some of his. Adalhard, his war chief, may well march with me. But I'm still none the wiser as to who it is doing all of this.'

'You should go and see my father,' Saxa said. 'I know you two don't exactly get along!' she cut in before I could protest. 'But he came north to save you last year, didn't he?'

'Only because you begged him,' I said sulkily. 'Besides, the Chauci are far away to the north. Whoever is doing this is in the south, I'd bet my life on it.'

'I'm more concerned that you are betting *my* life on it. Let alone our boys. Go and see my father. The Chauci are a powerful tribe, with many ears. If something is happening, my father would have heard about it.'

'But—'

'I am *not* asking you, Alaric. I am telling you!'

I sighed and looked to Eadger and Hilde for support. Eadger gave me a shrug, Hilde a knowing smile. 'Looks like I'm off to see Dagr then.'

* * *

It was a cloudy day. Misty rain hung in the air as my small celox beached itself on the shallows of the river close to Dagr's hall. Disembarking, I felt an unfamiliar twinge of fear in my gut as I stared up at the place I had once called home.

Last time I had set foot in that hall had been to kill Fridumar, Dagr's father. I could still remember it, the recent dreams bringing it to the forefront of my mind. What sort of reception could I expect? To Dagr I was the husband of his daughter. I was only that out of necessity on his part. He had offered me her hand out of desperation, fearing the noose of the Suebi growing tighter around his neck. He had thought then an alliance with the Ravensworn would be enough to save him. He had not counted on his treacherous son trying to take it all from him, too.

But I had killed that son, and that was another un-penetrative bridge that lay between me and the man I hoped could offer me salvation, or even just some answers.

'You waiting for an invitation?' Hilde said. She and Eadger had come with me, Sedric too, just for old times' sake. The three of them stood behind me as I looked up at the hall, lost in memory.

'I ever tell you I had a horse called Hilde once?'

'You did,' she said.

'I much preferred the horse.'

I was about to move, to force my ageing legs up the hill and face my fate, when the Spinners intervened and my fate came down the hill to face me. It looked as I had envisioned it would. Spear tips glinting in the rain, round shields and helmeted heads. A lot of them.

'Well, at least we know Dagr has plenty of warriors to spare us,' Eadger said. He brought himself up to his full height and drew his sword, moving to stand at my shoulder. Hilde did the same on my other side, Sedric beside her. It was good to have friends.

'You are not welcome here!' Dagr called to me from behind the safety of his shield wall. 'Just because we are family does not mean we are friends.'

Ain't that the truth, I thought as I took a step forward and stretched my arms wide. 'I come in peace!'

'Take another step and you'll be in pieces! What do you want? You old rogue.'

'I want to talk. Have you heard about what's happening in the south?'

Dagr merely shrugged. 'Word got to me of some battle with Rome, your old friend Balomar up to his neck in it. I assume you were with him. Got nothing to do with me as far as I can see.'

The rain got heavier, spitting off my helmet and running into my beard. I gave the sky a grimace. 'Has word reached you as to why there was a battle? There's some strange goings on in the south. My family has become mixed up in it. I need answers.'

'Saxa and the boys safe?' Dagr asked. He pushed himself through his shield wall so he stood face to face with me, concern etched on his face. He was my senior by a handful of years, though those years seemed to have treated him much kinder than they had me. Whilst I had spent my youth on horseback, roaming from one fight to the next, Dagr had spent his in the comfort of his hall. It was rare for the Chauci to involve themselves in the politics of Germania. Dagr kept himself to himself, only leading his men into war when all other options had been exhausted.

He was tall and broad, his waistline as trim as when he was a young man. His beard was sparse and streaked with grey, though it covered an unlined face that had never known hardship. I could still make out the white scar on his neck, though, where my sword had cut him the night his father left this world. 'Aye, they're safe. And I'd like to keep it that way.'

'So what do you need from me? I saved your worthless arse only last year! What sort of trouble have you got yourself into this time?'

I grinned at that. Some men just never change. 'Actually, it seems this time the trouble has found me. Why don't you invite us into the warmth of your hall, and we can talk about it without the gods pissing on us.'

Dagr looked back to his hall, tall and proud atop the hill. He seemed to weigh it in his mind. 'You have taken much from me over the years, Alaric. Understand it when I say you might not find yourself welcome in my hall. Family or not.'

'I know all too well what I have taken from you. But let us not forget what drove me to do it. You ever spent a night listening to your mother being raped to death, Dagr? I can assure you, that sort of shit leaves a scar.'

He hung his head at that. I could see the memory burning behind his eyes, just as it did in mine. Me walking into that hall, his smirking face greeting me. The jokes about my mother, the certainty that I could not hurt him. All of us had demons in our past, moments we wish we could erase from our memory. But always they were lurking in the depths, creeping out when you least expected it. Eventually, Dagr gave a small nod, as if to himself, and turned and walked back to his hall. He stopped halfway up the hill, turned to me, and waved me forward.

Taking a deep breath, I pressed on, my loyal friends grouping around me.

* * *

'So you've come to me for what? An army?' Dagr said. We sat on the dais in his hall, around the table where I had killed his father. Dagr feasted us with roasted boar and strong ale, then sent his guards away so we could talk in private.

'Just a small one,' I said with a grin. I had drunk too much, and I sat back in my chair, feeling more relaxed than I had in an age.

'Oh well, as long as it's just a small one!' Dagr scoffed. 'I lost ten men last year in that battle to save your arse. Men are hard to replace. As you well know.'

I nodded, as I knew it to be true. The nights I had spent tossing and turning after a prolonged war with the Ravensworn, wondering how I was going to fill the gaps in our ranks. One summer, I had lost a hundred and fifty men in one campaign. It had nearly been the end of us. Once my enemies knew of my weakened state, they bounded together and spent an autumn hunting us, when they should have been at home taking in their harvests. It had been a lean winter for many of our people.

'How long before these pretend Romans reach your lands?' I asked him. 'They won't stay in the south forever. They'll run out of settlements to raid. Balomar and the other southern chiefs will hunt them. Mark my words, Dagr, they'll come north. And when they do, your people will suffer.'

'And when they do, I'll deal with it. Until then, I cannot see how this is my problem.'

'You remember the bit where they nearly killed your daughter and grand-sons? Pretty sure that makes it your problem.'

Dagr sighed. 'Saxa sent you, didn't she?' I nodded. Dagr mused on that a moment. 'So she wants me to give you men, so you can hunt down whoever is doing this?'

'That's the long and short of it, aye.'

He looked around his hall at the banners that hung from the ceiling. 'There is something I need to discuss with you, but we need to speak alone,' Dagr said, with a pointed look at Eadger, Hilde and Sedric, who sat silently at the table.

'We'll get some air,' Eadger said, giving me a nod. Dagr waited until they had left before speaking again.

'I am an old man, Alaric. An old man who has no heir. Thanks to you, I might add.'

'Warin would have come for you, eventually. Power went to his head. You know that as well as I. Anyway, wasn't as if you had any great love for the boy.'

Dagr chuckled. 'You've more front than a Roman legion, I'll give you that. But there is a touch of truth in what you say. But I promised the boy's mother before she died that I would always have his back. I broke that promise, thanks to you.'

'Where are you going with this?'

'Can you not work it out? Your boys are next in line to be chief of the Chauci. I would have Ludwig, your eldest, here with me, so he can begin his training to lead my people.'

I scoffed at that. 'He's nine!'

'I was young when my father started instructing me. And just as well he did, given how young I still was when he was taken from me.'

Dagr gave me a pointed look, and I had sense enough to hang my head. Truth was, I could well picture Ludwig jumping at the chance. He was loud and brash, endlessly confident, and had a way of bending people to his will. Chances were, he would grow into a fine leader one day. But – and it was a big but – he was still my son. 'Saxa will not want to be parted from the boy.'

'I know. That is why she and Eric will have to accompany Ludwig here.'

That hit me like a hammer. 'You would take my family from me?'

'No,' Dagr said, though he tilted his head slightly, as if he were trying to think of the best way to sell his lie. 'You would be welcome any time. Though you and I both know how itchy your feet get when left to your own devices for too long. How long did you stick to being a merchant for?'

I raised an eyebrow at that. I had never told Dagr that's what I had been doing. The man had ears all over Germania. My resolve stiffened then. There was no chance he had been so ill informed as to the goings on in the south. It wouldn't surprise me if the old whoreson knew exactly who was behind it all.

'So you give me warriors, and in return my wife and children move back here. I am welcome to come and stay whenever I wish, but free to come and go as I please. That right?'

Dagr nodded. 'Freedom. That is all you have ever desired. I will not take that from you.'

I mused on it a while. 'How many men?'

'Ten.'

I scoffed. 'A hundred.'

'What do you think I am? Some great king? A hundred is pretty much all I have. I'll give you twenty, that should be enough with what you already have to see this done.'

'Fifty,' I said.

It was Dagr's turn to brood. 'Fifty,' he said eventually, spitting on his hand and holding it out.

I did the same and shook his hand, my grip more certain than my mind. Had I just given up my family? And for what? Was a small band of men pretending to be Romans really worth it? How long before someone else stepped in to deal with them? Balomar, or one of the other southern kings? But it was done now, and without another word I rose and headed out to the night. The rain had stopped, the sky clear and the air crisp. My friends stood in a small huddle, passing around a jug of ale.

I gave them a nod and walked off into the night. I needed time to think. And to perhaps take counsel from a man I had not seen in a very long time.

* * *

The farm hadn't changed much. Just a small scrap of land on the northern boundary of Chauci territory. The dawn light painted it in orange hue, and I stopped on the path and just stared for an age, my youth coming back to me in a flood.

The tarn glistened green. I could almost see myself splashing and thrashing for my life after my father had thrown me in. Our hound barking, sniffing the edge of the water, desperate to come in and save me, but held back by fear. My mother's enraged screams, berating my father, who stood, impassioned, on the long grass, seeing if his son had enough resolve to save himself.

I did. Just. I walked past the patch of dirt on which he had trained me on the arts of the sword, lessons that had paid dividends in later life. The barn had been rebuilt, no more the smoking husk it had been the day the weak sun broke after my mother's murder. Still, my father had not learned his lesson, though, and the walls were built straight onto the ground. Should have been built on stilts.

My father had always been a stubborn man.

And there he was, that stubborn old fool. He seemed smaller than when I had last laid eyes on him. Though I did admittedly still have two eyes that last time. He had seen me since, when I was delirious with pain after Silus had stripped me of an army and an eye. Saxa told me he had stayed for weeks, looking after me and my family. I remembered none of it.

As if sensing me, my father stood from where he had been kneeling, his back not straightening with his legs. His hair had thinned, his pale scalp showing through his wispy, greying locks. He did not turn to look at me. A spade fell from his numb hand, his eyes fixed on his boots. I don't know how long we both stood there, feeling each other's presence. 'Been waiting a long time for you to walk back down that path,' he said after a time. He did not raise his voice, but there was strength enough left in it for the sound to carry the distance.

'Me too,' I breathed, my eye still fixed on the stoop of his back. 'Somehow, I never thought I'd make it.'

'Me neither. Never gave up hope, though.' He turned then, and fixed me with a smile. It was still him, still the man I remembered, though age seemed to have softened his hard edges. His eyes were wet, lined with red, the whites faded to off yellow. His face a crisscross of wrinkles and lines, a fluffy beard clinging on to the underside of his chin. Took him an age to walk towards me, his steps reduced to a slow shuffle. We hugged when he did, and I breathed in his scent, the scent of my youth, and felt a tear prick in the corner of my eye. I was home.

'Come inside, we can talk,' he said, taking my arm and pulling me along.

He poured us ale, and I sat in the living space of my childhood home, staring around in wonderment. 'Not changed much, eh?' my father said, lowering himself onto a wooden stool older than he was. 'I'd always meant to spruce the place up a bit. Guess I never got around to it.'

On a chest by the fire was a collection of wooden figures I had played with as a boy. My father used to have a friend who was a carpenter. He had made them for me when I was young. I couldn't remember the man's name. There was a blanket my mother had knitted together, cooking pots hanging from the same hooks they had been on a lifetime ago. 'I feel as though I've gone back in time,' I said, and my father laughed.

'If only we both could. Oh, to have my time again.' He stared at me with those wet eyes. 'How are you? You look healthy.'

I almost laughed at that. I was covered in cuts and bruises, tired from travelling, and weary to my bones. I did not feel healthy. 'I've been better, truth be told. Been having a bit of trouble of late.'

'Well, the last time I laid eyes on you, you were half dead. That eye has healed well,' he said, pointing to the ruin of my left eye. 'Does it still leak pus?' I shook my head. 'Good. Seems I did something right, at least.' I winced at that. I knew he thought he had messed up with me. The thought must have been weighing him down through the long and lonely years. 'Tell me what is troubling you, boy,' he said, and so I did.

I spoke for an age. The sun rose, and the day passed us by. We sat in the gloom, he and I. He listened, I spoke, and to my surprise, I found the words tumbling from my mouth.

'So to save your people you must sacrifice your family?' he said when I had finished. 'It is a good home you have built for them down there.'

'Aye. It is. I do not want to live under the shadow of Dagr. I am not even sure I want my son to grow up and be chief. I have seen so much blood, all of it from men who sought power. Part of me thinks it better my boys grow up to be farmers, to live in peace and let the world pass them by.'

'That life was not enough for you,' my father pointed out. 'But you have come to the same conclusion I did once my fighting days were over. Sometimes you have to live through the bad times to recognise the good ones. I am not a wealthy man; far from it. But there is a satisfaction to be taken from an honest day's work in the fields. A sense of pride I never got from the sword.'

I nodded at that. 'I have been selling amber. I made friends in the north last year; they give me a steady supply. When this is over, that is what I shall return to.'

'Saxa came and saw me whilst you were in the north. Whatever took you up there, anyway?'

'Long story,' I grunted, in no mood to relive it all. 'Didn't start well, didn't end well. Let us leave it at that.'

My father chuckled. 'One day you'll grow up.'

'Saxa says the same thing. So what should I do, Father?'

He was not my real father, a fact that had hung over the two of us over long, absent years. I had been a man grown when I found out. Childhood memories long suppressed had surfaced in my mind as certain truths were made clear to me. But blood was only worth so much. He was the man who had raised me, the man who had stood by my mother as she raised the son of a king in secret. And he had loved her more fiercely than any man had ever loved his wife. I knew that to be true.

Loved her so much that even when he knew she was dying, when her screams filled the night and he was powerless to change it, he focused his energy on making sure her son got through it. Courage. It comes in many forms.

'Firstly, I think you should take Dagr's offer. I'll keep an eye on Saxa and the boys when they're here. Having their grandad around for them cannot hurt. You will find a way to make it work; you and Saxa always do. And secondly' – he paused a moment, taking a deep breath – 'you should go and see Haribert.'

That made me scowl. 'Haribert, as in chief of the Anglii, Haribert?'

'The same.'

'Why?'

'Because I think you'll find his son is the one leading the men you are looking for.'

My mouth blubbered like a fish out of water. I started ten sentences but never got more than three words into them. I thought about it a moment, remembering the little whoreson who had given me such a hard time the year before. And the more I thought about it, the more it made some sense.

'His father kicked him out last year. Word on the street was you had something to do with that,' my father said, giving me a pointed look. 'He went south, and from what I hear, he's trying to make a name for himself.'

'How have you heard that when no one else has?'

My father shrugged. 'I'm a man about town. I ask questions.'

'Son of a bitch,' I muttered, but I wasn't talking to my father. I was thinking about a spoilt brat, strutting in his armour on a beach, demanding I pay tax to sleep on his lands. 'How many times do I have to beat him?'

12

Haribert smiled at me like I had been expected. He was the bear of a man I remembered from the year before. A loveable rogue, a bit like myself. I had killed one of his finest men in single combat within a circle of shields in Tastris. Haribert could have felt well within his rights to finish me off, especially with his enraged warriors egging him on. But he had not. He shook my hand and congratulated me on my victory. A man of his word. If only the same could be said of his son, Sigimund.

'I know why you are here,' he said to me through a sigh. 'He's an industrious little bastard, you've got to give him that.'

'That little cur will be lucky if I give him a clean death. Where is he?'

'Truly, I do not know. We've not been in contact since that little incident in the north last year.'

'"That little incident" being your son using Roman gold to recruit an army of mercenaries to march north and seize the lands of another tribe as his own?'

Haribert rubbed his beard. 'Yes. That sums it up well enough.'

'What happened when you brought him back here?' We were in Haribert's hall. He had ushered out his people, and just four guards flanked the chief as he sat on a would-be throne.

'I tried to speak to him. He wouldn't listen. In the end, I threw him out. Figured he'd end up crawling back.'

'How's that working out for you?'

Haribert chuckled. 'Like I said. Industrious little bastard. Drink?'

'The strongest thing you've got,' I said in a scoff. 'What friends does he have in the south? Where would he have gone?'

Haribert blew air from his cheeks, took a cup of ale from one of his men and sat back on his throne. 'I'm not so sure. He had a small circle of companions once. You slaughtered most of them on a beach on the west coast last year.'

I rolled my eye. 'Don't make your son's crimes against our country about me.'

Haribert raised his hands in submission. 'Just saying, that's all! Apart from the dead, I would imagine he visited Filibert. You may not have heard of him. He rules a small tribe, not too far from your hall, I do not think.'

'Filibert?' I repeated, feeling a small smile spread across my thin lips. 'Oh, I've heard of Filibert. In fact, he and I have some unfinished business.' Sometimes the gods shat on you. Other times, they send you little reminders that they've been with you all along. I sent a swift prayer of thanks to Loki. I knew he hadn't abandoned me yet.

'Alaric, old friend. It would amaze me to find a chief anywhere in our land you did not have unfinished business with.' He raised his ale cup in salute, and suddenly, I had a plan of action.

* * *

'What happens if he hides in a shed again?'

'Fuck off, Faramund.'

A low crescendo of chuckles rippled through the men at my back until I turned and silenced them with a look. Still had it. I was still waiting on the promised men from Dagr, but I had the small group of warriors still loyal to me, plus Eadger, Hilde and Sedric. I thought it enough for this little endeavour.

'Seriously, though, what's our play?' Eadger asked me. He had his sword drawn already, a murderous glint in his eye.

'I need you lot to hold off any resistance whilst I press in and grab Filibert. Once he's told me all he knows, I'll kill the fool and we'll move on.'

'How many warriors does he have?'

'Fifty at most, I reckon. Though calling them warriors is a bit of a stretch. Remember the army we trained last year? Well, those men were hardened killers in comparison to anything you'll come up against today.'

'Well, that's comforting,' Hilde chimed in. She fastened the tie of her helmet and drew her own sword, giving it a practice swoosh through the air. 'So all *we* have to do is hold off fifty men whilst you torture their chief?'

'That's about the long and short of it. Ready?'

We moved in. I don't know if the stinking little collection of hovels we walked through had a name, but it would not be one worth remembering if it did. It was like the camp of a defeated army at battle's end, the last stragglers and hangers on who had not had the presence of mind to run away. No one challenged us, fourteen armed and mailed warriors strutting through the heart of their home. That in itself said a lot.

'You guys stay here. I'm going in there,' I said, pointing with my sword to a shack slightly bigger than the rest. I guessed that was where I would find Filibert.

Now you might remember Filibert from the beginning of this little tale. He was the rat who had promised me thirty cattle and delivered them – well, delivered halfway – thirty half-starved beasts so skinny they made your average small German child seem pudgy. I had been meaning to get back at him, since he had locked himself in a shed and the gods had stopped me from setting him on fire. Seemed now the gods had a plan all along. I smiled as I pushed back the flap to the shack and ducked inside. Everything works out in the end.

Took a moment for my eye to adjust. It was gloomy within, in contrast to the bright day I had just left behind. Two men sat by the door playing dice, another Roman custom that had snuck its way north of the border. Neither noticed me as I strolled past. I assumed they were the door guards. In fairness, they were no worse than most other door guards I'd come across up and down the country. Not the most exciting of jobs, after all.

A handful of people sat on the benches. The rushes on the floor were old, stinking, and half rotted to mush. An elderly lady knitted what looked to be a tunic for a child in one corner. The benches themselves were rotten, green moss growing where men were meant to sit and eat. The whole place, inside and out, spoke of a tribe on the brink of extinction. I felt a small pang of sympathy creep across me then as I pictured Saxa and my boys living such a life. Would I take offered coin to improve their lot, even if it meant betraying my people? I already knew the answer to that. I was called an oath breaker for a reason. But still, Filibert's decisions had put himself on this path. And it would end with me taking his life.

'How did you get in here?' a voice called from the shadows at the end of the shack. A man stepped forward. Short and slim, half-starved in truth, he wore mail forged for a man twice his breadth and at least four inches taller. His hair was patchy, seemed to be falling out in clumps, and his face was pale and gaunt, as if he were halfway to the land of the dead already.

'Hello, Filibert,' I said, flashing the man a grin. 'Thought I'd drop by and say hi. See if maybe you've got any more cattle you want to sell me.'

'G-get out!' He stumbled over the words. He drew his sword and held it before him with shaking hands.

'I will, gladly. Stinks all kind of rotten in here.' I scrunched up my face and made a show of being repulsed. To be fair, it wasn't much of a show. It really did stink in there. 'But first, you and I are going to have a little chat about Sigimund and a group of men running around our land dressed as Roman soldiers.'

'I don't know what you're on about!' Filibert screeched in panic, but already his eyes had betrayed him. There was another door at the rear of the shack, and as I spoke, his eyes darted to it. Whatever it was he was up to, the answers were back there.

'Oh, I think you do. See, you and Sigimund are old friends, according to his father, at least. And when old Haribert kicked him out, he came down this way, didn't he? See, Sigimund already had contacts in the empire, I found that out the hard way last year. So, here you were, half-starved, struggling to get your people through the winter. So when he made you an offer, what was it? Coin? No, you've no use for that. I'm betting grain, wine, furs and pelts; whatever he could get from the Romans, you took it. In return, your little shithole of a capital became their base. Quite central here, isn't it? Good tracks running south and west to east. I'm guessing Sigimund and his friends can get to wherever they need to go. I'm right, aren't I?'

I sat my fattening arse down on a stool, quite proud of myself. I hadn't been certain what I would find going there, but seeing Filibert and the state he and his people were in, it had not taken much for me to piece the thing together. 'Is he here? Behind that door?'

Filibert shook his head, eyes still wide. But I noticed, almost too late, that they weren't looking at me, but rather just behind me. I sprang to my feet, feeling the rush of air as one of the door guards swung an axe destined for my head. It whistled past my helmet and carved the stool I had been sitting on in two. It stuck on the floorboards, giving me the moment I needed to plunge my blade into the guard's back, ripping it free in a spray of claret.

'Get him!' Filibert shrieked, and the other guard was ambling towards me, spear held out before him. The man was no killer, that much was obvious. He came on too quick, wanting it over fast, adrenalin driving him. I batted aside the spear with ease, then let the man's momentum carry him on to the edge of my blade.

Two dead men in barely a dozen heartbeats. Who said I was past it? The shack had emptied, the few people who had sought shelter within streaming out into the daylight. I heard a faint clash of iron as the flap opened and knew then my men had gotten themselves into a scrap. I figured they could handle it.

'Filibert. What have you got yourself in to?' I asked the man, who stood shaking like a leaf on a winter wind. He didn't give me an answer though, just spun on his heel and ran through the flap out the back.

The fighting outside was intensifying, judging by the sounds. Forcing myself to ignore it, I pushed on through the flap at the rear and dropped down to a squat, ready to defend myself. I had no need. There was no one there. I found myself in a small chamber, cracks of light filtering through the gaps in the poorly built wooden walls. The rushes on the floor were fresher; the air smelt cleaner. But it was what lay on the rushes that captured my attention.

Bundles of discarded Roman kit. Shields and helmets, swords and mail. Enough to equip thirty men or more. All piled up neatly. I could even smell the oil where the armour had been greased recently. There was no doubt then that this was where Sigimund and his men had made their base.

I could still hear the fighting outside, and suddenly my mind put two things together. Sigimund and his men were not with their kit. And my men were fighting someone outside. With a curse, I sprang back through the flap and flew past the two corpses I had made in the shack Filibert called his hall. Blood was being spilt. I needed to make sure the right men were dying.

* * *

The sunlight dazzled me, and I had to blink rapidly to stop myself from going blind altogether. My world was light, dark, light, dark, for a few dizzying moments, until I could finally adjust my one overworked eye and make sense of what was in front of me.

I may not have found Sigimund in the back of the shack, but it seemed my men had. They formed a shield wall on the path through the middle of the rundown town and were in a fight for their lives. Twenty or more unarmoured men assailed them. I made out Sigimund immediately, his flop of dark hair and bright eyes wild in the melee.

They must have come back whilst I was in the shack with Filibert, seen my men on the track and decided to attack. Well, that suited me just fine. I charged, silent as a wolf, into the fray. My first slash cut a man from shoulder to waist, my second skewered an unknowing warrior through the back.

'Nice of you to join us!' Eadger called. He gave me a red grin slick with blood, and I pushed my way into our line, so I was shoulder to shoulder with him and Sedric.

'Get yourself into one of the huts,' I said to Sedric. 'This isn't your fight.'

I knew how much Sedric detested war. It had taken the young man months to get over what he had done in the north. But, to his credit, he simply shook his head and raised his sword. I knew then what he was thinking. He had seen Sigimund just as I had done. Sedric was thinking of Batur and Kai, the two friends he had lost because of that man's greed. He was staying for his vengeance. And that was something I could understand.

'They're going to turn our flanks!' Hilde called from the centre of our line. 'We're too thin! I suggest we move back.'

She was right. We were fourteen warriors, them thirty or more, but even as we stood panting ten paces from each other, another handful appeared to bolster their ranks. 'They've no armour, and I'd wager even if they had, they'd be no match for us!' Faramund called, and my men gave a rousing cheer at his words.

'We hold our ground!' I ordered, snatching the shield I had left with one of my warriors and hitting the rim with my blade. 'These bastards came to your home and tried to take your loved ones from you! They would put us on a war path with Rome! You want to live to see your children grow? Beat them now!'

And then there was no time to speak. Sigimund led the charge, to give the worm some credit. They slammed into our shields with the force of a charging bull. We were pushed back three paces, then five, before our boots found purchase on the dirt and we leaned into our shields and forced them back. Then we were snarling and growling, cursing each other over the tops of our shields as we sought an opening. Our enemy had no shields of their own, but they pressed into us so tight we could not find the space to bring our swords to bear. Something had to change.

'On my word, we break!' I said, battering my shield into a youth's face and following through with a sword thrust to the chest. 'We need space to move!'

I smashed my shield forward once more, cutting nothing but air with my blade. But it bought me the moment I needed. 'Now!' I bellowed, and as one, my men moved back and spread out, giving themselves space to fight. Our enemy was dumbfounded, unsure what to do. 'Get them!' Sigimund shouted, his voice shrill with uncertainty. They came for us, and they died.

I killed one with a feint high to the left, followed by a sidestep and a low sweep that sent the man's guts spilling to the dust. A second came for me with a spear thrust to the heart. I dodged it, spinning, knees creaking, and almost lost my footing as I swiped my sword across his throat. 'On your left!' I called to Eadger, who was hunched behind his shield, fending off axe blows fit to cut his head clean off. He turned at my shout, just in time to catch a thrust spear on his shield, which lodged in the wooden board. He used his strength to pull the spear man in, who hadn't the presence of mind to let it go. The man was dead in the mud a moment later.

With no one in front of me, I took a moment to look around the melee. My small force, outnumbered just heartbeats before, was now pretty much even. None of them had fallen, whereas at least ten enemies lay scattered on the ground. I grinned and sought out Sigimund.

The little shit hadn't changed much since I'd seen him last. A well-built youth, with the rounded shoulders and broad chest of a hardened killer. He still had a baby face though, hairless and pudgy with fat his youth should have melted away. He was flushed with anger, eyes scanning left and right, until they settled on me. I saw the fear then; the bowel-clenching terror he felt at the sight of me. He had not been able to kill me the year before, when he had an army at his back and me a small group of untrained farmers. There was no chance for him now, and he knew it.

Quick as thought, Sigimund turned and ran, letting his sword fall as he did.

With a curse, I set off after him. He was young, hale and strong. I was none of those things. I had covered ten paces, heart already pounding in my ears, knees, ankles and hips protesting, when a blur of shadow and air flew past me. The spear hit Sigimund in his right thigh, and he collapsed to the mud with an agonised howl.

Turning back, Hilde gave me a wink before spinning and finishing off the foe she had left sprawled on the dirt whilst she leant me a hand. I've met many great warriors in my time, killed my fair share of them. Not sure I'd ever met one more skilled than Hilde, though.

I pulled up once I reached Sigimund. Him bleeding on the ground, me with hands planted on knees, sucking in air like I'd just ran ten Roman miles. Gods, what a pathetic excuse for a war lord I had become. 'You and I... need to have a little talk,' I panted out, before sitting down on the dirt, blinking to try to clear the white spots in my vision.

* * *

'It's not what you think!' Sigimund squealed as I eased the heated blade closer to his flesh. The sun was setting. A clear night, stars glimmering in a purple sky. The sort of night to sit around a fire and share stories and ale with friends. In happier times, at least.

Faramund had found Filibert after the battle, the small-time chief cowering in a hut with a collection of women and children. A pathetic excuse for a man. I'd had him gagged and bound and put back in the hut. The women and children had been directed to my own hall, there to be fed and looked after. None had complained. Saxa, I knew, would take them in and see to their needs.

That thought distracted me for a moment. How much longer would that hall, that settlement, be mine? I'd been so proud of the place when it was built. Prouder still when we had extended and welcomed new settlers. We were not a tribe exactly, but neither had the Ravensworn been. And they had still been mine. How much would I miss it? The freedom it gave me. A bit, I conceded. But the opportunity to see my son as the chief of the Chauci pulled at me. So too, if I was being honest, the prospect of being nearer to my father. Hengist had aged a lifetime since I had last seen him. It had shocked me, turning up to his small farm and seeing the stoop of his back. The man who had once been a titan; godlike. Or so it had seemed to the small child who had looked upon him in awe.

So was the fate of us all. I shook my head to clear my reverie, the heated knife still inches from Sigimund. The youth winced, tears streaming down his face. 'How is it not what I think?'

'They made me do it! Said they'd kill me if I didn't!'

'Who?'

Sigimund just shook his head. His eyes were scrunched shut, and when he opened them, they were round with fear. Call me a fool all you want, but there was something in those eyes, *something* I had seen before. More than fear. More than desperation. They were the eyes of a man who knew he had no choice. I lowered the knife. Perhaps because I had been where Sigimund was once. Beaten, broken, a heated blade inches from my face. Knowing it was the end, knowing I would not see the sun rise again. What does a man in that position have to lose? 'Tell me everything from the beginning.'

I cut loose his bonds, helped him to sit up. Eadger and Hilde stirred in the firelight, each reaching for a blade. With a gesture from me, they sat back down.

Sigimund took a moment. He rubbed his wrists and ankles. His wounded thigh was heavily wrapped, the wound cauterised to stop the bleeding. He had passed out when Hilde did that, but it had probably saved his life. Pale, shivering, despite the night's warmth, Sigimund took a deep breath, and then spoke.

'All started last autumn. I was made homeless, banished from my tribe, thanks to you.'

I thought that a bit rich. Whatever the lad's father had done to him was not on my account. He had been lucky to survive going to war with me. But I kept my peace. I needed him to speak, not start an argument.

'I came south at first, not really knowing what to do. Word got to me of a new people migrating from the eastern steppe. A tribe in need of warriors as they sought to carve themselves a home in the west. Thought I'd go check it out.'

'Aye, bet you did,' I said. 'Carving out kingdoms seems to be a speciality of yours if I remember rightly.'

That got a scoff from Sigimund, but he carried on. 'I journeyed all the way to the Carpathians, passing north of them and into the wilds of the steppe. You ever been that far east?'

'I have not,' I said with a shake of the head.

'Grass that stretches from one horizon to the next. No forests, little water. Just endless plains. It is a sight to behold. And the people...'

'Sarmatians?'

'Aye. Sarmatians. Though they call themselves something different. Their tongue is different to ours. Harsher, less words. Some words mean the same thing in three or four different ways. It is hard to master.'

I thought immediately of the slave I killed in the *fabrica*, and the alien accent he had spoken in. 'I don't understand what a new group of people coming from the east has to do with your dealings with Rome. How are you getting Roman kit? And what have they been instructing you to do with it?' I knew, of course, where it was coming from and how it was getting out. What I needed to know was how it was being orchestrated from the outside.

Sigimund laughed, a mirthless, mocking, dry chuckle. 'You've got it all wrong. Rome has nothing to do with it. No knowledge of what we are doing. It is *they* who are pulling the strings. They who I answer to.'

'The Sarmatians? Why?'

'Because they said they would kill my tribe if I did not comply. Their numbers are endless. Men, women, all are warriors. They are a people born to horseback. All of them trained in the ways of the spear since childhood. They come not just to conquer us, but Rome too. Dacia will fall first. Then Pannonia and the other northern provinces. They are a plague.'

I rubbed my bearded chin, trying to make sense of what Sigimund said. He was leaving details out, that much was obvious. Whether through shame or fear, I did not know. Had he made promises he could not hope to keep? Or had he simply been threatened to follow their orders? 'Who is their leader?'

'Bahadur is his name. Cruel Spear, his followers call him.'

'Cruel Spear.' It was my turn to scoff. 'Seems like I shall soon be meeting with this Bahadur. Where will I find him?'

'Last I heard they were just west of the Carpathians, north of the lands of the Iazyges. But it has been some time since I have had communication with them. What will you do with me?'

'Take you back to your father. I need time to think, formulate a plan.'

'You will fight them?' Sigimund asked me. Again, there was something in his eyes. Disbelief, more than anything.

'Aye. Seems I will have no choice. If they come to slaughter us all, as you say, someone needs to stop them.'

'Not even you, the great lord of war, Alaric Hengistson, have the might to stand in their path.'

I gave Sigimund my wolf's grin then. The grin I would give my killer one day before they dealt me the final blow. Defiant to the end. 'I've been written off before, puppy. Underestimate me at your peril.' With that, I left the cur to his rest and walked off into the night, my scheming brain already hard at work.

13

The following days passed in a blur. I felt as though I had a thousand things to do, and no time to do them in. First, I went home. Saxa had indeed gathered the remnants of Filibert's people and taken them under her wing. But no sooner had they settled than I had them on the road again, this time heading north.

Saxa had taken the news of her father's offer badly, as I feared she would. She had no desire to see her son become chief of the Chauci, embroiled in the schemes of the land. Much better he grow to become a farmer or a blacksmith. A life of peace was no bad thing. But once I had explained all I knew to her, she conceded it would be safer to be amongst her people, at least for the foreseeable future. So north we went. Our people on foot, us by the rivers in my celox. I was in a rush.

At Dagr's hall, I swapped my wife and children for fifty warriors, which ranked among the hardest things I had ever done. But Dagr had been good to his word. The men I received were no beardless youths who did not know one end of a spear from another. Hardened warriors all, many of whom I recognised from battles past. I would need every one of them.

Next I went further north still and offered Haribert back his son. My offer, though, was refused.

'So how serious is this threat from the east?' he asked me as we ate a noon meal.

I could only shrug. 'Your son has not been honest with me. He's told me what he has to. The rest, I think, he was too ashamed to admit.'

Haribert chewed on salted meat, his head tilting as he thought. 'How many warriors do you have?'

'Sixty-five, give or take.'

The big chief laughed at me. 'Gods, brother. I thought what you did in the far north last year was reckless enough. You're going to stop an invasion with sixty-five men?'

'I will fight the gods themselves with sixty-five men if it ensures the freedom of our people.'

He considered me then, that bear of a man with hands big enough to crush skulls. 'You know, I never know what to make of you.'

'What do you mean?'

Haribert considered the question a moment. 'For years, I heard stories of the great Alaric Hengistson. Chief slayer, battle turner. The man who would sell his own mother for a victory. But then last year I meet you. And I find a man willing to die for a people he does not know. A man who will fight to the last drop of his blood for someone else's freedom. It was not an easy thing to condemn my son and march north to support you. But you wrote me a letter, asking me to. Why did you do that?'

I could only shrug. 'I trusted in your humanity. Plus, your reason. You need good relations with your neighbours. We all do. Like it or not, we are a community, and we thrive when we all get along. Just a couple of weeks ago, I saw a united Germani army fight off the might of the Fourteenth legion. No single tribe could have done that alone. Together, we are strong.'

'I wish someone would explain that to my son.' Haribert glowered across his hall, to where Sigimund sat in a corner, pushing around the food on his plate with his eating knife. He was not happy to be home, something I was ashamedly glad of. One day I would grow up.

'Well, your son seems to think these Sarmatians in the east are coming for us all. He was scared enough to do their bidding. Again, I do not know why. Perhaps he will tell you?'

'Perhaps. Though I do not think so. Our relationship is somewhat broken. I have a proposition for you, Alaric, lord of war.'

'Aye? Let's hear it.' I wondered what this one would cost me. The last proposition I had faced had cost me my family. What else did I have to lose?

'If Eadger and Isvilt agree to spare some of their warriors to keep an eye on my people, I will campaign with you to rid us of this curse my son has brought upon us.'

I started at that. It had been a long time since I had been able to count a powerful chief – or a weak one at that – as a friend. Balomar aside, the great men of our country largely despised me. In fairness, I had betrayed most of them, or their fathers, one too many times in the past. It was one of the reasons my hall was built in such an isolated spot. The fewer people that knew of it, the more chance I had of staying alive.

'Why would you do that? You are a long way from the east. This war will not be one of your immediate concern.'

'It surprises you, that a chief might think of matters outside his own immediate interests,' Haribert said with a chuckle. 'Truth is, Alaric, I am getting old. I was a feared man once. Not in your league, of course, but the tribes up here knew to keep their distance from the Anglii. I have been living on past deeds for too long. Last year, marching north to save your sorry little arse from my brat of a son, I felt *alive* in a way I had not for years. Even knowing what I would face at the end of the road! I want that feeling again. That bubble of excitement in my blood. You understand what I mean, I think?'

I nodded. I did all too well. 'I'm meant to be a fucking merchant,' I said, and the two of us broke into a fit of giggles. 'But I do believe in our country. Always have. I only got involved in tribal politics when there were no Romans around to fight. How many spears can you bring with you?'

'One hundred and fifty, give or take,' Haribert said, waving a meaty hand in a vague gesture. 'Enough to give you a fighting chance, I think.'

One hundred and fifty men would indeed give me a leg up. Indeed, it turned my small war band into an army. 'Let us speak with Eadger and Hilde. I'm sure they can get a message to Isvilt. The Cimbri are at peace. They should be able to spare some men.'

'And they will stay with you? That Hilde, she seems... formidable.'

'That she is! And yes, I think they're sticking around. They've a nose for trouble, same as you it seems,' I said with a wry grin. 'A toast then. To an alliance. And victory!'

* * *

Haribert needed ten days to set his affairs in order and muster his men. I agreed to meet him at my hall fifteen days after our meet. I was back in my celox before nightfall, heading south. I had over two hundred men at my beck and call. I would need more.

'Where are we going?' Hilde asked me. I stood on the prow of the celox, the wind rushing through my thinning hair. I had always loved life on a ship. At sea was the best. The salt spray, the waves, the sheer freedom of it. But a river was a good second. The celox sailed smoothly, a gentle wind ushering us along with the current.

'To see Balomar first. And then to set up a meeting with the Romans.'

'Why?'

'Because this is their fight as much as it is ours. These Sarmatians, whoever they are, have infiltrated their empire. Do you think they will stop at taking our land? As soon as they have it, they will look south or west over the Rhine. They will fight with us. They must.'

Hilde grunted something non-committal. She and Eadger had never had dealings with the dreaded empire. That would change soon. 'I am grateful you and Eadger have stuck around,' I said. 'I need people I can trust around me.'

She gave me a smile. 'You were there for us at our darkest hour. Neither Eadger nor I will leave you alone in this.'

'Won't Isvilt miss you?'

Hilde and Isvilt were lovers. A secret now out in the open among the people of the Cimbri. I was happy for them both. Isvilt led her people well. Not that I had time to go north and see it for myself. And Hilde led her war band ferociously. They were a good team, with Eadger at their side to chip in with advice. It just went to show how far a people can move forward in a short space of time. I wondered where I would be in a year. If I was even alive at all.

'Did you get any more out of Sigimund?' she asked me.

'No. I'm hoping he will talk to Haribert. Though I wouldn't mind another crack at Filibert.' As much as I would have dearly loved to nail the whoreson to the nearest tree, I had left Filibert alive for now. There were bigger issues at play than my revenge for a coward who hid behind a reinforced shed door. We had left Sigimund with his father. Haribert had vowed to bring his son south with him. There was a good chance we could use the ill-advised youth in some way. I was the Trickster reborn, after all. If there was a scheme I could cook up to bring our nameless enemy out into the open, I would do it. It felt as though my brain wouldn't switch off. Different scenarios whirled through my mind. What would I find in the east? How could it be possible no word had reached us of this Sarmatian migration?

In the end, there was only one way to find out. South, then east. To meet friends and enemies alike. I felt the butterflies in the pit of my stomach. Looking up into the clear night sky, I smiled. I was Alaric, lord of war. And this was what I lived for.

* * *

It took a total of sixteen days for me to prepare. A trip to Goridorgis and a meeting with Balomar had led to a jaunt over to the land of the Quadi and a meeting with their leader, Areogaesus. From there, riders had been sent out as far east as the Iazyges on the Dacian border and north to the myriad tribes that lived in the middle of our vast land.

A meeting with a reluctant Silus had taken place in Carnuntum, though the veteran soldier had been hesitant to offer any support. 'Germani problems should be handled by the Germani,' he had sneered at me over a cup of wine. I had left with a smile, knowing a seed had been planted. Whatever the big man said, I knew he would report to his seniors in the Fourteenth legion, and I knew too they would report to the leaders of the *frumentarii*. Agents would be worming their way north through Dacia within a day or two of our meeting. All would depend on what they saw.

And so it was I marched on a mud road on a beautiful summer's day, an army of over six hundred men at my back. Both Balomar and Areogaesus had sent men, even if they had not come themselves. The two southern kings were not exactly friends, but there was a companionable rivalry that I had unashamedly exploited. In private, Balomar promised me one hundred spears and Adalhard, his war chief, to lead them. I had taken that to Areogaesus, and told the leader of the Quadi that Balomar was giving me one hundred and fifty spears. He immediately offered me two hundred.

Not to be outdone, Balomar had ended up giving me two hundred and fifty. I smiled to myself as I marched. Loki would be proud. So four hundred and fifty men marched with me from the southern tribes. Haribert had kept his word and arrived at my hall with one hundred and fifty men, and with my own small war band plus the fifty warriors from Dagr, I felt as confident as I could that we would hold back whatever storm was rolling in from the east.

My good mood did not last, however. We were a few days into our march. An army marches on its stomach, as the old saying goes, and therefore our army could only march as fast as the supply wagons that trailed us could travel. Which was not fast at all. Through valleys and forests, the scent of pine resin lingering in my nostrils, we marched, and our wagons groaned. Twelve oxen had been given to us by Balomar; the carts had come from my own hall. They were usually laden with amber, but for this journey, they were filled with grain and salted meat, nuts and berries, ale and wine. Six hundred men burned through a lot of food.

The Romans, of course, had men employed to keep their armies fed. They travelled ahead of a marching force, securing water and grain and whatever else was needed so the army that trailed them could just pick it up as they marched. It was another infuriating example of their efficiency, and what we lacked. How could we ever hope to beat them?

But it was not those thoughts that dampened my mood, and not Rome I marched east to face, rather our destination. I had not been back to Parienna since the fateful day the Romans had taken from me my army and my eye. It was the darkest day of my life, one that still haunted my dreams. The ground seemed familiar to me as we marched, and I realised my army was following the same track I had that day years before. There was the forest I had been led into, where my men and I had fought off a group of fanatics. The same open plains of grass that led to the same small rundown town, with its rickety wooden walls.

'We don't need to go in,' Adalhard, Balomar's battle chief, said to me as I stared.

The place was abandoned. I had heard it had remained uninhabited since I had fought out an epic battle with the Fourteenth legion within. Locals had referred to it as a haunted town, the ghosts of the dead still roaming the streets. It had been home to a tribe once. The Arsitae, a small tribe that had been allied with Rome. They had been folded into the Quadi not long after the battle, Areogaesus sensing an opportunity. I wondered briefly if any of the men the Quadi had provided had originally come from here. 'The men need a rest, and we will need shelter tonight.'

'It is warm. We can sleep in the open. Come, let us move on another few miles.' I knew what Adalhard was doing. Whether out of politeness to me, or because there were mutterings from the men about wanting to avoid the place, I did not know. But either way, I appreciated the gesture.

'No. We go in.' I needed to go in. It felt as if the gods themselves had led me there. I had to see it again, to relive the lowest moment of my life. It was something I could not explain.

The western gates had not been repaired. They had hung open when my men had ridden through. I could not remember if it had been my men or the Romans who ripped them from their hinges, but they lay rotting in the long grass.

* * *

The gates are open.

All worries of assaulting the walls, of keeping my men organised and in unison throughout a brutal assault, dissipate to dust. The gates to Parienna are wide open, and I feel the touch of Loki in the sun's warming rays.

'What did I tell you?' Ruric says with a savage grin. He has a single-headed war axe loose in his right hand, and he swings his arm in a circle, the silver blade gleaming in the red and orange light of the dawn. 'One last day, Alaric. One more battle. Gods, I'm excited!' He grins again then kicks his horse hard in the flanks, urging the beast towards the gates, which still hang seductively open.

* * *

The memories flood back, a wave of suppressed emotion I could not hold down if I wanted. It was to be Ruric's final battle. One last dance in the storm of iron and blood before he hung up that axe of his for good and rode off into the sunset. It had proved to be his final fight, but there had been no retirement for him to ride off to. No small farm in the middle of nowhere where he could grind out an honest living and sit with his feet up as the sun set in the evening.

Gods, I missed that man. His surety, his willingness to stand up to me when he knew I was wrong. Which of my young warriors would do that for me now? Faramund? I did not think so. The problem with being a living legend is that people want to make you happy. They want to tell you yes, even if they know they shouldn't. Ruric never worried about what I would think of him.

Never had any issues telling me I was wrong. I couldn't count on all my fingers and toes the number of times he had saved the Ravensworn from disaster just by standing up to me. A finer man there never was.

I walked through the dilapidated town, following the path I had once ridden Hilde, my old trusted horse. What a servant she had been. I hadn't bothered naming horses after I had lost her. In fact, since I was last in that gods forsaken place, I had avoided making attachments to almost everyone outside of Saxa and my boys. There had been Sedric, of course, and Batur and Kai. Their deaths had hurt. Eadger, Hilde and Isvilt had surprised me, but none of them had gotten as close to me as the captains of my Ravensworn had been.

The path led to the hall that sat in the centre of the town. Last time I had been there, the roof had been beginning to cave in. The thatch had fallen away, but a rotting support beam still clung on to the tops of the walls. And hanging from that roof beam...

* * *

Gerulf hangs from the wooden beam that runs vertically from the east wall to the west. It is the beam that should hold up the highest part of the roof, but judging from its darkened and uneven state, it appears it could fall at any moment. And yet it supports the weight of a man. Poor Gerulf's face is as blue as the ocean; his eyes bulge from his head and his tongue hangs uselessly from his gaping mouth. He still wears his armour, arms held behind his back with thick rope. His body has not been defiled like the four men of his command we had found back west. For that, I feel oddly grateful. I step forward until I stand directly underneath him. I reach up and touch the foot of one of my most loyal men and feel a burning shame mixed with anger.

* * *

That was it. The thing I felt more than anything else, coming back to the place of my greatest defeat. Shame. It was the reason I had shut myself away from the world for so long. I stood looking at the half-collapsed hall, images of Gerulf running through my mind. Him strong and hale, leading his men in a charge. And then him hanging in that hall, his face as blue as a frozen lake.

No one had cleaned up the town after the battle. From the looks of it, no one had entered since. Skeletons littered the ground. I could make out the dead from my army. Tattered shields still clung to the once proud red paint-work that had marked them out as men of the Ravensworn. It had been some-thing to brag about once. Men had been proud to fight under my banner. All knew only a true warrior made the cut. To fight for me was to be a killer. And there was nothing our people respected more than killers.

I turned from the hall, unable to look at it any more. Unable to look anywhere. Almost too scared to walk, in case I crushed a rotting skull, I care-fully picked my way through the battlefield. It was clear where my men had fought. A great line of dead ran north to south through the centre of the town. Even in death, they held their ranks.

'Why do all the good men die?' Ruric had said, slumped on his knees when we found Gerulf's body. And why indeed? Why had all these men died and yet I still lived? The Allfather must have needed to extend his hall when they all showed up at his door, ready to feast until the last battle. Were they there? Waiting for their lord to arrive and lead them to glory once more? I hoped so. But if they were, if they greeted me with open arms, it would be a gesture I could not earn in a hundred lifetimes. Five hundred men had once trusted me to lead them to glory. All gone now.

Rusting weapons littered the grass, some still held in skeletal fingers.

* * *

'And me?' Ketill is at my shoulder. Loyal Ketill, brave Ketill.

I grab him by the shoulder and pull him back to the hall's entrance. 'Get your men out of here, brother. Go over the northern wall, get back to your lands and live your life well. I cannot ask you to fight this fight, I will not.'

He says nothing. He stares at me with such ferocity that I think he will strike me. He does not, though; just shakes his head meekly, grips my wrist in the warriors' embrace and whispers in my ear: 'Wait for me in the Slain One's hall, brother.' And with that, he is gone.

* * *

I was standing right in that spot when the Romans came through the gates. I could still picture it, their bright-red shields, silver mail, spear tips like a forest of iron. Ketill had no reason to be there in the first place. He had just brought his men to support his friend. And I had led him to his death. If only he had left when I said. It would be me in the Slain One's hall, and not him. I wondered what sort of life he would have had. Would he have taken a wife? Sired children? Found peace? I knew he would have done none of these things. The reasonable part of my mind knew if he had not died in Parienna, he would have met his end on some other battlefield. It was just who he was. But still, he had died for me.

Tears spilt freely. I took a step forward, and then another. I wanted desperately to be away from there, and at the same time did not want to leave. Hilde and Eadger stood five feet from me, each of them unwilling to come any closer. Two more friends with no reason to be in that place with me. Just there to offer their support. Would I get them killed too on this trip to the east?

'I have never seen such a sight,' Adalhard said. If even a man such as he – a man devoted to war – had never seen a sight like this, then it was as bad as I thought. The dead were everywhere, stretching across the barren ground.

'You have never seen a battle like this one,' I said in a quiet voice. 'Truly, there has never been one like it.'

I walked. Careful footsteps avoiding the bones of my comrades.

* * *

'Ruric, the banner,' I say. Ruric gives a nod to a man at my back and he unfurls the beautiful banner. It is a glorious red, deep, rich and striking. The raven is blacker than the night, its head bigger than mine. Its one eye seems to look straight at me as the standard billows in the wind. What is it trying to say to me, that raven? Is this to be my last day on this green earth? Only time will tell.

* * *

I stood at the spot where my line was formed when the Romans advanced on us. Looking left and right, I could see the holes in the skeletons, where Roman *pila* penetrated armour and bone, snatching away the lives of my men. I closed my eye and relived it, the whistle of the javelins in the air, the crunch as they bit home. My heart hammered, palms sweaty, hands shaking as it all came back. Worst thing was, I knew I had not seen the worst of it yet.

* * *

'Wounded to the rear,' I say as I turn to Ruric. He is pale, is Ruric, paler than death. His eyes are red rimmed, and a trickle of blood runs from the corner of his mouth. 'Ruric?' I say as I lumber to him, holding him by the waist to prevent him from falling.

'Never... forget... lad. One day... you must answer... for your sins.' He dies in my arms. It is only as I hold him that I realise my hands are slick with blood. High on the right side of his chest, a Roman spear has bitten deep, penetrating his mail and driving deep.

* * *

Was Ruric one of the corpses at my feet? I didn't know. In my memory, the man was larger than life. A colossus so great even the Valkyries could not fly him to the Heroes Hall.

'We cannot stay here,' Haribert said. I had not heard him approach.

'No,' I agreed.

'I have just been told...' He trailed off, trying to find the words. 'About what happened here,' he finished. 'I am sorry, Alaric. But it does none of us any good lingering in this place. Especially you. We have a war to fight, a nation to save. And you are our leader.'

I nodded, half listening. 'Take the men outside the walls and set up camp. I'll be with you shortly.'

I sat down on the half-dead grass as the others left. My body in the present, mind lost in the past.

14

I stayed in Parienna all night. I did not sleep.

As the dawn sun painted the world in red and orange, I rose and staggered out of the ghost town. My army was stirring. I stopped a moment and took it all in. We had no tents, there had not been time to either make or buy what we needed, so the men had slept in the open, grateful for the warm night air.

My eye roamed over the warriors who had entrusted me with their lives. Just as another army had done in the past. I had let that army down, spent the lives of those men as if they were nothing more than Roman coins. What would happen to these?

I caught the eye of Sigimund. The youth was rolling up a blanket, storing it away in a cart. His eyes fixed on mine. What was he thinking? Was he too reliving his own great defeat to me? Picturing the corpses of his men decaying on the ground outside the southern gate of Tastris? A vengeful part of me hoped he was. He had been taught a lesson much younger than I had been. It appeared, though, he had not learned from it.

'You've got to talk to me eventually,' I said to him as I approached. 'We get nearer to these Sarmatians with every step. I need to know what we're going up against.'

He would not look at me; instead, he looked back to the gates of Parienna and stared for a time. 'Was it as bad as it looked?' he asked me.

'Worse,' I said. 'Worse than anything you could possibly imagine. I reckon over a thousand men died in those walls, Germani and Roman. It was the fiercest battle I have ever been involved in.'

'And you've been in a few.'

'Aye. That I have. How did you end up doing this people's bidding?'

'I've told you this!'

'No you haven't. You told me some man named Bahadur would kill your tribe if you refused to do his bidding. You did not tell me how that came about, or why.'

Sigimund looked back to the dilapidated walls of Parienna, and the horrors that lay within. I let him take his time. Out of the corner of my eye I saw Haribert hover into view, the big chief wanting to stay quiet, not alert his son to his presence.

'I went east. I met them north of the Carpathians like I said. I was riding up to their camp when three men came to meet me. I was bound and hooded, led into the camp and into the tent of their leader.'

I could feel the shame burning off him. A young man, reckless with ambition. What had he thought, riding up to this alien tribe? That he would be welcomed with open arms? The naivety of the young.

'I was put on my knees in front of Bahadur. He bade me to tell him my story. I offered my services as a warrior and as a leader. He mocked me.'

'He speaks our tongue?'

Sigimund nodded. 'Aye, to a degree. Enough to carry a conversation, anyway. He ordered me to form a small group of warriors, outlawed men I could find to do my bidding. Even gave me coin to pay them.'

'Roman coin?'

'What other kind of coin is there? So I did, I went back west, scoured the land for every man I could find. Had over fifty when I was done.'

'And then what?'

'I took my men back east. We found Bahadur and his tribe in the same place. When we got there...'

He trailed off, tears brimming in his eyes. 'You need to spill it all, my son,' Haribert said. He put his arm around Sigimund, bringing him in close. Fathers and sons. Didn't matter the crime of your child, they were still your child. I thought of my own boys then, far away back west. I knew I would be the same.

'We were... branded.'

'What?' Haribert roared in disgust. I scowled in confusion, before memories of something I had seen in the Roman *fabrica* came back. 'With a horse? On your back?'

'Yes.' Sigimund sniffed, wiping tears away with his hand. 'That's when we were told that we were now the property of Bahadur, and if we failed to comply with his orders then our tribes would be slaughtered.'

'Show me,' Haribert said. 'Show me this instant!'

I thought back to the slave I had killed at the weapons factory. I also thought back to the others he kept company with, those men now mining in Dacia. Their skin had been darker than ours, their eyes like narrow slits. But those men had spoken our tongue, and I had not appreciated the scale of the issue at the time.

Sigimund had removed his mail, and his tunic was half over his head when I saw it. The clear markings of a horse burned onto his back. The flesh was seared; I could not imagine how painful it must have been, or how long it had taken to heal.

'So some of your men were sent as slaves into the empire, there to source the weapons. And you were to use them to sow discontent between the tribes and Rome north of the river.'

'Yes,' Sigimund whispered.

'And this Bahadur sent some of his own men with yours into the empire? I saw them at the *fabrica*. I'm sure of it.'

'Yes.'

'How can this Bahadur reach so far? He is just another tribal chief from the east. There must be a hundred of them.'

'I don't know,' Sigimund said. 'But I know he is determined to find a home for his people in the west.'

'Hmmm.' I mused on that a moment. Haribert fussed over his son, running one of his paw-like hands over the brand. I had seen many such before, though Sigimund's was a fair size. The Romans branded their slaves as standard, many on their faces so they could not hide it.

'What are you thinking?' Haribert asked me, his hands still on his son.

'I'm thinking that no matter how big or tough this Bahadur thinks he is, he and his people are running from something. Why else come west now? With such plans and conviction? What is chasing them from their home?'

'That does not bear thinking about,' Haribert said.

'No,' I agreed. 'One fight at a time, I suppose.'

We broke camp soon after. The path we had been following ended, so we marched over wild grass, keeping the river just visible on the southern horizon, on our right.

'We need a plan for when we get there,' Adalhard said to me as we walked. 'We have no idea what we are walking into.'

I could see the Carpathians well enough in front of us, their snowcapped peaks striking against the deep blue of the sky. We had passed no one, not a single village or settlement since we had left Parienna, and I thought that telling. No one seemed to want to live out that far east. There were always tribes coming west, looking for land and willing to kill whoever got in their way to get it. But no tribe ever went east. There were the Iazyges, nestled on the north side of the Danube between Pannonia and Dacia, but they had always been a people to keep their distance. I had sent a messenger east to see if they had news of the invaders. No message had come back.

'How can we form a plan if we have no idea what we are walking in to?' I countered Adalhard. 'We're going to have to wing it. Trust our instincts.'

Adalhard scoffed. 'Did your instincts tell you to march into Parienna without properly scouting it first the day you lost that eye?'

I bristled at that. In truth, I thought those open gates had been a sign from the gods. The Allfather giving me a gift, Loki working his cunning from the shadows. How wrong I had been. 'You have a point,' I said through gritted teeth. 'What do you suggest?'

'I think the men should march battle ready from now on. Armour, helmets, shields strapped to their backs. They can carry water in a skin but nothing else. Everything they don't need goes back to the carts and we send ten men out in front to scout ahead.'

It all sounded reasonable. I was angry I had not said it myself. It had been something I had been considering. But in my mind we had a day or two before we needed to worry about bumping into the enemy. Still, it couldn't hurt. I called a halt and had Adalhard and Haribert relay the orders. The men grumbled, and I smiled at it. Sedric brought me the cuirass he had made me, and as I put it on, I noted the scars from the battle with Rome had been knocked out, and it shone just as it had when newly made. The man really was a marvel.

Just as we were preparing to set off again, Haribert appeared at my shoulder, a wide grin splitting his beard. He pointed to the centre of our formation, where I saw the blood-red Ravensworn banner flying proudly on the breeze. 'You are our commander in this endeavour. Which I believe makes the rest of us the Ravensworn,' he said in a loud voice, and the men cheered. 'The finest fighting unit in all Germania!'

With a grin wide enough to bridge the Danube, I ordered our force on and we marched in good spirits. I sent Faramund out with ten of our younger men as scouts. I thought it a good opportunity to give him a chance to lead men in war. He had done well by me so far, even fighting Sigimund and his band of would-be Romans twice. This, though, would be a whole new challenge.

All was well after we stopped for a noon meal. The carts made good progress over the grass, and the summer sun warmed us as we walked and talked. It was mid-afternoon when I first felt a twinge of doubt run up my spine. 'Can you see Faramund?' I said to Hilde, who walked alongside me.

She paused, squinting to scan the horizon. Short of the distant mountains, there wasn't much to see. Grass plain rolled across shallow valleys off to the east. A slight rise to our left, concealing what I knew to be a clutch of trees I had seen earlier in the day. Apart from that, there was nothing to remark upon.

'No. But could be he had passed that rise up ahead. No point him scouting just a few hundred feet ahead of us, right? He's just doing what you wanted.'

I grunted, but still the feeling wouldn't shift. 'Adalhard, could you send a couple of men up that rise? I want to know if there's anything to see.'

The war chief nodded and moments later two of his men disappeared over the crest of the hill. I stood in tense silence as my army marched by.

'What's got into you?' Eadger sniffed, looking around in confusion. 'There is nobody here.'

I looked to Adalhard, our gazes locking together. I could tell he was thinking what I was. We were both experienced warriors, probably the most experienced out of all with us. 'Perhaps that is the problem, friend,' he said in a quiet voice.

Then two things happened at once. Adalhard's two warriors appeared on the hilltop, waving their arms and shouting something incoherent. An arrow hit one in the back and the man collapsed, falling head over arse down the hill. The other threw himself to the ground before the same could happen to him. And then the ground began to shake.

'What the fuck is happening?' Eadger muttered, eyes on his feet.

'Shields!' I bellowed, ripping my own off my back. A moment later, all was chaos.

* * *

Horsemen charged over the hill to our left. Too numerous to count, no time to prepare. They streamed down towards us and smashed into the men nearest.

'Fuck!'

'Shields!'

'Form up in a line!'

Adalhard was roaring, Haribert bellowing, me yelling. I couldn't say who said what. It all happened so quickly. I just had time to think that the last time I had come east I had sleepwalked into a disaster. And I was doing it again.

'Form a circle!' I called eventually, the cry echoing through our army. I'd been here before, not long ago, though it was Roman cavalry that surrounded me then. A circle gave us the best chance of fighting the bastards off, whoever they were. I had no time to take them in. There was just shining armour and faceless helmets. Arrows zipped into our shields, spears littered the sky. Men fell around me, their bodies becoming trip hazards as they slumped lifelessly to the long grass.

'We need to move back towards our wagons!' I called over the din. Fighting cavalry can be infuriating, mainly because as an infantryman you feel so impotent. Horsemen can ride around you out of reach of your sword, whilst they pick off whoever they can with missiles and spears.

'No, Alaric! We should hold our ground!' Haribert called back. Even as he spoke, the big man darted out of our circle of shields and cleaved his sword through a horse's neck. It was a move that made me think of Ruric.

'If they get to our supplies, we're screwed!' I called back, hacking out at a leg and being rewarded with a splash of blood on my face. And it was true. We had maybe one week's supplies left in those wagons. I had been banking on us being able to buy supplies from the Iazyges on our journey east, but they had not replied to our messages. It was another nagging concern that had been bothering me.

We backed up, slow and steady, until shouts from the rear told me the wagons were in sight. 'They've killed the horses!' one man called, and I despaired. How were we supposed to move the wagons without them? 'Then let us take some of theirs!' I snarled back in anger, getting a rousing cheer from my men.

But then, just as soon as the enemy had appeared, they vanished. A horn sounded in the distance, a long and mournful note, and the cavalry simply rode away, back up the hill they had come down. The whole thing had lasted moments. The damage done, though, would last much longer. We had thirty dead, sixteen wounded. Three of those were not expected to see out the day. The rest would need patching up. I had the men stay by the wagons, rest up and take on food and water, whilst I and a few of those closer to me walked off to take in the devastation.

'Killed a few of the fuckers,' Haribert said, nodding at the dead enemy on the ground. We had not managed to capture any of their horses, the riders taking their dead mounts with them. There were six enemy dead left on the grass, and Eadger was stripping one down to get a better look. I left him to it for the moment, more interested in walking up the hill to see if I could see where they went. Or if they were coming back.

The two men Adalhard had sent up the hill lay where they had fallen. I stopped by the bodies of both and checked for a pulse. There was nothing. Atop the hill, I paused a moment and took three deep breaths in. Sweat streamed down me and I was still breathing hard. All was quiet. A track through the long grass showed where the cavalry had come from and where they had retreated. Two beaten paths ran to the forest and back. I could tell which one they had attacked us on, and which one they had used to retreat, judging by the way the grass was flattened.

When my heart had slowed and my breathing returned to normal, I looked long and hard at the clutch of trees in front of me. Should I send men in there? If I did, would they come back out alive? Looking back to my men, my army, I saw Adalhard leading a small team of diggers. Shovels had been collected from wagons; graves were being dug. At least those men would be buried, not left to rot like the last army I had brought out here.

I was still pondering what to do as I walked back down the slope and joined Haribert, Eadger and Hilde as they stood over the corpse of the man Eadger had stripped. 'Get a load of this,' Hilde said to me as I approached.

Pushing through the three of them so I could see, I found I had nothing to say for a good long while. There was something almost arcane about the body. So very like us, and so very different at the same time. The man's eyes were slits in a sun-darkened face. Dark hair topped a clean-shaven face, the hair shaved around the sides, the top allowed to grow long, tied up in a topknot. Huge, hooped earrings hung from both ears, what appeared to be small fragments of bone looped over the golden thread. But it was the body that struck me hardest. The man's back was arched terribly. I got the impression of someone who had spent a lifetime stooped in the saddle. The hips, too, bowed wider than a mother who had just given birth to twins. It looked bizarre, as was the curve of the legs, which seemed to have curved around the saddle the warrior must have spent every day on.

'Who are these people?' I muttered to myself, rubbing my beard with a bloodied hand.

'They are horsemen, born and bred. That seems obvious to me. Remember the men we fought last summer?' Hilde asked me.

'Aye, of course.'

'Remember how huge and rounded their shoulders were? They were a people of the sea, men who had spent their lives working an oar. These men' – she gestured to the corpse – 'are horsemen. Their bodies have adjusted to their way of life. There is nothing for us to fear here, no weird sign of the gods or any other stupid superstition for the men to fixate on. They are just people.'

'Ferocious people,' Eadger muttered. He had drawn the dead man's sword and ran a hand along the blade's edge. It was a sword to match mine, long and straight. The hilt was hooked at the end, and I wondered if that made it easier to draw whilst riding a horse.

'What was their number, do you think?' Haribert asked. He, too, had cuts on his arms, and I could not work out if the blood on his face was his or someone he had killed.

'Four hundred,' Hilde said with certainty.

'How could you tell? It all happened so quick.'

'It's my best guess. Plus, I counted the hoofbeats left on the grass.'

I had nothing to say to that. Some people had a knack for certain things. Eadger had once had a knack for carpentry; Sedric had a knack for working iron. Hilde's was war; she was a warrior through and through. If she said there had been four hundred horsemen, who was I to argue with her? 'We need a plan,' I said. 'We can't just sit around here waiting for the bastards to come back. We can't move the wagons, and we can't move far without them.'

'So what do you suggest?' Adalhard said. He approached with a shovel on his shoulder, Sedric in tow. He, too, had been digging, and I was pleased to see no blood marked him. Clearly, he had kept a distance from the fighting. I very much wished he had stayed at home.

'We need a camp,' I said. 'A base. Somewhere we can call home, return to every night. We could be out here a while.'

'Parienna is not so far behind us,' Adalhard said, and everyone groaned. 'What? It has walls!'

'It is full of ghosts,' Haribert said and shuddered.

'Ghosts,' I mused. 'Do we have a priest with us?'

The others looked at each other in confusion. I am a man of the gods. Not as devoted as I was as a young man; I had seen too much blood and death for that. But I still believed the Slain One walked among us. In fact, I thought I had seen him one night on the beach on my doomed venture in the north. Had spoken with him, even. I still believed Loki sat at my shoulder, the Sly One guiding me through life. Fenrir the feared stalked the shadows, his growls heard through the wind in the trees. I still believed the Spinners wove the fabric of my life. Every step I took was because they had laid out the path. But I was doubtful in my old age. Something had changed in me at Parienna, when Silus had burnt out my eye and my men had been slain in droves.

'Why would we have a priest? You disdain them for one!' Adalhard said. And that was true. It was common knowledge that I had no love for priests. They stank, refused food and water and spent their whole lives in some form of drugged-up trance they claimed made them closer to the gods. I looked to Hilde and Eadger, saw the naked fear on their faces. It had been a fanatical priest, along with a treacherous chief, who had seen to the deaths of many of their people. Including Eadger's wife and daughter.

Having said all that, throughout the height of the Ravensworn, I had always kept a priest or two in our ranks. It gave the men some solace, to know they could speak to a man close to the gods. It also came in handy in battle on occasion. 'Ghost fence,' I said, suddenly full of inspiration. 'We make a camp in the woods over the rise there.' I pointed up the hill where the enemy had come from. 'We cut off the heads of the three dead enemies and form a small ghost fence on the eastern edge of the forest. It might slow them down if they come for us again.'

Ghost fences were common practice among the western tribes. Some tribes even had them up permanently around their villages, warding off raiders and thieves. To walk through a ghost fence was to bring about your demise. All knew. All feared them.

'Three heads is hardly a formidable fence,' Adalhard grumbled, though I saw him stroking his beard in thought.

'What if we used—'

'No!' I cut Haribert off, sensing what the chief was about to say. 'We cannot use the heads of our own dead. Do not even suggest it.'

'To do so would be to anger the gods,' Adalhard agreed with a nod. 'Not to mention the effect it would have on our men.'

'So we build a base in the trees. How do we know the enemy is not within?'

'They aren't.' I shook my head. 'The trees gave them cover to pass through undetected. They'll be out on the plains somewhere. Remember what Sigimund said? They live in huge tents, and the grass plains are their home.'

'Well, what are we waiting for?' Haribert said, clapping his hands together in enthusiasm.

* * *

The sun was setting somewhere in the west when I was alerted to a rider approaching from the east. The man was bathed in gold and red, the last of the daylight making him appear as some sort of god as he approached. We had made good progress throughout the afternoon. The forest was dense, the trees packed in tight, though under the command of Adalhard and Sedric, the men had carved a clearing on the eastern edge, wooden huts roughly formed with thick canopies of leaves and vines above. If it rained we would still get wet, but we had made it as comfortable as we could. Our carts had been painstakingly pushed through the long grass. I had insisted on helping with this, and three great fires roared in the centre of our makeshift camp, my dead horses cut up and roasting above them. We would eat well that night, at least.

'Has he said anything?' I said to the lookout as I exited the forest.

'Nothing, Lord.' The man shook his head.

The horseman waited fifty paces from the forest's edge. He gave me no acknowledgement as I approached, just stared dully at me, as if the sight of me bored him.

'What do you want?' I asked, not bothering to give the man my name.

'You are Alaric Hengistson?' the rider asked, his accent thick, clumsy with the words of our tongue.

'I am,' I said, somewhat put out. How could this man know who I was?

'My lord summons you to his presence. Please follow me.'

The rider turned and made to leave. I did not move. He had covered perhaps fifty paces when he stopped and turned his mount back to face me. 'Perhaps I did not make myself clear,' he said. 'I am still learning your tongue, after all.'

'Oh, you were clear enough,' I said, then hawked and spat. 'I need to get a couple of bits, and I'm bringing a guard with me.'

'You will not. My lord has requested your presence, and you alone.'

I considered it a moment, then gave a nod. 'I'll bring one companion with me. A young man by the name of Sigimund. I believe your lord knows him?' The rider nodded. 'Fine. Wait here, I'll be back presently.'

Turning to leave, I grinned at the disgusted frown on the rider's face. Clearly not a man used to being made to wait. Walking back under the canopy of the trees, I was immediately surrounded by Adalhard, Haribert, Sedric, Eadger and Hilde.

'Who is that?'

'What did he say?'

'Have they come to fight again?'

'Get me Sigimund,' was all I said in reply. I walked to where my armour lay on the detritus-ridden forest floor and scooped up the cuirass Sedric had made for me. If I was going to meet this Sarmatian lord, I would do it dressed as a lord of war.

Sigimund appeared, a fearful look in his eyes. He had read the room, so to speak, and knew what was coming. 'You and I are off to meet your boss. Bring a cloak; it will be cold once the sun drops.'

'He does not want to go,' Haribert said to me firmly, resting a hand on his son's shoulder.

'I bet he doesn't! But your lad here made his bed. Now he needs to lie in it. He has had dealings with this Bahadur before. I want him with me.'

Sigimund was an insurance policy, more than anything. In my mind, I believed this Bahadur may see Sigimund as one of his men, mercenary or not. I thought having the lad with me might boost my chances of survival. With my armour strapped on, helmet in place and sword at my hip, we left. I told Haribert and Adalhard that if we were not back by dawn to come looking for us, and be ready to fight, and then Sigimund and I set off under the darkening sky, our impatient guard riding up ahead.

15

'It's cold.' Sigimund's teeth chattered and his shoulders shook as we walked.

I tutted. 'You need more meat on your bones, lad. It isn't *that* cold.'

In truth, I was just as frozen as him, but determined not to show it. The endless grass plains stretched off into the night. The sky was clear, stars twinkling down on us from above. A savage wind assaulted us from the east, blowing directly into our faces. It was bracing, to say the least. I knew the temperature dropped harshly overnight, the grass plains being far away from any sea, but to experience it firsthand was horrible. I kept clenching and unclenching my fists beneath my cloak, not wanting my sword grip affected if I had to fight.

'How much further do you think?' Sigimund asked through quivering lips.

'I've no notion of where we are. You're the one who has been here before. You tell me.'

We must have been walking for over a Roman hour. My legs ached from the exertions of the day, the small of my back twinging with every step. Just another of the gods' reminders of the poor life choices I had made. 'They set up camp somewhere different every night. Their tents are on wagons, so easily moved.'

'That is useful information that you should have told me before,' I grumbled. 'Tents on carts?'

'Aye. You have to climb steps to get into them. No need to pack them away the next day, see? You just hitch your cart up and ride off. It is clever.'

It was, I had to admit. I found myself curious, almost looking forward to seeing them for myself.

We did not have long to wait. Within a matter of heartbeats, I saw the glow of cook fires on the horizon. We were walking down a gentle slope, into what appeared to be a long, shallow valley that ran north to south. I found it a curious place to camp, surrounded by hills, with no clear line of sight as to what might be over the horizon. It gave shelter from the wind, though, I guessed. And what did these people have to worry about? There was no one around for miles to threaten them. They had made sure of that.

As we approached, our guide decided he was bored with waiting for us, and kicked his mount in the flanks and disappeared into the night. 'Guess we're on our own,' I mused as we walked. 'Anything else you'd like to tell me at this point? Can I expect to be branded as you were?'

'I think that honour is reserved for the men who fight for him,' Sigimund said, and then he gulped. 'He is going to think I have betrayed him.'

'Well, you kind of have,' I said unhelpfully. 'But I don't think he'll kill you.'

'You don't?'

'No. If I was him, I'd let you live and then kill you in battle. He just wants to size me up. He got a look at our men this afternoon. Now he wants to know who leads them.'

'All about you, isn't it?' Sigimund muttered. 'Nothing changes.'

I had to laugh at that. 'Did you ever hear of the Harii?' I asked, changing the subject.

'Of course. Black-clad warriors who stalked the night. They would cover their faces and arms in soot so be invisible in the darkness. My men would talk about them often when we were in the forests looking for prey.'

His prey happened to be my family, but for the moment, I let it slide. 'Did you ever hear of how they used to play dead?'

'No?' Sigimund threw me a quizzical look.

'Their chief, a friend of mine, Ketill, once got his men to cover themselves in blood and lie on the ground. They had fought a skirmish that morning, and were waiting to spring a trap on another enemy later in the day. They covered themselves in blood, lay down on the cold ground next to the men they had killed, then when their enemy rode up to find the aftermath of the morning's battle, they simply sprung up and took them by surprise. That is what we are doing here, lad.'

'I don't understand?' Sigimund frowned.

'We are playing dead. Circumstances are slightly different, I'll grant you. But it amounts to the same thing. When we meet with this Bahadur, I want him to think we are already beaten. He would have seen us this afternoon, gauged our numbers and our mettle. Make no doubts about it. If he had wanted us finished, he could have got it done. But he didn't, and that makes me curious.'

I had been thinking about that as we walked. Why had the Sarmatians retreated? They had us surrounded, our supply horses slaughtered. We had no hope. But the man had simply ordered his cavalry to retreat. Was it a mere flex? This Bahadur showing off how powerful he was? Had he left us to stew, knowing he would come back and finish us off come the dawn? That had been my first thought, and my reason for wanting the men to make camp in the woodland. But this summons had me thinking. What else could this Bahadur want from me?

Sigimund and I silenced as we approached the camp. Even in the murky light of the night, it was a mightily impressive sight. The camp was encircled with carts turned onto their sides. A makeshift barricade, with men armed with bows on top. These men scowled at us as we walked through a small gap between two carts, but they said nothing. I imagined there would be warriors bracing the chill night air on the eastern and western high points of the valley, though I had seen no one on our walk. Clearly, Bahadur had his men well organised. They were no strangers to war. They had proved that to me already.

Once through the carts, the temperature rose. The wind whistled above us, but did not reach down to strike. Fires roared, dotted around the carts that littered the long grass in no particular order. In a Roman camp, even many Germani ones, there would be some form of order. Tents pitched in rows so men knew where to walk. The commander would usually be in the centre, in theory the safest place if under attack. In the Sarmatian camp, though, there was no order whatsoever. It appeared that the huge carts with tents on top stopped wherever they wanted for the night. In and out we weaved, slit eyes peering at us through tent flaps as we walked. The night air was rich with the tang of roasting meat and wood smoke, a not unpleasant smell that had my belly rumbling.

'Where do we go?' I asked Sigimund. All the tents looked the same to me. And they were impressive. Huge structures of wood and leather, built on great carts that must have taken at least four horses to pull. The tents were round, small holes at the summit where smoke from fires within rose lazily to the stars.

'That one,' Sigimund said, pointing to a tent twenty paces to our front.

'How can you be sure?'

It looked no different to the others to me. 'There is a warrior on top, look,' Sigimund said. Looking up, I saw he was right. A warrior stood above the door, bow nocked and trained on us.

'That one it is.'

As we approached, the tent flap was opened and three men came out, all with swords drawn. 'No weapons inside,' the first of them said, and I saw it was the messenger we had followed here.

'How do I know you won't just kill us as soon as I give you my sword?'

'You don't,' the messenger said.

I looked at Sigimund, who gave me a fearful gaze in return. 'Play dead, remember,' I said quietly, hauling my sword free and handing it over, hilt first, to the Sarmatian. Sigimund did the same, and then the two of us were frisked. Once satisfied, the Sarmatian warrior nodded to his comrades and the tent flaps were thrown back open. We were ushered inside.

The tent was not what I would have expected from a great chief or king. It was plain, but well appointed. Rugs lined the floor and walls, keeping in as much heat as possible. They were dull reds and blues, aged over time. The sort of rugs I had seen in common homes in the Roman empire. I had been expecting fine tapestries woven with gold, intricate designs depicting some famous victory or other. Many Germani chiefs had similar in their halls. Roman generals, of course, had mosaics and paintings covering their stone walls.

But the rugs insulated the tent well enough, and I felt none of the biting cold I had outside. The three warriors followed us inside. I could feel their presence at my back. I had to squint slightly as I looked around the tent. There were a few wooden chests, a simple straw pallet laid out by the fire that smoked in the tent's centre. Beyond the fire, a man sat cross-legged on a rug, his eyes closed. I stood and waited, unsure whether I was expected to approach the man. A nudge in my back made my mind up for me, and Sigimund and I walked around the fire to stand in front of the sitting man.

I studied that man as we waited for him to open his eyes. In Germania, the most feared warriors are men with the strength of gods. They stand a head above everyone else, with thick arms and rounded shoulders. They can cleave an axe through bone, dance through four or five enemies, slaying them all without taking a cut. I had fought with such men. Ketill of the Harii, Ruric, my trusted second. Their exploits became legend, and every warrior in the land whispered their name in fear. This man, though, appeared to have none of that prowess.

He was short and slim, with neatly trimmed dark hair above a clean-shaven face. Wearing just a sleeveless tunic, he showed off bare arms devoid of scars or muscle mass. His skin was sun kissed, not dissimilar to the colour of Romans who hail from the south. I wondered then how far this man had travelled to that wind-swept plain in eastern Germania. And again, what had driven him there. How could this man be the fearsome war lord come to take over our lands? He looked as though he would be blown away by a gust of wind. 'So you are Alaric,' the man said, opening his slit eyes and fixing me with a murderous glare. 'It is good to finally meet you. I am Bahadur.'

'Honoured, I'm sure,' I said with a sniff. I sat myself down opposite him and stared into his eyes, flashing him a grin. 'Got anything to drink?' I've often found meetings such as those were nothing more than a posturing show, with two men each determined to prove they had the biggest balls. I liked to think my balls were pretty impressive. And I would never show fear to an enemy. A lifetime of dealing with Rome had left me well equipped.

Bahadur said something in his own tongue, and a cup was placed in my hand, quickly filled with water. 'Well, that's disappointing,' I said, frowning into the cup. 'You make me walk all that way in the freezing cold and don't even offer me some heated wine when I get here? Not great hospitality, that.'

Sigimund was rigid with fear. I glanced up to where the young man still stood, stiff as a plank. The only part of him that moved was his eyes, quivering, never leaving Bahadur. 'Sit down,' I said to him quietly. 'You're making the place look untidy.' Bahadur's three men stood spread out behind us, hands on sword hilts. Not for the first time in my life, I wondered at the logic of my decision making. Had I just walked freely to my death?

'We do not drink wine or ale. I know it is customary for you to do so. We find it dulls our senses. And it is our senses that keep us alive.'

'What do you want?' I asked, setting down the cup of the useless water. 'It is late and I wish to sleep. Get to the point.'

Bahadur chuckled at that. His men moved a step closer. I could feel how tense they were. 'I have heard word of your deeds, Alaric. Your reach is greater than you could ever know. Alaric the battle turner. Alaric the chief killer. Men tell tales of your exploits in our lands.'

I have to admit I sat a little straighter at that. Pride had always been my enemy. I was sure one day it would get me killed. 'Too right and all,' I said, throwing Sigimund a wink. 'I'm not a man to mess with. Today, though, you messed with me. I do not make a good enemy, Bahadur, chief of no lands.'

Bahadur chuckled again, running a hand over his smooth face. 'I believe you. But it seems our paths are destined to cross. What do you suggest we do about it?'

'You turn around and fuck off back to where you came from. I'll do the same. Deal?' I spat on my hand and held it out.

The Sarmatian shook his head, with what appeared to be genuine sorrow in his dark eyes. 'That I cannot do. Believe me when I say I wish we could. The lands we have left were warm and fertile. The soil rich and the woodlands thick with game.'

'And now we get to it,' I said, my one eye fixed on his. 'What is it you are running from?'

Bahadur shifted, and his eyes glanced to the three men at my back. I felt them all shift in turn. They understood our tongue, for what I had said made them uncomfortable. Both facts were good to know.

'There are some horrors in this world that do not bear speaking of. Believe me, Alaric, famed enemy of Rome. You do not want to cross paths with the people we flee from. They are demons. Killers. Burners. There are some men whose sole ambition is to see the world burn and chaos rule. I trust you have met with such men in the past?'

'I have been one in the past,' I said, smirking. 'Though I prefer the term disrupter.'

Bahadur returned my smile, though his was tight and full of sadness. It did not reach his eyes. 'Disrupter is a rather tame term for the men we flee. Pray they do not follow us. We seek to carve ourselves a home in the west. There is much we can bring in trade and comradeship. We hope your people will embrace us.'

'Have you reached out to the Iazyges? Their lands are just south of here. If you wanted to make friends, you should have started with them.'

There was a flicker of something in Bahadur's eyes, I couldn't make out what. And then I thought of the messengers we had sent to the tribe, the odd fact that they had not returned. And then it clicked into place. 'You did seek out the Iazyges. They were suspicious of you. As a tribe they have always been a warlike people. Did you kill them all?'

Sigimund was practically shaking with fear now. I could feel his body pulsing. It wasn't doing my nerves any favours. Gods, where was the wine when you needed it?

'Yes. We visited the Iazyges. And no, they were not hospitable. There was a battle; we were victorious. Though we did not slaughter their women and children, for we are not animals. We won the battle, and then we turned our mounts back north and left them in peace.'

'You left widows and children to bury their husbands and fathers you mean?'

Bahadur merely shrugged. 'Such is war. So you and I, we will not be friends?'

I shook my head. 'We will not. I will do all I can to stop you moving further west.'

'I have four hundred horses with me. I could simply ride around that makeshift army you have brought to defeat me.'

'You could. But you won't. You know the importance of not leaving an enemy at your back. And you know I will hunt you for as long as it takes. Fight me tomorrow, or in a year or two. Makes no difference. It will end with you at the mercy of my blade.'

The Sarmatian considered that a moment, and then his gaze flickered to Sigimund. 'And then there is a decision to be made about you, my young friend. You, who promised me a war between the western tribes and Rome. You, who said you could orchestrate it all, with that clever little plot of yours. And now you come back to my home in the company of my enemy. Did I not make it clear that I expected total loyalty from those who serve me?'

'I... I... err...' Sigimund was a quivering wreck. Sweat streaked down his face, his hair matted to his head.

'Was I not clear that the punishment for betraying me was death?'

The three men behind us drew their swords. I rose swiftly to my feet, wondering if I was really about to die for that little shit. The same cur that had tried to have me killed just the year before. I had pretended to be a slave because of Sigimund, thrown myself at the mercy of my enemy and spent months away from my family. Men I had known had died; the tribes had lost thousands of men fighting the Fourteenth legion. All because of him.

But then I thought of Haribert, awaiting our return in the stand of trees where we had made our camp. I could picture the big chief spending the freezing night at the edge of the woods, eyes desperately scanning the eastern horizon. Haribert had been good to me when he had no need to. He had given me men, accepted my command and rode to war when he should have been tucked up in his hall. He had also marched to my aid to stop his son killing me the summer before. I sighed inside, knowing I could not let Sigimund be killed.

'Seems there is a deal to be struck here, Bahadur.'

'Is there?' the Sarmatian asked. He was still seated, hadn't moved a muscle. A picture of calm, he held out an open palm to me, inviting me to speak.

'The lad here betrayed you. Only because I caught him. His men are all dead; there's just him left. I would say that is punishment enough.'

'I'm not hearing your deal.'

I turned to look at Sigimund, his ashen face looking halfway to the Heroes Hall already. 'Remember the Harii?' I said very quietly to him. He gave me the smallest of nods. 'Trust me,' I whispered.

'That brand you gave him. What does that mean to your people?'

'It means he is a warrior of the Sarmatians. Under the sky god's realm he is commanded to fight until his last breath. It is an oath he has broken. For that he must die.'

'How will you kill him?'

'I will slit his belly and watch as his intestines spill to the ground. His head will then be cut off, followed by his arms and legs. There will be nothing of him left to greet his gods when he passes to the other side.'

I puffed out my cheeks. 'And there was me thinking you were quite civilised. Here's the deal. I'll kill the boy myself, outside this very tent. It will be swift and merciful. You will give me a horse so I can take the body back to his father. The two of us will agree on a truce for the next ten days, so a proper mourning period can be observed. After that, it is a war to the death.'

I was talking out my arse, obviously. We had no mourning period, not like the Romans. We had very little customs at all when it came to death. We came from the earth, and when the three spinners cut the thread of our lives, we returned to it. Simple. But I needed to buy some time.

Bahadur took his time considering. 'There seems to be very little for me to gain in this deal.'

'Ten days to plan your attack? To scout further, understand more of the land you ride into? Seems to me you have plenty to gain. If you use your time wisely.'

'What are you doing?' Sigimund hissed. I glanced to him, saw the dark patch spreading down the front of his trousers. The coward had pissed himself in fear.

'Shut up,' I hissed at him.

Bahadur rose to his feet, seemingly coming to a decision. 'You will have your ten days. But the traitor dies now.'

I shrugged. 'Then give me back my sword.'

We were ushered outside. Sigimund half dragged as he screamed in protest. 'Take off your mail,' I said to him, taking my sword from one of Bahadur's men and holding the blade out.

'Why are you doing this?' he said to me, teeth chattering.

'We're playing dead. Remember?' He nodded at me again. Still shaking like a leaf in a storm, he shrugged off his mail.

'Do it now,' Bahadur said. He stood at the entrance to his tent, looking down at us from the top of the wooden steps.

I gave the chief a nod, then aimed my sword at Sigimund's chest and drove it home with all the strength I could muster.

16

We were suitably sombre for the following ten days. A funeral pyre was built on the eastern edge of the trees that sheltered our men, and we stood around it as the sun set on the day I had arrived back, a shrouded body placed atop and burned in a blaze that lit up the night.

But we were not idle either. Haribert had men out on patrol every day. He led the men himself, calling insults to the Sarmatians that came within earshot. He told them they had killed his son, and that his vengeance would rain down upon them. He was a ferocious-looking man, Haribert. Built like an ox with a voice that carried well on the wind. The Sarmatians heard what he said, and I think even if some of them could not understand all the words, they got the message.

I drilled the men every day. I brought out what I called to Eadger and Hilde my greatest hits. We dug pits, staked them, covering them back over with earth. I laid huge stones out at paced intervals between the edge of the trees and the rolling hills we knew the enemy would come from. Ghost fences were built from the rotting heads of the enemy we had slaughtered in our first battle. All this we did in sight of enemy scouts. I cared not one bit.

And so, ten days after I had returned back with Sigimund's body rolled in a rug, thrust atop a borrowed horse, the enemy came.

They streamed over the hilltop and came for the trees at a trot. I think they had been expecting us to sally out and meet them in the open. They had certainly been expecting a barrage of arrows, for why else would I have bothered with the rocks to gauge the distance? What they had not been expecting was for us to do nothing at all.

Bahadur would have been able to make out the lines of helmets in the shade of the trees. He would have seen the glinting spear tips pointing up to the gods. But those helmets did not move, and the spears were not launched into the sky. It took them half the morning to send three runners into the trees to investigate. All they found were helmets propped on shafts of wood, spears buried butt first in the ground.

I watched the charade from the south, feeling quite content. I had indeed been drilling the men. We had split them into three groups. A third scouted with Haribert as he raged at the injustice of a slaughtered son. The second third dug and heaved stones. The final third trained with sword and shield, but on the western edge of the small forest that gave us shelter. Away from prying eyes. West had been the direction we had moved before daybreak on the tenth day, leaving behind us anything we could not carry. Sedric had been in charge of a small party of eight. Men who were not warriors, but smiths and cooks. These men had repaired what armour they could and ensured the men were fed. But in between those duties, they had performed another task.

Sedric was a man I knew I could trust with my life. I also knew that I had bought ten days' grace from the war to the death I knew was coming. I needed that time to get some comradeship between the men, to get them fighting as a unit. I have learned many lessons from the Romans in my life. As much as I despise the bastards, I am constantly amazed at the wealth of knowledge I have still left untouched. But one thing I had caught on to pretty quick was that a body of men who fights like one will more likely be victorious than a band of heroes who fight alone.

And I needed to win. We drilled. The men were split, so they drilled not with their brothers from their tribe, but so a Marcomanni stood shoulder to shoulder with an Anglii. Cimbri fought alongside Quadi, and so the factions of our army began to melt away. I didn't want them thinking they were going into battle to fight for their tribe. I wanted them to think they were fighting for their country. They would be Ravensworn. They would be mine.

'So that's the easy part done,' Eadger said to me as we watched from behind a small clutch of bushes that littered the open fields.

'Seems so. Wonder what he'll do next,' I mused.

'There'll be riders out searching for us before noon. We should get back.'

I nodded, still smiling to myself. It was as we ran across the open ground, out of sight to the horsemen to the north, that I saw the plume of smoke to the southeast. 'Three figures on that hilltop,' Eadger huffed out as we ran. He pointed, and I followed his finger. Three silhouettes in the distance, their armour glinting in the sunlight. One of them was a giant of a man, and I had an inkling who it would be. Whether it was good news for me or not, I did not know. But it meant that my diversion into Carnuntum before we marched east had not been a waste of time.

'Will they intervene, do you think?' Eadger asked me. He had figured out who they were.

'Certainly,' I said. 'But will they fight with us, or against us?'

* * *

Sedric and his men had found a narrow path that ran between a crop of thin woodland. Beech trees intertwined with pine, both providing little shade, but the surrounding ground was rocky, unsuited for cavalry, and that was perfect.

'It was the best we could find, Lord,' Sedric said to me, nervously tossing his weight from one foot to the other.

'I could have asked for nothing better. Well done, my friend. Where will we camp?'

'I've got the lads there now. It's half a Roman mile back west. The ground is level and there's tree cover. Not as good as the last one, but it should serve.'

'I hope they've got the cook fires lit. We'll be hungry tonight.' I asked Haribert to have three of his men serve as scouts, and they went off to the south and east. It was not Bahadur I wanted information on, but anyone else that could be coming at our rear.

And then we settled in for a wait. It would not take long, I knew, and the men stood in the formations I had been drilling into them, eating, drinking, pissing, whatever they needed to do to prepare themselves. There was no wine, another lesson I had learned from Rome. A sober man fights better than a drunk one. Too many of our warriors filled up on wine or ale before a fight, seeking courage at the bottom of a skin. All they found was an early death.

I ate a meal of hard bread and cheese, olives and dried fruit. I stretched, and then Sedric strapped me into the cuirass he had made me. Then I sent him away. 'Go back with your men, get ready to help with the wounded later. And get those cook fires going!' Sedric had seen his fill of war and blood, and there was a lot of that coming our way. It was just before noon we first heard the horses. Silence spread among us. Men ceased their idle chatter and snatched up spears and strapped on helmets.

'Remember your training,' I said to them, taking my place in the centre of the front rank. We had a raven banner propped up at our backs, though there was no wind. So the banner hung limp. But it was still the black raven on the red field, and I was just as proud to fight under it as I had been the first time I had seen it raised. The ground quivered under the charge of horses' hooves. Through the gaps in the trees we saw flashes of flesh and metal, and then as they rounded the corner, the full might of the Sarmatians came into view.

'Shields!' I bellowed, and my men raised their shields high, showing the enemy nothing but the slits of their eyes. Arrows hissed through the air at us. We caught them on our shields then cut their shafts off with our blades. None of my men moved an inch, and I grinned. I had bought myself ten days, and used the time well. Arrows spent, the horsemen levelled their spears and charged.

'Now!' I called out, dropping to my knees and bringing my shield close to my chest. The men in the second rank stepped forward and raised their shields above ours, the third rank doing the same, their shields held over head. The Sarmatians saw nothing but an unbreakable wall of wood, no gaps for their long spears to punch through. A horse will not charge a well-made shield wall; it will get within a handful of paces and try to turn away. The problem the enemy had was they were forced to come at us on a narrow track, their mounts unable to loop around us due to the rocky terrain.

I waited as long as I could. Until I could feel the breath of the horse to my front on my face. 'Ravensworn!' was my battle cry, echoed by hundreds of men around me. As one, the front rank launched themselves up, our swords licking out and slashing out at the horses rearing at our unexpected movement. I hacked wildly, blood hot on my face, the scream of a terrified horse ringing in my ears as it threw its rider and tried to back away. Poor thing had nowhere to go. Our second rank held the last of our spears, and they launched these in the air now, whistling in a low arc to slam into the second and third ranks of the enemy.

All was chaos. 'Push forward!' I called, bloody sword held high as a beacon for my men to follow. I ducked under a slashing sword, knocked aside a thrust spear and carved my blade down a horse's flank. Another rider was thrown to the ground. With the stamping of hooves all around me, men screaming, blood on the air, I took a blow to the top of my helmet and dropped to one knee, dazed. With blurred vision in my one remaining eye and fog in my brain, I rose unsteadily to my feet and was quickly knocked down by a spear thrust hammering into my shield.

'Don't move!' a voice called from above me. I had my eye closed, trying to clear my head. Pain lanced through me, from the top of my head to my jarred left shoulder. Heart hammering, blood thick in my ears, I opened my eye to see Eadger and Hilde fighting side by side. Eadger was ramming his shield up into a rider's face, Hilde stabbing the same man in the side before wrenching her blade free and slashing open a neck.

'Get up now!' Hilde shouted to me, turning to me with a snarl. She swung back to the fray, pushing past a riderless horse and hacking away at another Sarmatian. Gods, she was ferocious.

I rose unsteadily, taking a few steps back to survey the battlefield. Our line had broken. Where I had pushed forward in our centre, the flanks had not followed. Adalhard had our left, and he and a clutch of men were surrounded on three sides, horsemen oppressively forcing them into a half circle. Haribert was faring better on the right, but even with his great bulk leading their charge, the men could not push forward enough to catch up with the centre.

Sarmatian cavalry were beginning to encircle our advanced position in the middle and get around the men we had left on the flanks. 'Hilde! Eadger! We need to get these men back and reform a line!' I shouted, though my voice was hoarse, throat like jagged rocks.

They heard me though, and within moments the men were pacing backwards in organised fashion. I grinned, thinking again what a bonus having those ten days had been. And then we sprung our trap.

Once our line was reformed across the narrow pass, I turned to the warrior holding the Ravensworn banner. 'Give the signal!' Before I had even finished speaking, the banner was hoisted up in the air, the man waving it from side to side. The Sarmatians must have seen that and wondered what was happening, as it felt as though there was a momentary pause in the action. I saw heads turn from side to side, questioning frowns exchanged. And then with a cheer to wake the gods, Sigimund, back from the dead, rose from his concealed position far to our left flank, a hundred men at his back, and slammed home a charge into the enemy flank.

The day was ours.

* * *

I had, obviously, not killed Sigimund ten days before outside Bahadur's tent. I'd rammed a sword through him, but through the gap between his arm and torso. I had nicked his torso enough that a long, thin cut had spread and blood seeped through his tunic. But it had been dark, and I have often found that men only see what they want to.

Bahadur had wanted to see Sigimund killed. Therefore, he had. I had also made sure that only I had touched his body once the deed was done, wrapping him myself and throwing him over the mount they had provided. And so we had 'played dead', and Sigimund got to live on.

He had been terrified on the journey back to our camp, constantly squirming and calling out. Bahadur had sent two men to follow me, I guess to make sure I really was leaving. Thankfully they hadn't bothered getting close enough to notice.

Haribert had helped with the deception, though he didn't realise it at the time. He had come storming out of the trees when we arrived, shouting and cursing every god he could think of. He had even tried to hit me, which was a nice touch. Many tears had been spilled once the enemy riders had turned away, and Sigimund was finally freed from his blanket.

I wish I could say I had seen Bahadur's face when he saw young Sigimund charging downhill to smash into his army's right flank. But such was the press of men forced onto that little path through the woodland that I could make no one out. The Sarmatians were pressed in tight, unable to move forward due to the line of shields facing them. Dead horses and men littered the surrounding path, making manoeuvrability even harder. And the riders at their rear could not make out the threat coming from their right flank, and therefore, they did nothing to help their comrades.

The slaughter was horrific to watch, even for one who had seen as much blood as me. Sigimund and his men were in a frenzy, stabbing and slashing at anything that moved. The whole thing lasted mere moments, but there were a hundred or more corpses on the ground by the time it was over. The Sarmatians tried to fight back, but their courage failed them, and one by one they backed off, before turning their mounts and streaming away back east.

We watched them go, a raucous cheer echoing to the heavens from our lungs. To call it a victory would have been generous, but we had stopped them in their tracks, and that was good enough.

'Alaric! Over here!' Hilde called to me over the cheering, and looking around, I saw her on her knees, leaning over Eadger, who was as pale as winter snow.

'No,' I whispered to myself. Letting my shield drop to the ground, I ran over to where Eadger lay. He had a spear wound high on the right side of his chest. Blood pumped from it.

'The fuckers... got me,' Eadger wheezed. He gave me a bloody smile, a trembling hand reaching up to grab mine. 'Don't mourn for me, Alaric. I'm going to my family.'

Tears streamed into my beard, but I returned my friend's smile. In the time I had known him, he had proven himself to be one of the finest men I had ever met. He was not a warrior by trade, but from necessity. He had been a wood-worker before the ships had landed on the beach of his home. Before his wife and daughter had been murdered. A man of peace and principle. And now he was to die, fighting for nothing more than his principles, those being that you stood by a friend in need. That friend had been me. I have lost many brothers in my time. In that moment, losing Eadger would almost seem worse than losing Ketill or Ruric. Those men were warriors to their core.

'We need to get him back to Sedric and the others. There are medics there, Alaric. The wound is deep, but he might yet make it.' Hilde forced me to look at her with her words. And slowly I found myself coming back to my senses.

Haribert and Adalhard took over, getting the healthy to aid the wounded, and soon we were moving back to our new camp, leaving the desolation of battle behind us.

* * *

Eadger lived on, though none of us knew how long he had left. One of Sedric's men had sedated him with a concoction that stank worse than his wound, and was currently cleaning and stitching his chest. I worked my way around the rest of the wounded, talking to men for whom the end was coming. The dying lay with swords in their hands, their paths to the Hanged One's Hall guaranteed. It was all we could do for them.

'How many have we lost?' I asked Haribert, who slumped down on a tree stump beside me as the sun set. The chief looked haggard, a ragged cut running down his left cheek. He had refused all efforts to have it seen to.

'Around a hundred, give or take. Another fifteen won't last the night. Of the wounded, thirty are good for nothing. We've got no horses or mules or wagons, for that matter, to get them back west to safety. Sedric has sent a man to Balomar, asking him for aid.'

'He will help,' I said with more certainty than I felt. I had been disappointed Balomar had not come with us on this journey. My friend was a battle king, and kings like that only stayed in power as long as their warriors knew to fear them. True enough, he had fought and been wounded in the battle against the Romans. But I still thought he would have wanted to be a part of this. But there was the ongoing feud with Rome for him to consider, coupled with his difficult relations with his neighbours. With him gone, and most of his army too, it was not impossible that an opportunistic chief would seek to take some of his lands.

'But that will take time. We need to decide on our next plan.'

I nodded. 'How many do you think Bahadur lost?'

Haribert tilted his head in thought. 'About fifty more than us, I'd guess. Adalhard left three men to watch the battle site. They've just returned to say the Sarmatians are there collecting their dead.'

'We should do the same.'

'Aye. Tomorrow. No wagons or horses will be an issue.'

'Then we'll burn the bodies where they are. Moving them a mile or so beforehand won't make much difference.'

A silence settled between us. Two old warriors who had done and seen this all before. Never got any easier, though.

'Gods, I ache,' Haribert said, rolling his shoulders. 'When I was a young man, I could have fought all day, slept a little, then rose and done it all again.'

'Aye, I know the feeling. I'd have managed to squeeze in a skin or two of wine in between and all.'

We both chuckled. I was still in my blood-stained cuirass. There were dents on the left side and low on the right. I had no memory of being struck in either place. I shrugged it off, mainly thinking to hide the thing before Sedric saw it and gave me what for. It would be hard work for him to beat the dents out whilst camped in a forest clearing. I walked away from our camp, skin of water in hand. There was a small stream half a mile or so away, and my feet took me there without thinking. Stripping off, I submerged myself in the icy water, revelling in the shudders that ran through my scarred and ageing body.

When I rose, I breathed in deep and wiped my hair from my face, feeling somewhat refreshed. Setting to washing the blood and grime from my body, hissing at the stings from the litany of small cuts that dotted my arms and legs, I eventually rose out of the water and lay down on my cloak, looking up at the night sky. Sporadic clouds dotted what was otherwise a relatively clear night. A cool easterly breeze had me shivering slightly, but it was not unpleasant. Stars twinkled, and my thoughts drifted to Saxa and my boys. Were they sitting outside Dagr's hall, looking up at the same sky I was? I liked to think so.

Life was a funny thing when you took the time to stop and think on it. The paths it took you down, always turning, changing. If you had asked me as a young man what I thought the future had in store for me, I would have said that my name would rise so high it would sing down the ages. In a hundred years or more, warriors would still be talking of the great Alaric Hengistson, and the endless battles he had won against Rome.

The thought made me smile, sardonically, at least. There I was, an old man, lank, greying hair plastered over my face, leading a small army of misfits against a mighty enemy, seeking to conquer my homeland. Except the army was not Roman. In fact, I still hoped Rome would prove to be my saviour, remembering the three men I had seen on the hilltop, the plume of smoke behind them in the distance. Surely Rome would not stand by and do nothing, as a potentially dangerous enemy came closer to their lands? Better the devil you know, as the saying went. I was praying it translated to Latin.

Rising wearily, still damp, but judging myself dry enough, I shrugged on my tunic, struggling to get it over my left shoulder. An old wound given to me the night I lost my army and my eye. It had never healed well. I was just beginning my walk back to camp when the first prick of sound caught my ears. Stopping in my tracks, I cocked my head. As still as stone, I stood, eye closed, just listening. There was another rustle in the undergrowth, somewhere off to my right. What I thought was the sound of a distant horse nickering. But we had no horses. Opening my eye, turning right, I saw a small hare, three babies in tow, emerge from beneath a bush and move off through the long grass. I smiled at my paranoia.

Moving off, spirits somewhat lifted, I had walked another twenty paces when I heard the noise again. I was in no doubt this time. It was no small animal moving across the forest floor. It was a horse, and it was close. And then the screaming began. A flash of flame ahead, silhouettes illuminated in its glow. My heart sank as I registered what I was seeing. Bahadur had not waited until the following day to resume our battle. He had come for us in the night.

17

I ran, lungs aflame, aching legs pumping as hard as my tired body could force them. Men were screaming. I could hear Haribert bellowing orders, my name being called. I ran for what felt an age, until I reached the camp, breathless, swordless, my one eye taking in the destruction of my army.

Bahadur's riders had stormed through our camp. I had no idea how they had managed to sneak up on us with no one noticing and had no time to ask. Arrows flew in the murky light. Men died where they fell. Haribert had a small body of men formed up on the far right, a half-circle that bristled with spear points. The rest of the men were in turmoil. They fought in small knots, some naked, others just in tunics. Most had shields and swords to bear, but they were of little use in open ground against well-armoured cavalry. It was a massacre.

I staggered through the mass of horseflesh and men. A Sarmatian lunged at me from atop his horse and I grabbed the man's arm and pulled him from his mount. He hit the ground hard and rolled, the wind knocked out of him. Before he could recover, I snatched the blade from his numbed hand and slashed it across his throat. The sword was alien to me, the curved blade and heavy hilt leaving the weight unbalanced on the wrist. It was a blade designed for slashing down from horseback. But the edge was sharp, and it would serve me as good as any.

'Ravensworn to me!' Haribert was shouting from the centre of his ring of shields. Slowly I saw men flocking to him, and was once more very grateful for the big chief. I staggered that way myself, using my stolen blade twice more to even the odds a touch. When I got there, we had around one hundred men in a tight formation. They were all the warriors we had left.

'Lord! Thank the gods! I thought you dead,' Sedric said to me as I squeezed in between the shields. He had a cut below his right eye, another running up his left arm. My sword was in his right hand, a hammer in his left.

'Looks like we all will be soon. Thanks for saving my sword.'

'Take it, Lord.' Sedric offered the blade to me, but I shook my head.

'You keep hold of that for now. It was my father's, that blade. Look after it for me.'

His face swam into my head then. His, my mother's, Saxa, my boys. All of them. The faces of the men I had lost over the years. I could almost hear them urging me on to take my place at the feasting hall, to eat and drink with my lost brothers until the end of time. I snarled. One day, I would greet them all again. But I was not quite ready yet.

'How many shields do we have?' I called out. Men lifted theirs high, and I counted sixty. That would have to do. Around us, our camp burned. Bahadur had come with fire and sword. He had been counting on us to be licking our wounds, more focused on tending our wounded and recovering our wits than on the lookout for another attack. He had been right. The thought made me sick. Somewhere out there in the firelight, the Sarmatian leader was smirking to himself, patting himself on the back for getting one over the great war lord Alaric. I ground my teeth. Two could play at that game.

'What's the plan here, Alaric?' Haribert asked me. I tried to make out Hilde or Adalhard, but couldn't see them. I called their names and was told they had not made it to the shield wall. Cursing, for losing the two of them was the same as losing twenty warriors or more, I breathed in deep, closed my eye for a moment, and calmed myself.

'Boar's snout,' I said once I had collected myself.

'Are you mad?' Haribert called back. 'We're heavily outnumbered here! You want us to go charging into that lot with no protection? We'll be encircled after our first charge!'

'Not if we scatter them. Push them back into the trees. It will be just like the battle we've already fought.'

'Except this time we don't have men hidden in the trees to ambush them.'

'Then we'll just have to win it ourselves!' What I didn't say was that I had hoped Hilde and Adalhard were out there somewhere, lurking in the shadows. Both were seasoned warriors, and I did not think they would have been taken by surprise so easily. If they were there, they were bound to have more of my men with them. If we could just link up, we could make a fight of it yet.

'On me!' I called, and pushed my way through to the front, setting off at a run. I had no shield, but the men formed up around me well enough, and we charged across the small clearing. The Sarmatians were scattered, chasing down remnants of my fleeing men, and they had no time to react as we hurled ourselves out of the flame light and smashed into them. My first kill was a thrust through the back, the rider falling without ever knowing what killed him. The sword stuck in the man's back and I let it go, snatching up a spear and jabbing it into a horse's face. The beast shied away, rearing up, tossing its rider, and I speared the Sarmatian through the chest as he lay strewn on the ground.

Haribert threw himself at one enemy, forcing his weight on a horse's flank so it toppled sideways, tossing its rider, flailing legs kicking up into the air. Sedric was beside me, using my sword to block a blow whilst his hammer crunched a rider's leg. I sensed the battle turning. The predators had become the prey, and uncertainty engulfed the Sarmatians like winter fog.

A horn sounded in the night air, the same mournful moan I had heard days before on our first engagement with the Sarmatians. Sure enough, they backed away, streaming into the night. I caught sight of Bahadur then, a picture of stillness amongst the chaos of battle. He locked his eyes on me, and I expected him to turn away and flee with his men. Instead, he lowered his spear and charged right for me.

I had time enough to sidestep his charge and feel the rush of air as his spear cut just past my face. Turning, ready to launch my own spear at his back, I was staggered to find he had already stopped and turned his mount, and was once more charging right at me. I threw the spear anyway, but it whistled just to the right of Bahadur's head and then he was hanging low in his saddle, leaning to his left, ready to strike the killing blow.

A sudden cry at my back, and heavy footfall on the earth. Two figures rushed past me, a spear flying from one, two others with swords bright in the firelight. Adalhard emerged from the shadows and plunged his blade deep into Bahadur's leg, the blade sticking. Hilde had thrown the spear; it bit into the Sarmatian's mount just below the neck. Horse and rider were sent crumbling to the earth. Around us, the cacophony of battle roared on. Blades clashed, men fell; the air was rich with the tang of blood and smoke.

'Grab hold of him!'

'Don't let him go!'

'We've got their leader! Let the rest of them go! Rally to me now! Rally to me!'

My men fell in around us, a circle of shields slowly encircling the fallen horse and its wounded rider. I limped up to Bahadur, who lay writhing on the ground, blood spilling from the wound in his leg. 'I don't mean to brag,' I said to the Sarmatian, squatting down beside him, 'but I did suggest to you that you were better off leaving us alone.'

* * *

Warm sunshine and a cool, southerly breeze. It was a beautiful day for grim work. Felt like we had cut down half a forest to build funeral pyres enough for all the dead. We burned the enemy as well as our own. Not out of respect or good will. It was a simple fact that disease spread quickly when bodies were either left in the open or not buried deep enough. We were not yet ready to pack up and leave, and the last thing I needed was men getting sick.

We were down to just over a hundred in men in any state to fight. 'There's a rider coming from the east, Lord,' Faramund said. I turned to the young man. He had his left arm in a sling. It was bruised and swollen, and we had all assumed it broken. Faramund said he had been kicked by a horse sometime in the night. He was the last remaining warrior who had come with me from my hall. More benches had been filled in the Allfather's hall. At the rate I was going, the One-Eyed Wanderer would need to build himself a new one, just for all the brothers I had sent to him over the years.

'I bet there is. He said anything?'

'No, Lord. He's just waiting out in the clearing. Looks like he's alone.'

I grunted. Snatching up a hunk of bread and some hard cheese, I walked out, aware of the stares that followed me. Morale was low among the survivors, despite the fact we had beaten the Sarmatians off twice. Reality dawned on all of us. Didn't matter how many battles we won against this enemy, we would ultimately lose the war. Battles were won by courage and leadership. By supply routes and equipment, morale and organisation. Wars were inevitably won by numbers.

Could be we would fight again that day, in the warm sun and the cool breeze. Could be we would win again. But if the enemy came back the day after, there would surely be no one left for them to fight. I trudged from under the canopy of the trees, black smoke from the pyres rising lazily to the summer sky. We may as well have put out sign posts telling everyone where we were. It didn't matter, not really. The Sarmatians had found us in the night. They'd have done it again in daylight.

I nodded to the rider. It was the same man who had come and fetched me the night I met Bahadur in his tent. I sat down in front of his mount, laid my cloak out on the ground and broke out the bread and cheese. 'Hungry?' I asked him, gesturing to the food.

'You think I will eat your poisoned food?' The rider sniffed, not moving from atop his horse.

With a sigh, I broke off some of the bread and cheese, putting both in my mouth. I shrugged up to him, chewing. The rider took a long look at the tree line, seeing my men staring out at us. Eventually he dismounted, moving with care to sit down opposite me. He broke himself off some food and ate thoughtfully, his eyes now fixed on me. 'Is my brother dead?' he asked in a quiet voice.

'Bahadur was your brother?' I asked, careful to use the word 'was'.

'Aye. Three years my elder. I have followed him my whole life.'

I turned to the black smoke, still snaking its way up to the sky. 'You'd have a hard job following him now. We burned his body with the rest of the dead.'

The rider was quiet a moment, pinching the end of his nose and contemplating. 'You should not have burned his body. It is not the way of our people.'

'Fuck the ways of your people,' I spat. 'You come to our lands with fire and sword. You know how many of our people have died because of the actions of your brother? You have put us on a war path with Rome, not to mention the men I have lost out here fighting you. All this is on your brother. I should have taken his eyes and ears before I burned him, left him to meet your gods blind and deaf, and never know the truth of what comes after we pass.'

'Even for a man of your reputation, Alaric the chief slayer, that would have been despicable.'

'Despicable? I'll tell you what's despicable! The bodies of dead women and children we found in the wake of Sigimund and his little army. All in the name of stirring up a war on your brother's order! Despicable is the children that will grow to adulthood without their parents. The men who came home to find their family corpses. Don't speak to me of despicable acts, you whoreson.'

'You know nothing of the plight of my people,' the Sarmatian said, though I noticed he kept his eyes downcast. Could be he was not proud of what his brother had ordered. I couldn't blame the man.

'Seems to me it's awfully similar to the situation you would put my people in.'

The Sarmatian sighed. 'You may well be right. I came here to recover the body of my brother. If there is no body to recover, then I shall return to my people. We will mourn, but mark my words, Alaric. When our mourning is done, we will come for you.'

'We'll be waiting.'

* * *

'Time to cut and run,' I said to Hilde, Adalhard, and Haribert as I returned to our camp.

'How do you expect us to do that?' Haribert scoffed. 'We've more wounded than we have fit men. How do we transport them?'

I pawed at my face, bone tired. 'Did we capture any of their horses in the battle?'

'Six. But we'll need to slaughter them for food.'

'How many wounded do we have?' I asked this to Hilde, who had been working with them tirelessly since the end of the battle.

'Eighty-nine. Forty or so of them won't make it. We don't have the equipment to treat them. Eadger included.'

'He's still alive?' I asked, shocked. I had purposely stayed away from the mound of dead bodies as the sun rose after the battle. Eadger and the other seriously wounded men from our previous fight had been in one place in our camp. It had been in front of them that Haribert had formed his circle of shields.

'Aye. Though he worsens by the moment.'

I took pause at that, breathing and thinking. I would not, *could* not, leave good men here to die. There had been a time where I would have made that decision without thinking, all in the name of the greater good. But I was not as sentimental then. 'I will go to him. Where are Sedric and his men?'

'Sedric is sleeping. He's got a cut below his eye and I reckon he took a mighty blow to his head. Only three of his men are left alive. They're still doing what they can for the rest of the wounded.'

'And our new friend?'

'Passed out. We sealed the wound on his leg with fire. But he won't make it.'

'Good. Get some rest, all of you. I need to think.'

I walked through our small camp, dismayed at the few men left standing. We had marched east with just over six hundred and fifty men, an army sizeable enough to stop an invasion, or so I had thought. Half those men were dead, another hundred or so laid out on the earth, each dying a slow and painful death. Dagr's fifty men were all but gone, a handful remaining, stretched out around a campfire. The men I had brought from my settlement, led by the curious and talkative Faramund, were now in the Heroes Hall. Balomar's men had fared better. But the men of the Marcomanni were seasoned warriors, not easy to kill. I was grateful I could still count on them. The Quadi, sent by Areogaesus, had lost over half their number. Their chief would be furious with me, but that was an issue for another day.

Haribert, too, had lost the bulk of his warriors. But his son was still casting a shadow, and I could see the old chief with his arm around the youth, sharing a skin of water. They had at least put their differences behind them on this trip. I found Eadger, awake but pale as winter, lying in a pool of sunlight. 'I thought you dead, old friend,' I said, slumping down next to him.

'Still here,' he whispered, giving me a faint smile. 'I'm trying to hold an image of my wife and daughter in my head. Funny, I can't seem to make out their faces. Guess I'll see them soon enough.'

'You should be holding your sword,' I said to him, moving to grab the weapon and put it in his palm.

'No! There will be no feasting at the Allfather's hall for me. I will go to my family. That is my wish.'

I nodded, putting the sword down. 'I am so sorry, Eadger. You should never have come here.'

'I've a few regrets. Coming here with you isn't one of them. I should have died last summer. In truth, I was already dead inside. You helped bring me back to life. I am grateful. You should go now, brother. You have much to do. I have a wish to die in peace, the sun on my face.'

He closed his eyes then, a soft smile dancing across his lips. I hoped he was picturing his wife and daughter and seeing their faces with clarity. I left him then to his rest. It was the last time the two of us spoke.

I moved through the camp, chatting to wounded warriors, comforting those who were seeing the sun for the final time. It was all I could do. Five men guarded a secluded corner of the camp, and slowly, inexorably, I made my way there.

'He awake yet?' I asked one of the guards.

'Aye. He's muttering away. Can't understand anything he's saying, though.'

With a nod, I passed them and came face to face with Bahadur. 'I'm disappointed to see you're still among the living,' I said to him. 'But not surprised.'

The Sarmatian lord gave me a weak smile. His face was gaunt, bloodless. The whites of his eyes had soured to the colour of an egg yolk. He raised a limp hand towards me, but it fell after a heartbeat or two. 'If you wanted me dead, you would not have sealed the wound.'

'I didn't!' I scoffed. 'Some of my men thought keeping you alive would make for a good bargaining chip. Seems to me it was a waste of effort.'

'I will go to my gods soon enough,' the Sarmatian said matter-of-factly. 'I was a fool to charge you at the end.'

'Aye, you were. Good idea though, to ambush us in the night. Got to say, I hadn't been expecting it.'

'A man who is not as cunning as he is cruel does not get to rule for as long as I have. You know this, Alaric, the man who once led the finest fighting force in the west.'

I gave the man a tight smile and sat down beside him. 'If I had had those men at my back, Sarmatian, you and your army would have perished on our first engagement. Truly, for a time, we were unbeatable.'

'What happened?'

'Rome. That's what happened. What always happens. I always thought I would die fighting that cursed empire. Seems instead it will be your tribe that does for me,' I said.

'I have heard many tales of the men of Rome. I had hoped to see them for myself. Believe me when I say they are far from the most formidable fighters in the world.' Bahadur closed his eyes a moment, seemingly lost in his past.

'You speak of the people you are running from? The reason you have come west?'

The Sarmatian nodded. 'They are a ferocious people. They were born on horseback, and their arrows darken the sky. We never stood a chance. The sky has always been precious to us, where the great god rules and looks down to us all.'

I had no interest in getting into conversations about gods, especially with a man about to meet his, and when it was looking as though mine had deserted me once more. 'How long before I have to fight them too?'

'I pray you never have to. Truly,' Bahadur croaked out in a weak voice. 'They are a plague on the peoples of the eastern plains. But one day they will come west, they will have to. But not for many years yet.'

'Are there more people from your tribe still to join you in the west?' It was something that had been bugging me. I had heard many times of the great swathes of people that lived on the eastern steppe. Men said their tribes numbered in the thousands. It seemed incredulous to me that Bahadur and his army were all of them. Strong as they were, I did not think them numerous enough to have survived so long out in the lawless grass plains.

'There are more. We had to leave another army to watch our rear. There are more women and children too; they needed to be defended. We could not be sure of feeding so many people at once on our great migration west.'

I gave a resigned nod. It seemed even if we were to survive our next battle with this tribe, or even triumph over them, there would still be more to come. 'It is the custom of our people to show respect to great warriors. I have come to show my respect to you. I will leave you now to your rest. I do not expect the two of us will speak again.'

'No, I do not think we will. Goodbye, Alaric. And good luck. Go back west, get away from here. You cannot stop what is coming.' He was asleep before I rose, and dead before the dawn. We wrapped his body in a cloak and left it out in the open for his men to find and honour as they wished. Haribert wanted us to burn it and be done with it, but out of respect, and in the hope it would buy us a bit more time, I left Bahadur's body for his brother.

And come dawn the next day, we were off.

* * *

Balomar had sent transport for the wounded. Not horses and carts, as I had asked, but barges sent along the Danube. It took a whole day to move the injured men the couple of miles south to the river, but we got it done without any more losses. The king himself was aboard one of the barges, his left shoulder still heavily bandaged after the battle with Rome. 'There's a Roman army north of the river. Care to explain?' he said to me as I boarded.

'Give me a break,' I muttered as I slumped down on deck and snatched a wine skin from a slave.

'Where are the rest of your men? Where are my men?'

I didn't answer, just glugged greedily from the skin. Adalhard, boarding behind me, shared a look with his king that spoke more than words ever could. 'You've lost so many,' Balomar said, turning back to me.

'We have been in a battle like you have never seen, my lord,' Adalhard addressed his king, head bowed.

'Did you win?' Balomar asked. The question was greeted with silence. 'Gods,' he breathed when neither of us answered. 'So what is your plan now?'

I held up the wine skin in one hand and pointed to it with my other. My family was gone, traded for an army that had been defeated. I had lost a friend, more men than I could count. And it had all been for nothing. I don't think I had ever felt so low. Not even when Silus had taken my eye and destroyed the Ravensworn. I felt every one of the winters I had seen. I thought then of my father, of how tired and weary he had looked when I walked down the path to his farm. Had he reached this point after his last battle, where the thought of going on seemed unbearable? Perhaps that was how all grey-bearded warriors felt, those who had lived long enough to have the fight sucked out of them. I felt as though I could have slept for a week.

Balomar hissed. Not a man who would relate to my glum feelings, I knew. He was a rare man, with a zest for life and battle like no other. He shrugged off defeats as easily as a winter cloak, and was back up the following dawn, ready to do it all again. 'Wouldn't have happened if I'd have been there.' He sniffed.

'Then perhaps you should have been,' I said sullenly, before returning to my wine.

We sailed in silence. A clear day, sparse cloud in an otherwise blue sky. I watched the walls of Carnuntum come and go, saw the weary looks of the garrison atop their high walls. Why had the Fourteenth legion marched north to just do nothing? I was certain they would have had scouts watching us, and therefore watching the desperate battle we fought. How naive, how stupid I had been to think Silus would insist his men come and support mine, right after we had just fought them to a standstill.

In hindsight, it made perfect sense for Rome to sit and watch, then pick off the victor when they were at their weakest. Perhaps that's what they were doing, as I sat on that barge and got drunk. I didn't know it then, but I was about to find out. We reached Goridorgis, capital of the Marcomanni, as the sun waned in the west. Our wounded were unloaded first. Balomar had erected hospital tents on the riverside, and men were at hand to start treating them straight away. I made a note to thank my old friend.

I was staggering up to the city, belly growling, head already thumping, when a runner sped past me, making a beeline for his king. I turned, nearly falling as I did, and squinting with my one eye in the murky light, I saw Balomar grow flustered as his messenger passed on whatever news it was he had to share. 'What's going on?' I slurred, making unsteady progress over to the king.

'The Sarmatians have met the Fourteenth in battle, just a few miles west of here. Damn it, but we sailed right past them! Seems there were more of the wicked horsemen waiting in reserve. My man tells me nearly four thousand of the bastards met Rome in the field. It was a rare battle.'

'Who won?' I asked and hiccupped.

'No one. They disengaged as the light began to fade. Reckon there'll be another battle tomorrow.'

We stared at each other, my old friend and I, in the silence that followed his words. 'Might be our one chance to beat them,' I said, suddenly sobering up. 'Bahadur told me he had more people back east. Another army watching their rear. Seems to me that army has come west with the rest of them. That can't be a good thing.' I remembered then what the Sarmatian had said. About there being worse threats than them in the east. It was a chilling thought. Had the second Sarmatian army been defeated? Why else would they be here now?

'Aye. But can we trust Rome not to turn on us when the deed is done?'

'Nope,' I said and giggled. Perhaps I hadn't sobered up after all.

Balomar turned to Adalhard. The war chief of the Marcomanni loomed giant in the half light. Hilde appeared at his side. She'd spent the river journey sobbing soft tears for Eadger. Her eyes were red raw. 'I think we should fight,' Adalhard said. 'If you had seen what we have, Lord King, you would agree. We cannot afford an enemy as powerful as them, not with Rome on our southern border.'

'And Rome cannot afford another power north of the Danube,' Balomar mused. 'What's that saying about your enemy's enemy being your friend?'

'Reckon you just said it,' I muttered, before my vision blurred and I vomited uncontrollably on the grass, splashing my boots in the process. 'Fuck,' I groaned as pain lanced through my head.

'Well then, old friend,' Balomar said to me with a grin. 'Looks like we've a march ahead of us come the dawn. Let's get some food in your belly.'

18

I think it would be fair to say that I was not a happy man when Sedric roused me the following morning. The sun had not risen when I staggered from his small hut outside Goridorgis and vomited once more on the long grass. Sedric had repaired my cuirass whilst I slept off the wine. Judging by the weary look in his eyes, he had not slept a wink, and I hugged him even as he recoiled from the stench of me, regaling him with my gratitude.

Finding a tub of cold water to immerse myself in, I plunged my head in and stayed under until I could take the cold no more. Heaving myself back out, I felt a little more alive. Conscious that I needed to wash more than my face, I then stripped off and scrubbed myself with the cold water, wishing I had the luxury of a Roman bathhouse to hand. As clean as I could get myself, I dressed in my armour and forced down a handful of figs with some bread and dried meat, and drank as much water as I dared before I thought I might actually drown myself.

And then we marched.

Balomar had not been idle as I slept. Runners had been sent to Areogaesus, his neighbour to the east. The Quadi supplied us with a further three hundred men. Balomar himself brought every warrior the Marcomanni could muster, leaving his people entirely defenceless. It seemed, though, the king had realised it wasn't important. There was already a Roman army north of the river, and for once they had not marched to seek him out. Instead, we would fight alongside them.

'We need a plan for when we get close,' the king said to me as we walked.

The piercing pain behind my eye had subsided, and I was feeling more human again, despite being baked by the high summer sun. I nodded. 'Rome needs to know we are coming to support them before we engage. We don't want them thinking us another enemy. It will stretch their lines too thin if they turn to face us and give the Sarmatians the edge in battle.'

'You must go ahead,' Balomar said. 'You are known to them, and you can therefore relay messages between us and them.'

'Send a runner,' I scoffed. 'It doesn't matter who you send, as long as they have some Latin. You know as well as I that the men of the Fourteenth legion have no love for me.'

'Ordinarily, I would agree. But these are exceptional circumstances. Take a horse and a few men and ride. Seek out Silus, let him know our plans. He will determine where is best for our force to deploy. We must strike at the optimal moment. I want it to be Germani warriors that turn the battle. Understand? It is us coming to save them, not the other way around.'

I nodded at that, already seeing the bigger picture my old friend was painting. He wanted to make sure Rome would not use this intervention as a bargaining chip in their favour in the future. As much as they were our enemy, our people had come to rely on trade with the empire. If Rome decided to up tariffs on our goods, or to raise the price of the food and wine they sent across the Danube, it could be disastrous for us. We were, as much as I hated to admit it, reliant on the goods they sold us. There had been a time when our people lived off the land we farmed and roamed. But that time was long gone. Now we consumed dates and figs, other fresh fruits from the Mediterranean and went to war with iron swords and armour made by smiths far to the south. It was Rome's way. Even if they knew they could not conquer us, they could still make sure we were in their pockets. In many ways, we were a province in all but name.

But if Balomar succeeded in this endeavour, he might well have been able to turn things back in our favour. If Rome would acknowledge our role in keeping a new enemy from their border, then perhaps certain trade deals could be re-negotiated, better terms set in place. It would be about money, riches, as all things were when powerful men were involved. Much depended on the battle's outcome.

'Fine. I'll do it. Who's coming with me?' Hilde volunteered herself immediately, as did Sedric. I had tried to persuade my former warrior to stay at home, but the young man said he had come this far and would not miss the end. He still had his head heavily bandaged, the wound beneath stitched. It was the second head wound he had received fighting for me, the first coming the year before at Tastris.

We mounted and were on our way swiftly, the three of us giving the beasts their heads, eager to make contact with the Roman army as quickly as we could. It did not take us long. Battles are easy things to find if you're looking for them. Dust clouds rise even on the dampest of days, and they're not exactly quiet. It looked as though this one had not been going for long. We reined our mounts half a mile or so to the south of the battlefield. The Roman army was formed up in traditional fashion, with the first cohort on the right flank, its standard swaying in the light breeze. The legion's eagle took pride of place in the centre, three ranks behind the front. Roman soldiers would die before they let their eagle be taken by an enemy. If it was, the legion faced decimation, and then the indignity of their legion number being wiped from history.

Caesar had once taken a legion that had suffered that fate, renamed them the Tenth, and made them his own. There had been no more zero-to-hero stories since, though. You lost your eagle; you were finished. I pondered once why then they put the thing so close to their front ranks. For surely the closer it was to the enemy, the greater the risk. I had spoken the thought out loud to Ruric, who had understood it in a moment. 'Why do you fight in the front rank?' he had asked me.

'I am a symbol for our men to follow. The harder I fight, the harder they do.' I had shrugged at him. 'That is leadership.'

He'd given me one of his beard-splitting wide grins. 'Aye, lad. You are a symbol, and the men around you fight harder not because you do, but because they want to keep you safe. It is the same for them and their eagle. Their men push themselves harder to ensure no harm comes to it. They fight for that eagle, for everything it symbolises. They would rather die than see it be taken.'

I had understood then. And I understood it as I watched the Fourteenth legion march ten steps forward and pause, shifting their shields to pull back their javelins. 'Here we go,' I said to Sedric and Hilde, and before our eyes, the sky darkened as thousands of javelins whistled into the air and smashed into the Sarmatians with a crunch. The Sarmatians were all mounted. The battle-field was not one of their choosing, I guessed. Trees blocked the north and a steep bank to the south. They were forced to charge head-on into the Roman infantry, with their huge rectangular shields and deadly swords. I thought it possible they would not need us at all.

'This is madness,' Hilde said, thinking the same as me. 'Why have they given battle here? The cavalry need open space, room to manoeuvre. They'll be cut to bits like this.'

They have no choice, was my first thought. Their numbers were far greater than the army Bahadur had led against me. That told me that the men he had left behind as a rearguard had encountered trouble. Which told me there was another force coming from the east. It also told me that the Sarmatians were now in a do or die situation. To get away from whatever it was they were running from, they had to go west. And to go west, they had to get through anyone in their way. Their time for clever movements and night attacks was over. It was win or bust, their chief leading them or not.

'Look there,' Sedric said, pointing back west. A dust cloud swirled above the tree line, and all of a sudden I understood.

'That's not our men, is it?' Hilde asked.

'It is not,' I said, knowing Balomar could not yet be so close. 'That is the other half of the Sarmatian army.'

'They will attack the Roman rear, or even the marching camp the Four-teenth left this morning. They'll spoil their food, kill the slaves and civilians, probably burn the place to the ground.'

'Aye, and the Fourteenth will have no option but to retreat. They aren't trying to win here, just distract the Fourteenth for long enough to win the battle out of sight. Hilde, ride back to Balomar and tell him what is happening. Tell him to make for the Roman marching camp and help defend it. Sedric and I will inform our friends down there what's happening, and then we'll meet you there.'

With that Hilde left, her own small dust cloud swirling in her wake. Sedric and I rode closer to the battle, so close I could see Roman soldiers pointing in our direction, calling out to officers. I slowed the pace then, letting the Romans send a man to us. The last thing I wanted was to be attacked. A man did come eventually, grinning at me beneath his black beard. 'Alaric, as I live and breathe. You just won't die, will you?'

'Salve, Habitus,' I said through a smile of my own, giving the man the traditional Roman greeting. 'You're having yourself some sport, I see.' Habitus was blood spattered, his bow strung over his left shoulder.

'I was in with the front rank, of course. We've just rotated. Silus spotted you, sent me out here to ask what the fuck you want. His words, not mine.'

I pointed to the dust cloud looming above the trees to the Roman rear. As quickly as I could I outlined what I knew, and where Balomar was and how quickly he would be able to attack. 'Looks as though you and I will finally get to fight on the same side, my friend.'

'We sort of have already, have we not? Fine, brother, I will pass on the message. You and your comrades deal with the rear, we'll sort this lot out.' He hooked a thumb at the massed Sarmatians. And with that, I was gone.

* * *

Our ride was desperate. Never before and never since had I wanted a Roman army to be victorious. But that day all I could think of was that the Fourteenth must stay on the field and win the battle. The future of my people depended on it. Sedric and I pushed our mounts until I could feel the beast laming beneath me. She was a chestnut mare from Balomar's stable, greying on her flanks. She did not have much left to give, but she strived, feeling my urgency, and gave me the last of her strength.

We did not make for Balomar, for Hilde was already on the way. I calculated she would have reached the king by the time I was riding away from the battle, and therefore Sedric and I headed straight for the dust cloud. Which, in fairness, was a horrible mistake.

I don't know if you've ever witnessed two riders charge an entire army before. It seemed so glorious at the time, so heroic. The Sarmatians were making their final approach to the Roman camp. The Fourteenth had at least built a proper one, with eight-foot wooden walls and men to man them. An officer called for the gates to be shut as the enemy came into view, and they were striving to do just that as Sedric and I charged, though they faced overwhelming odds as the Sarmatians were trying to force an entry.

Freeing my blade, the sword my father had wielded as he sought to defend my mother and me the night Rome came for us, I roared a wordless battle cry and launched myself at the nearest Sarmatian, cleaving my father's blade through the man's neck. We smashed into the enemy's left flank, their eyes fixed on the closing gate. I say smashed; we were two men against hundreds. We were no more than a ripple in the ocean. But men died under our blades. Two, then three and four. The enemy knew we were there then, and they turned to face us.

That's when I realised we were fucked.

'We need to turn back!' I called to Sedric as our mounts were forced back. Spears lashed out at us, and I frantically tried to control my horse with my knees as my hands fended off blows with shield and sword.

'No... shit!' Sedric snarled through gritted teeth, himself defending for his life. Problem was, we couldn't just turn our mounts and run off into the sunset. Our enemy was fixed on us, the gates almost forgotten. That itself was a small victory. Even over the cacophony of battle, I heard the gates slam close, the locking bar fix into place. A small cheer went up from the men inside. We had succeeded in keeping the Sarmatians from taking the camp. Now we just had to survive.

Step by step, my mount retreated. She, too, fought for the right to live to see another sunrise. She snapped at the mount pressing into her, then rose onto her hind legs and kicked a rider from his horse. I was almost thrown off, having to drop my shield to desperately claw at her mane to stay upright. Laughing as the beast dropped back onto all fours, I rubbed her flank and praised her. By all the gods, I did love a beast with spirit. She had also bought the few precious heartbeats Sedric and I needed to turn and flee. Which I'm unashamed to say we both did without encouragement.

The tree line to the south of the Roman camp was a hundred or so paces away. I reasoned with myself that if we reached it, the enemy would not pursue. They had not ridden there for two inconsequential riders. They had come to destroy Rome. I leant over my trusted steed, willing her to make the trees. Sedric's mount was younger than mine, a beige gelding that strained with all its might to be away from the battle. My own mount was nearly finished now, her breath loud and shallow. Sixty paces to go and I turned back, seeing nothing but a storm of metal and horseflesh riding for me. They were mere paces away. We weren't going to make it.

Could I stop, turn, and hold them off? Would Sedric make it if I sacrificed myself? I reasoned he would. Picturing Saxa and my boys for one last time, holding their image in my mind's eye and finding courage from it, I turned my lame beast, brandishing my father's sword. One last time.

A spear raced past my head in a rush of air. It startled me for two reasons. One, because it was so close to me. And two, because it had not flown at me, but come from behind. I had not time to turn, the first of my pursuers already on me. I was just raising my sword for the first killing blow when an almighty roar sounded behind me, and men streamed from the woodland, crashing into the incoming cavalry.

Balomar had come. It seemed I might yet live after all.

* * *

In a confusing few moments, I went from exultant relief at still being alive to terror at the thought of the oncoming battle. Then to shame and foreboding as I realised that even if I did survive, Balomar would be holding it against me for years.

His army was a terror. They ravaged the Sarmatian cavalry, foot soldiers leaping onto enemy horses and killing their riders before anyone could react. It was a slaughter. Grim. Gruesome. I fucking loved it. Buoyed by the unexpected joy of being alive, I leapt into the fray. My mount seemed rejuvenated too, and she snapped at the nearest horse even as I slashed at its rider's face. We were stepping again, but this time forwards instead of back. The Sarmatians were in shock. They had been expecting easy pickings against unarmed civilians whilst the Romans fought a half mile to the west. But they had never fought Romans before, and they underestimated two things.

First, the Romans always built marching camps. They were infuriatingly well built. Take it from me; I had tried to take more than one in my time. Second, they always left a small force behind. It was never more than eighty men, and was usually made up of the weaker men they had available to them. But they were still soldiers, behind high walls. And they were about to show the Sarmatians what they could do.

Spears rained down on the enemy from above. Seemed the commander of the fort was not content to sit and wait for us to do their dirty work for them. There were a hundred or more men in a line. Cooks, clerks, slaves and soldiers alike. Seemed whatever was left in the Fourteenth's mobile armoury was being utilised. Cooking utensils slapped off helmets, tent pegs soared from the sky like arrows. The Sarmatians had us at their front and high walls to their rear. The only way they could run was west.

'Don't let them get away!' Balomar roared to his men, sending Adalhard with whatever men he could muster to cut off the enemy's retreat. It worked. Hemmed in against the walls, the Sarmatians fought on for a while, but they were being cut down like wheat at harvest time. Eventually one of their riders threw down his sword and shouted something, I assumed it to be some form of surrender in his native tongue. The rest followed his lead.

Dismounting my trusted mount, giving her a kiss on the nose and rubbing her face, I pushed her away gently and let her walk off to find fresh grass to munch on. Gods knew she had earned it. Balomar was already organising for the Sarmatians to be disarmed, their mounts taken from them. 'We must press on, Alaric,' he said to me as I caught up with him. 'I haven't marched all the way out here to take care of a few stragglers. There is a battle happening just behind those trees. Let us be at it!'

I smiled at my old friend. Leverage was what he wanted. I had a mind to ensure he got it. The gates to the marching fort opened and an ageing camp prefect emerged and offered his name. I don't think I heard it in the first place to remember. He offered to take care of the prisoners, his small army of cooks and clerks coming out to assist. We happily left the man to it.

Sedric was left behind, much to his disgust. But I needed someone who would not antagonise the Romans, and Balomar needed men to stay and care for the wounded. Sedric was no warrior, though he had fought well in the last weeks for me. I had asked of him all I could, and I explained that as I asked him to assist the Romans in rounding up the prisoners and making sure they got up to no bother. Reluctantly, he agreed, and I set off in the fine armour he had made me, hot on the heels of Balomar and his men.

I was on foot, as were all of Balomar's army, and Hilde and I jogged along a wooded path to catch up with the king's men. 'What's the plan?' I said as I came alongside him.

'We'll judge the state of the battle and throw ourselves in where we are needed. We *must* win, Alaric. Too much is at stake!'

'Almost like someone was trying to explain that to you a few weeks ago,' I said with a wry grin. 'Could have done with the rest of your army, then.'

'Oh, you'd have just got more of them killed,' Balomar scoffed. 'Nice work back there, by the way. Don't think I've ever seen two men charge an entire army before.'

'You were watching from the tree line, weren't you?' I asked, spirits sinking.

'Aye, that I was. Got to say, I thought for a moment there you almost had them.' He fixed me with a look, but couldn't stop the smile spreading through his beard. We laughed as we jogged, and I felt some of the weight that had been resting on my shoulders ease. The pressures of leaving my family, the defeat we had suffered in the east, had all been weighing heavy on me. But all I had before me then was another battle, and despite the tiredness that ravaged my body, battle was something I knew all too well.

We came out of the trees to see the battle unfolding before us. It was a very different scene to the one I had left just a couple of hours before. The Roman line had been intact for starters, their legionaries presenting an unbroken line of shields. Now, though, they were bent so far back I could see the left wing was moments away from breaking off from the centre. When that happened, the Sarmatian cavalry would be able to stream through the gap and surround them. And that would be that.

'Look there!' I pointed to the growing gap. 'That's where we need to go!'

I was off without another word, charging into the fray with my sword held out in front of me. 'After him!' Balomar called, and I heard the stamping feet behind me as the Marcomanni army raced into another battle. We smashed into the Sarmatians, our initial charge as devastating as in the battle outside the marching fort. I ducked under a stamping hoof, cleaved my blade through a horse's belly and blocked a jabbed spear all in one fluid motion. Rising from under the horse, sheeted in blood and gods knew what else, I hacked at an unhorsed rider and rammed my shield into the man's face, sending him sprawling.

'For Germania!' Balomar cried as he barrelled into one rider, skewering another on the end of his sword. His men took up the cry and step by bloody step we forced the Sarmatians back. I heard Roman trumpets blasting, but had no time to look and see what they were signalling. We had to trust in the Romans to play their part and not turn on us. That would not happen until after the Sarmatians were defeated, I knew, but it was something to be weary of.

A spear point broke through my defences and clanged off my helmet. Dazed, I staggered back, caught by the man behind me as we pressed forwards. Muttering my thanks and letting more warriors press past me, I removed the helmet to see the great dent on the top. Gods, what a blow that had been. Had it have been to my chest, I was sure it would have gone straight through, fancy armour or not. I took two deep breaths and for a blissful moment thought I had recovered. But then my stomach churned and before I knew what was happening, I was on all fours vomiting up the remnants of last night's wine. I sank to the grass, oblivious to what I was lying in. The sound of battle dimmed with my vision.

* * *

I stand on a mountain, the breeze cool on my cheeks. Carrion birds circle above, their squawks an insult to my ears. Looking around, I realise my vision is not impaired, and tentatively I hold a hand up and cover my right eye. I can still see. My left eye has been returned to me.

'A marvel, is it not, to see once more when it has been denied to you for so long.'

Spinning on my heels, I am at first shocked at the speed of my reactions, my light- ness of foot. And then I see him. I have seen this man before. On a beach to the far north, when the stench of burning buildings was hot in my nostrils. When my life had turned to blood and fire, and I felt as lost as I ever had in my life. I say man; he is no man, and I know that too. He is the Allfather. The All Knowing. The Hanged One who gave up his eye for all the knowledge of the Nine Worlds. He has come to see me once more.

'How did I get here?' I ask him.

Beneath his wide-brimmed hat, the god smiles at me. 'You are not here. Not really. You will awake, covered in your own vomit, back on that battlefield down there and think this a dream. Just like you did the last time you saw me.'

I follow the god's outstretched finger and see through the thin clouds two armies waging war on a flat patch of ground surrounded by trees. One army fights under red banners, their infantry trying and failing to keep their tight lines in formation. The other is a mass of cavalry. No order to their approach, just chaos and death wherever they ride. 'I knew before it was no dream,' I say. 'When I awoke, I had a waterskin. I had not had that on me when I fell asleep. You gave it to me.'

'That I did.' The god nods. 'Do you remember what we spoke about?'

'Destiny,' I say.

'Aye, in a way. And we spoke of legacy and fame. You have used the sword to

forge your path. Not the first man, won't be the last. But we also spoke of other ways to live your life, to pass your name on to the generations that will follow. You made a decision, I think, on that far-flung beach to the north. A promise to yourself. You have gone back on that promise, Alaric.'

'I have,' I breathe. *I remember the pain of missing my family, the same pain I feel now. The promise I had made to myself to return home and be a better man. Be the father my boys need, the husband Saxa craves. In my defence, I had tried it for a time. But a man cannot run from who he is, cannot lie to his heart. I look at the god with two eyes and shrug.* 'A man can't run from his nature.'

The god smiles at me, a wicked grin that makes my stomach churn. 'Stop lying to yourself, Alaric. A man can be whatever he wants to be. It is not a question of can or can't, but what you have the will to do. You consider yourself to be a disciple of my son, so I believe?'

I nod. Loki has always ridden at my shoulder, guiding me through life. Or so I have always believed. I am the Trickster reborn, more cunning than any man alive. That is how I have survived, how I have triumphed in war and turmoil. 'Tell me, where is it your hero lies right now as we speak. What is his fate?'

Smiling, I rub the raven on my cuirass and recall the stories I had been told as a child. 'He is chained in a cave, unable to escape. He cannot change form, cannot run. There you will leave him for all eternity.'

A nod from the All Seeing father of the world. 'And how is it he came to be there?'

'You caught him after he had angered you for the final time. He tried to run, of course. Slipped into a stream and took on the form of a salmon. He was caught in a net as he tried to swim upstream.'

'That he did. Do you know how we knew which salmon was him? The stream was full of them, after all.'

I did not. But I reasoned the Trickster would think as I would, and I gave my best guess. 'He was the biggest salmon in the stream. Twice the size of the others. Loki would consider himself to be no less, therefore he was.'

The god chuckles. 'You are correct. He is chained thanks to his own hubris; nothing more, nothing less. A fate I think you would do well to dwell on.'

I think on that, and see the truth in his words. Was it hubris that led me east at the head of an army? Was I too sure of myself, thinking that defeat was impossible? I concur that the god is right. He is always right. All Seeing. All powerful. 'What should I do?' *I ask with a sigh, knowing I have dug myself a hole I cannot escape from.*

'Return to your family, of course. Do what you promised you would a year ago.

But that is for tomorrow. Today you must win this battle. And from what I can see down there, that will be no easy task.'

The god has moved to the edge of the cliff, and looks down on the chaos on the ground. I move to join him, and spy two ravens circling the field, each the size of an eagle. One of those ravens decorates my armour, and I know they are the Allfather's spies, bringing him all the knowledge of the worlds.

'Tell me what you see,' he says, still looking down.

I concentrate. I make out the thinning lines of the Fourteenth legion, stretched too thin as they try and fail to fill a breach in their formation. The Sarmatians are a storm, their horses whirling across the battlefield. Arrows dart into any gap that appears; a thunderous charge follows. 'They are goading the Romans into advancing. To the untrained eye, it looks as though they have no discipline, no cohesion. But these men are used to fighting in the wide-open plains of the east. They know exactly what they are doing. Eventually the Romans will be surrounded, and once the Sarmatians can get at their rear, it will be over.'

'Just so.' The god nods. 'What then can you do to turn the tide of the battle?'

I look until I find where Balomar and his army fight. They are on the left of the Roman centre, keeping the left wing of the Fourteenth from being cut off. But their armour is weaker than their allies, and the losses taken are much worse. Even here, from so high up, I can see the mounds of Germani dead that heap the bloody ground. They cannot have been fighting for long, but in a short while they will be decimated. There must be something I can do.

'We need to encircle the Sarmatians. Restrict their manoeuvrability. To do that we need to reset the lines and then envelope the enemy, the left and right wings pushing forward as the centre holds its ground. It will be risky, as the Sarmatians will try everything to break through the centre. But it is the only way. Box them into a corner and the day is ours.'

'A good plan,' the god says, then he plants a meaty hand on my shoulder and stares deep into my eyes. 'I will send you back now, and then it is up to you to get it done. This will be the last time I come to you, Alaric Hengistson. One day we will meet again and feast together in my hall. Until then, remember the promise you made to yourself on that beach. Remember where your priorities lie.'

I give a solemn nod. 'I will do just that.'

The Allfather runs a hand over my face, and I feel my eyes forced closed, a weariness seep over me. And then I am falling, hurtling back towards the earth, to the maelstrom of battle below.

19

I awoke, groggy, confused, stumbling to my feet. And then there was a moment of startling clarity.

'Are you well?' a hazy voiced called to me, seeming to be very far away.

Turning, I squinted into the face of Balomar, the Marcomanni king frowning at me over his beard. 'I know what we need to do.'

'Do you now?' the king said, his voice coming clearer along with the roar of the ongoing battle. 'Looks to me you barely know your own name.'

'He came to me!' I blurted out.

'Who?'

'Him!' I said, pointing to my missing eye.

Balomar, the heat of battle on him, blood spattered and red faced, sighed. 'Brother, I know you have always thought of yourself as close to the gods, but this is no time for one of your fanciful dreams. We are on a knife edge here!'

'Please, just trust me! Keep our line in tow for just a while longer. I will be back.'

'Alaric, wait!' I heard my old friend cry as I ran off, sprinting as fast as my old legs would carry me, around the back of the Roman line. I saw it all as clear as I had standing on that mountain top, the Allfather beside me. The Fourteenth legion teetered on a precipice, their line fit to cave at any moment. Trouble with Roman armies was they were unaccustomed to defeat. They marched, they fought, they won. Came. Saw. Conquered, as the infamous Caesar had once said himself.

I ran past the command post of the legion, their banners fluttering in the air, a stream of messengers galloping to and from a clutch of men who sat astride powerful mounts in colourful cloaks. Each sat straight as an arrow in the saddle, no hint of panic or fluster on their stoic faces. Roman patricians to the end. It brought a wry smile to my concussed face seeing a couple of them frown in confusion as a Germani warrior streamed past them. I'd have given them a wave if I hadn't been so focused on my destination.

It was not hard to make out First Spear Centurion Silus in the midst of the battle. He stood under the banner of the first cohort, bloodied sword in hand, roaring his men forward. 'Fancy seeing you here!' I called out as I approached. Habitus was on his right flank, the wiry Syrian with an arrow strung on his bow. He shot me a wink before loosing. I didn't stop to see if he hit his mark. From what I knew of him, he probably had.

'Little busy at the moment, Alaric,' Silus said, turning to me for a moment to give me a disgusted glance. 'Though we appreciate your support.'

'You'll appreciate it even more in a moment. We're losing this battle, but I know how we can win it.'

Silus stopped berating his men and turned to face me proper, giving his optio Vitulus two swift orders before walking towards me. 'Speak quickly,' he said.

As briefly as I could, I outlined my plan. Once I had finished, Silus considered it a moment, before reluctantly nodding in agreement. 'It will be as you say. Get back to your men, Alaric. You and I will speak when this is done.'

With that, I was off again, trudging back the way I had come, though admittedly at a markedly slower pace. I was an old man, and a very recently concussed old man at that. I thought as I ran of what I had promised the one-eyed god on his cloud-high mountain. Why had I not stuck to it the year before? This time I would, I promised myself. A man can change his nature, adjust the path the Spinners had woven him. He must be able to. My people have long since believed that all is pre-ordained. We live and die at the will of the gods. When our time has come, it is just that – our time. But why could a man not set his own path? Gods be damned. I did not want my children to be raised in the hall of Dagr. Despite my love for his daughter, the man had proven to me who he was that distant day he had laughed in my face when I went to confront his coward of a father for failing to protect my family in their hour of need.

Did I wish my blade had cut deeper into his neck? Part of me sure did. But then I would have no Saxa, no two boys scurrying around my legs like excited hounds every time I came home. No. I could not wish the man dead. But that did not mean I wished him well. Reaching our own forces, squashed between the Roman centre and left flank, I could see how stretched they were. The Sarmatians were pushing the Romans further away from us to our left, and our line was growing thinner with every action as we fought to hold them back.

'Adalhard, Hilde, to me!' I called out as I saw them. Balomar came over too, though his eyes never left our front line. 'The Roman left is going to fall in on us and reconnect to their centre. They are more disciplined than us and better at holding their ground with those big shields. When that happens, our job is to fall back and encircle their lines and take the left flank. Once there, we will push forward with all we have, forcing the enemy back. Silus and his first cohort will do the same on the right flank. Together, we will give these bastards nowhere to go. Hemmed in, they won't be able to use the speed of their horses. Then we crush them.'

Balomar blew air from his cheeks. 'That's bold,' he said.

'Should work, though. Alaric is right, we're getting massacred just holding our ground here. We don't have the shields or armour to defend ourselves against spears from horseback. Attack is our best form of defence. Catch them off guard and win the day.'

I gave the man a nod. Persuading Balomar to go along with the plan would be much easier if his trusted captain was onside. Hilde said nothing, but gave me a nod and squeezed my shoulder. And then we set off, each of us pressing into the front rank so we could dictate the tempo of our withdrawal. To say I was confident would be overstepping it. Despite my fervent belief that I really had seen a god in my dreams, it did not necessarily make it true. I was also still not confident Silus and the Fourteenth would keep their word if we won the day. Would their legate sense an opportunity to rid himself of another enemy north of the Danube? The honours a man who vanquished two foes in one day could win in Rome were enormous.

But we pressed on. I yelled at our men to keep our ranks tight, shields overlapped, as the Sarmatians rained down spears and arrows upon us. It was a storm of death, a torrent of blood and iron, and my heart thrummed to its beat. One last battle. One last victory. And then I would find peace.

Trumpets blared behind our backs, and at once I felt the left wing of the Fourteenth step to their right. The centre formation forced themselves up three steps, and all we had to do then was hold our ground, men retreating two or three at a time as the Roman left inched its way closer. I stood and sweated, batted away spears with my shield and even took down two riders as I waited for my turn to back off. It came eventually, after what felt like a lifetime.

Gods, but battles were long events when you were old. In my prime, I could fight all day and it would feel like no more than a morning had passed. From dawn to dusk I could ride and march, wield sword and spear and always death stalked to my enemies. Panting, sweating, desperate for water, I was more relieved than I care to admit when I finally got the tap on the shoulder. I turned, stumbled back as a wall of red shields slid in to take my place. Stage one was complete.

We moved off around the back of the Roman line, already under intense pressure. We had to be quick, plug the gap on the far left before the Sarmatians noticed what we were doing. They missed their king in that moment. Bahadur had been a fearsome opponent. Intelligent, ruthless. He would have spotted the move and exploited it. But Bahadur was dead, and I guessed the man's brother led now. The brother had not struck me as a natural leader. I doubted he would last long in his position if he was not victorious. And I was seeing to it that he wouldn't be.

Balomar and I stood shoulder to shoulder and urged the men on. It was then I noticed Sedric with Hilde, lurking at my back. 'Why are you here?' I called to Sedric over the thrum of running men and galloping horses. Iron clashed, men screamed, a raucous I was sure could be heard for miles around.

'It's all under control back at the fort. Thought I'd come and see how the battle was faring.' He flashed me a grin. 'Besides, needed to bring you this.' Sedric and Hilde together unfurled the blood-red banner. It was a bit tattered, wearing at the edges. In fairness, it had seen plenty of action in recent weeks. I smiled at my friend. If this was to be my last battle, I could think of no better way of going out than fighting under that banner.

'Hoist it high, brother,' I said to Sedric, clapping him on the shoulder. 'And stay close to me. I'll see you safe.' With a grin, Sedric was off to fit it to a spear, and Hilde moved with me as we prepared to charge home to victory.

'Men of Germania!' Balomar called, holding his sword high. We were in position, on the left wing of the Roman force. I could make out the Roman right-wing lead by Silus already moving forward, trumpets blaring as the soldiers beat their swords on shields. 'Today we fight not just for our freedom, but for our future! After today we will no longer be held under the yoke of Rome! But free to make our own decisions, strike our own trade deals and forge our own path. One more battle, with me now, my brothers!' Men roared, me with them, my sword held high as we moved off.

'Ravensworn! Ravensworn!' came the cry, and I craned my neck to see Sedric at my back, the blood-red banner streaming in his wake. I grinned, one of my famous wolf grins. I was charging into battle, the symbol of my fame above me. Was the Allfather still watching from atop his mountain? Did the sight give him a thrill? I hoped so.

Then there was no more time for thought, for with a mighty cry we smashed into the Sarmatians. One last time.

* * *

I leaped to kill my first foe, a quick slash across his throat before he could respond. Forcing myself onto the saddle, I grabbed the reins in my left hand and urged the beast on. Together we smashed the flank of one warrior, me piercing the man's back as my new mount bit the other beast. Then we spun and I took another life on the half turn, my sword slashing and cutting open a chest. I revelled in it. One last battle. One last roll of the dice of death.

Our army moved liked a tidal wave, unstoppable. The Sarmatians saw the space around them shrink, and they tried and failed to control their panicked horses as they retreated further and further back. Their problem was they moved towards thick woodland, just a narrow track running through its centre. That had been fine for them as they rode to battle in the morning, able to take their time and form up once through. But now the men at the rear jostled for position to be the first into the trees. I could see them fighting among themselves from my elevated position, terrified men killing their own kin to be the first to escape the slaughter.

It was one of the finest sights I had ever seen. Roman trumpets blared in the air once more, and the centre, which had been holding its ground, moved towards the battle, two waves of thrown spears followed by a charge. It was over. I knew it, and so did the enemy. I had turned my back on the enemy and was watching the Romans move forward to finish the battle. Still grinning, bloodied sword hanging loose in my right hand, I didn't see the rogue rider charge me, just heard a muffled scream from Sedric, and had managed to half turn to see what my friend was pointing at.

A huge crash on my back had me tumbling from the horse. I hit the ground hard. My head, still swimming from the blow taken earlier in the day, rebounded off a discarded shield and my helmet was thrown to the dust. Groggy, winded, I rose to my feet and realised I no longer held my sword. Squinting through the dust, I saw a man rising in front of me. Bahadur's brother, come for his revenge.

'You will die if it is the last thing I do!' the man called in his thick accent. I nodded, blood leaking from my mouth as I smiled. It certainly would be the last thing he did. Men streamed past us. Some Roman, some Sarmatian. None paid us any heed. Through the dust my attacker ran, sword held high before him. I ducked his first blow, my head feeling heavier than my armour.

As I rose, another man came for me from the dust cloud. Bearded, helmet-less, a sword in one hand and a dagger in the other. I jumped back, the dagger grating on my cuirass. I lost my balance, slipped on the blood-slicked grass, and a sword cut the air just above my face. Scrambling for purchase, desperate for a weapon, over the clamour of charging hooves and screaming men, I heard someone yell 'Get down!' and I threw myself back to the ground, the wind driven out of me.

My attacker grinned in triumph, rose his sword for the killing blow. But it never came. An arrow thumped into his chest, then another, and blood spilt from his grinning lips. He slumped down, weapons falling, face first into the dirt.

'Told you I was a good shot!' Habitus said to me as I turned. The Syrian flashed me a grin. 'That's the last favour you'll get from me, old man!' he called, giving me a mock salute before disappearing into the mob of men and metal that streamed across the battlefield. Swaying as I rose back up, a tired smile beneath my beard, I looked around for my original attacker, Bahadur's brother, and saw he was coming for me once more. I heard a call from my right and saw a flash of light. Sedric had planted the raven banner and thrown me my sword. Good lad, Sedric. I've always said it. I snapped into action. Taking three steps with the speed of a wraith, I feinted a high blow to the right then swept the sword left and cleaved a bloody path across the Sarmatian's chest. The man staggered back, mouth hanging open, and his weapon slipped from his grasp.

'Say hi to your brother for me,' I spat, before ramming the blade home.

The battle was over. The day won. I looked up to the blue sky, my one eye fixed on two ravens circling the field. The Allfather would know of my victory.

* * *

A battlefield stinks at the end of a day's fighting. Blood and decay taint the air, an undercurrent of excrement as the living and the dead both void their bowels. Luckily for us, the Romans had taken the initiative on clearing the field. It was another lesson in their efficiency. Slaves walked the dead and took what weapons and armour could be saved. Centurions paraded their surviving men, a scribe noting down the names of those missing and passing it on. Each of the deceased families would receive a letter signed by their legate, stating their son or husband or brother had died valiantly defending Rome. Usually it wasn't true.

Corpses were piled for the pyres, more slaves already building them high. The Sarmatian dead had not been stripped, but their bodies were thrown under the eastern tree line to clear the field. I very much doubted their surviving kin would return to give them a proper sendoff. I couldn't bring myself to care. Balomar was already in his element, locked in negotiations with the legate of the Fourteenth legion, making his demands and furiously batting away any concessions Rome tried to make to him. I could hear him where I sat, just outside the command tent, a skin of wine in one hand, a bloodied bandage held to my wounded head in the other.

'Got enough of that to share?' a voice said in the gloom, and Silus appeared in the light of a brazier, slumping his considerable weight down opposite me. I gave him a wry grin and offered the skin.

'Quite a day, eh?'

'It's been quite a season, all in,' Silus said with a nod. 'Didn't think I'd start it fighting you lot, only to end it fighting alongside you.'

'Aye, me neither,' I agreed, taking back the wine skin. 'Tell you one thing, though. That's not the last we've heard of these people from the east. They'll be back in greater numbers next time.'

'They will. And Rome will be there to deal with them once more.'

I smirked at that. 'Not sure I'll be around to bail you out when they do.'

Silus barked a laugh. 'Going off into retirement, are you? I've heard that one before.'

'So what if I am? Got a life to live. You can't be far off yourself. You must be looking forward to spending more time with that son of yours.'

'Trading amber?' Silus scoffed.

'So what if I am?' I said, wondering how he knew. Rome had spies everywhere. 'Will you miss me?'

'I'll miss having the chance to kill you. Don't kid yourself into thinking we're friends, Alaric. And as it happens, I'll be retiring next year. Vitulus and I are going to build ourselves that nice little retirement settlement east of Carnuntum I told you about. A few of the lads are going to come with us. Should be a good place to settle down with young Albinus.'

I stood, wiping dust off my armour. 'Do you remember the first time we met?' I asked him.

Silus scrunched up his face. 'In the lands of the Marcomanni. You were causing trouble between them and the Quadi. I was sent north with a couple of cohorts to put a stop to it.'

'No. That was the first time you met Lord Alaric of the Ravensworn,' I said. 'When was the first time you met *me*?'

'You speak in riddles,' Silus said with a scowl. 'Just spit out whatever retort you're holding in.'

I took a breath. 'You were young when we first met. Me younger still. I had been at home, sleeping, with my mother and father. When we awoke to flames and screaming. Rome had come, and no one was safe. My father fought you lot off best he could. Me with him, but I didn't know my way around a spear back then. Not how I do now. My mother was taken from our home. Some of your friends took turns to rape her whilst the rest held my father and me down and forced us to watch.'

A shadow fell over Silus's face, the wine skin slipping from his bear-like paws. I knew what it was he was seeing. Flames in the night, a woman's screams in the air. And a father and his son, dragged around the back of a dilapidated barn, fear and sorrow etched on their faces.

'I've got business in the north. I'll leave you with Balomar to discuss how he is going to be recompensed for saving your worthless arses. Don't think I've gotten soft, old wolf. You and I will have our reckoning one day. You still owe me an eye, not to mention what you did to my family. I won't forget. Ever.'

With that, I was gone.

* * *

Hilde and Sedric joined me as we trudged through woodland in the darkness. I tried to wrap my head around another quiet summer in Germania. All had been going well until that scoundrel Filibert had locked himself in a barn and refused to come out. Since then, it had been one of the toughest seasons of my life. And I'd lived through some real shit ones. Laughing to myself, I shook my head and blew air from my cheeks.

'What's up, chief?' Sedric asked me in the darkness.

'Just reliving everything that's happened. You know, I didn't think I'd experience anything crazier than our adventure in the north last year. This might have topped it though.'

'Not even close,' Hilde said. She was walking with a slight limp, having taken a wound to her left calf in the battle. True to form, she hadn't muttered a word of complaint about being made to walk through the night.

'You're just getting old, chief,' Sedric said. I could hear the smile in his voice. 'Might be time for you to finally hang up your father's sword.'

'Aye, you're not wrong. Though I reckon I've got one fight left in me. Whether I want it or not.'

'Silus?'

'No. But that will come one day. Has to, really. I'm on about a man who has long had a reckoning coming. Come on, let's keep moving for now. We'll rest in an hour or so.'

We walked then slept, and repeated that for what felt like an age. It pleased me to observe the peace across the land as we travelled. Farmers toiled their fields, children playing in the swaying crop fields. Traders walked the mud roads, carts in tow, each with a cheery greeting as we passed. I felt my spirits lift, the stresses of the summer evaporate like morning dew. Eventually, we reached our destination. I saw them before they saw me. Saxa was kneeling at the river, scrubbing a small tunic and tutting to herself. Ludwig clashed wooden swords with another young boy, each roaring challenges at the other. Eric was close to his mother, playing with a small wooden horse in the long grass. I stopped, just taking in the sight of them. Sedric and Hilde eased away, each sensing I needed some time alone.

My face split into a wide grin when she saw me. She had lifted her head to say something to Eric, then saw me from the corner of her eye. Leaping to her feet, Saxa covered the ground between us in moments. Her scent was otherworldly as she wrapped her arms around me, squeezing me so tight I could hardly breathe. I didn't mind. Burying my face in her hair and scrunching my eye shut, I laughed as two small bolts of impact struck my legs.

'Father! Father! Where have you been?'

'Look at my horse, father!'

'Was there another battle? Did you win?'

I detached myself from Saxa and eased down on my knees, grabbing each boy in turn and smothering them with kisses. 'Aye, there was a battle or two. And of course your father won.' I winked. 'And now I'm here to take you home. Our hall has sat empty for too long. It's going to need a good clean. And we have stables to fill with new fine horses,' I said to Eric, cupping his cheek. 'What do you say?'

'But I am to be chief!' Ludwig said. 'Grandpa said I am to be a famous warrior like you, Father! I cannot leave!'

'Well, I'm going to have a bit of a chat with your grandpa about that. What do you say, my love?' I asked as I rose, taking Saxa's hand in mine.

'I'd like nothing more than to go home,' she said. 'It has been difficult being back. But... he won't be happy.'

'I'll deal with him,' I said. 'Where is he?'

'In his hall. Alaric...' She paused, reaching out and taking my hand. 'Promise me there won't be blood. I know what lies between you. But he is my father, and for all his faults, he has my love as much as you do.'

That stopped me in my tracks. For a long time I had pushed down the sour feelings I held towards Dagr. I had smiled when I had seen him, even married his daughter, but always there had been the young boy, standing in that hall, broken at the loss of his mother. And the smirking youth in front of him, safe in the presence of his mighty father. My hand trembled just at the thought of it. Asking Hilde and Sedric to wait with my family, I set off towards the hall, and a reckoning that had been too long in coming.

* * *

The same door guard nodded me in, just as he had the night I came and killed Fridumar. He was older, balder, fatter, but I reckoned I saw a hint of the same smirk a younger me had seen with two eyes. I growled as I passed him, then smiled as I saw the man flinch out of the corner of my eye. Before, I had been nothing but a worthless pup. Now I was a lord of war, and all men feared me. The rushes on the floor were lank with age, just as they had been that night. Dagr was on the dais at the end of the hall, his arm around the waist of a plump serving girl, a lazy smile on his bearded face. He pushed the girl away when he saw me, rising unsteadily to his feet.

'Alaric Hengistson, well met,' he slurred, raising a wine cup in salute. The group of hangers-on that sat around his table gave a small cheer. Six in total, each armed and armoured, I noted. 'News reached us of your battles in the east. I toast to your victory! Have you brought back my men?'

I shook my head. 'None lived to travel with me, I'm afraid.' I meant what I said. Despite the hatred that lurked between us, the men Dagr had given me had fought well, and proven themselves a match for the fierce reputation of the Chauci. 'It was a fight like I have never before seen. Most of my force perished.'

'Haribert?' Dagr asked. I smiled at that. There was no remorse for the fifty men Dagr had sent to their deaths. He cared not a jot for the wives and children left behind. He would not lift a finger to help them, I knew that. Like father like son. No, Dagr's first thought was for his northern neighbour. For if Haribert had fallen, there would be an opportunity for Dagr to extend his lands and wealth.

'He is as hale and strong as ever. I left him behind with Balomar. The two of them are negotiating new terms with Rome.'

Dagr blanched at that. All the tribes had a treaty of sorts with Rome, even the ones in the north. Dagr would not like that Haribert might be getting in on something he was not. I smiled wider. 'After all, we have Rome in our debt now. The empire will not forget those who fought to help keep their borders safe.'

I knew too well Dagr would not have heard the whole story. I had left the battlefield the same day the fighting finished. There was no way word could have got to him before me. Just as I wanted. News had obviously spread of our earlier battles against the Sarmatians. But Dagr would not know of the last one.

'What in the gods' names are you talking about?' he asked, staggering slightly.

'You'll hear about it soon enough, I reckon. I've just come here to tell you I'm taking Saxa and my boys home. Their place is with me, and mine with them. They'll be back to visit soon enough, I'm sure, but for now, they come with me.'

Dagr reddened with rage. 'Now listen here, you maggot! You and I had an agreement! Saxa and Ludwig go nowhere. Do what you want with the other whelp. I have no interest in a weak little boy.'

I took a step forward at that. Dagr's men roused themselves, drawing swords and flanking their chief. I wished I had brought Hilde and Sedric in with me. But the two of them had done enough bleeding on my behalf. 'Do you ever think about the night your father died?' I asked in a cool voice. I took another three steps forward, just ten paces from the Chauci chief. 'He sat right there at that table, mocking me for being the son of a foreigner. Untouchable was how he thought of himself. Safe, in his own hall surrounded by his men. Tell me something, Dagr. How safe do you feel now?'

Unconsciously, Dagr's hand went to his neck, his finger tracing the thin white scar my blade had given him many years before. I saw the moment he registered he could not beat me in a fight. Even flanked by six of his men I could smell his fear. I was Alaric the war lord. Chief of the Ravensworn. A killer of men. An old wolf I might have been. But a wolf was still a wolf. He gulped, nodded, some colour coming back to his cheeks once his decision had been made. 'Take your family home, Alaric,' he said through gritted teeth. 'But know that you are not welcome in my lands. Son of the Chauci or not.'

I had the grace to give the man a nod, which he would later tell revellers in his hall was a small bow, once he had granted me permission to leave. It did not bother me. Killing the cur would bring me some satisfaction, but would inevitably drive a wedge between Saxa and me, and that I did not want. Turning without another word, I emerged into bright sunshine, the scent of Germania's rich earth in my nostrils. I strolled back down the hill to my family, hugging them all one by one. 'Gather your things,' I said to Saxa, kissing her softly on the head. 'We are going home.'

EPILOGUE

And so we have reached the end of my tale. But what are endings if not new beginnings?

It's not been a bad one, I don't think. From the dizzying heights of the mighty Ravensworn, the indestructible army I built for myself, to the lonely lows of a man skulking in his hall, hiding from the world. I have seen it all, lived every moment of it.

I have been a mighty war lord, feared and respected by all. A beacon for men to follow, a rallying call when a battle danced on a knife edge. Let no man say I have not reached greatness. Even in the twilight of my life I have fought for my people and seen victory. I have sailed to the far north and fought foreign invaders from across the sea; I have marched to the great plains of the east and stood in defiance of a distant people who came to take my home.

All of this I have done under that red banner. That symbol of victory, of terror to my enemies.

Deep down, though, I know this is not the end. Even then as I stood there by the river, Saxa in my arms, my boys playing in the sunshine. A man can't run from his nature, and mine has always been war.

A grudge such as the one I hold against Silus is not something that can just be put to bed. Not without blood being spilt. An eye for an eye, as the saying goes. Well, that bastard had one of mine. The time will come for me to get my revenge. For a lifetime of hurt, of nightmares. A man does not live through what I have without some scars. As with all scars, it is the ones inside of me that hurt the most. Patience is something that comes to us all with age, and I am not a young man. So I will wait, watch, listen. The time will come for me to march again, of that I am certain.

Until then I will content myself with trading amber, living in peace and watching my boys grow. Might be I finally find some peace at last, contentment in the simple life. But deep down, I'll know what is coming, and look to it with relish.

Balomar, King of the Marcomanni, still harbours dreams of leading an army south and taking the war to Rome. One day he will realise those ambitions. When he does, when the time comes for the people of our country to unite and finally fight for the freedom that is ours, I will be there. Sword in hand, a black raven on a red field flying above me.

* * *

MORE FROM ADAM LOFTHOUSE

The first book in another series from Adam Lofthouse, *The Eagle and the Flame*, is available to order now here:
https://mybook.to/EagleandtheFlame

HISTORICAL NOTE

I always wonder where to start these historical notes with this series. So much of them are purely creations of my imagination. But there are some facts nestled into the fiction.

Roman weapon factories (*fabricae*) were commonplace throughout the empire. From northern Britain to the eastern front, slaves and craftsmen alike were put to work to keep the armouries of the legions full. I can only imagine at how much kit a legion would get through in one campaign season.

Just think on all the swords and shields, caltrops, spear tips and daggers that have been found over the last two hundred years of archaeological digs alone. There must be so much more waiting under the earth to be discovered.

The factory in Ratiaria is known to have been there, though its design and makeup are my creation. This, then, was one of Rome's secret weapons when it came to war. How to keep their armies in ready supply of arms and armour, as well as food and other provisions. Battles were won on full stomachs and well-prepared kit; I would guess that much is still true today.

As to the makeup of a Roman legion, the Fourteenth as I have described it in this novel is how every legion in the classical age would have been formed. Ten cohorts, each split into six centuries of men, eighty men per century. The first cohort would have consisted of five double-strength centuries, each with one hundred and sixty men. The highest a non-commissioned officer could hope to rise was to command the first century of the first cohort. These centurions were known as First Spear (*primus pulis*)

Camp prefects were taken from the longest-serving senior centurions. These were often men at the end of their career, and they served as a second in command to the legate of the legion.

Senior officers were mostly made up of tribunes, the sons of senators in Rome who had bought their heirs their first commission. Most would not stay in the army, but serve the mandatory three years before returning to Rome to take up a civilian post. The *cursus honorum*, the Romans called the ladder all aspiring politicians had to climb. A tradition that dated back to the Republic and carried on for hundreds of years after the events in this novel take place.

So, 5,200 men all told, with a small detachment of one hundred and twenty cavalry attached to every legion. The difference between these legions and the barbarians they faced was training and discipline. Each centurion had the autonomy to make their own decisions in battle. There was no need to wait for orders all the time; if an enterprising officer saw an opportunity on the battlefield, the expectation was he seized it.

Roman legionaries served for twenty-five years. Their discharge would come with a pension they had paid into throughout their tenure in the army, also often with a small plot of land close to where their legion had been based.

From these small plots of land, communities developed of retired soldiers, who would settle down and seek to find a wife and start a family. One can only imagine the stories they had to share around evening camp fires!

The Sarmatians began their migration west at some point in the early first century. By the end of it they had been defeated by Rome and Emperor Marcus Aurelius, when they were taken into the army as auxiliaries and sent to Britain as well as other provinces far from the German front.

Little enough is known about the Sarmatians, their customs or their gods. They were not a people to record their history, so what we have is made up from Romans' writing at the time. Their accounts will inevitably come with some bias.

The same can be said for the Germani tribes as a whole. Tacitus wrote quite extensively about them. You can still pick up a translated copy of his work *Agricola and Germania* today. I recommend you do; it's a really interesting read.

Rome never fully conquered the lands east of the Rhine and north of the

Danube. The tribes were too numerous, their leaders too hostile. For a time they held on to bits, but the disastrous defeat of Varus in the Teutoburg forest in AD 9 pretty much ended that. Three legions were wiped out in that battle. It remained one of Rome's worst defeats, right up until the collapse of the empire.

Alaric and his Ravensworn are of course my own creation. This will be his last outing. I think I've put the poor one-eyed old rogue through quite a lot in the last three books! He deserves some rest. *War Lord* is dedicated to my dad who, much like Alaric, is heading off into retirement! Hope you enjoy it, Dad, and thanks for everything.

You may have already picked up *Eagle and the Flame* that came out in July. That series will run for six books (at least), with three pencilled in for publication in 2026. Hopefully that will be enough to keep you all going!

I'll end with a huge thank you to the wonderful team at Boldwood Books. It's been nothing but a positive experience working with them on this trilogy. Special thanks to Vic Britton, my editor, whose sharp eyes and encouraging comments keep these books flowing and me typing when I feel I'm writing myself down a road to nowhere.

Thanks also to the eagle-eyed Jennifer Davies, who has once again shown me how little I still know when it comes to correct grammar, capitalisation and a hundred other things that don't even cross my mind when I'm hammering out a draft!

A huge thanks is due to the wonderful Jacqueline Beard MBE who proof-read the novel and found among other things a continuity error on my part (she's also great fun to get drunk with!).

To my three sons, Archie, Jack and Ralph, thanks for occasionally behaving yourselves so I can escape to a quiet corner to get some words down! And the biggest thanks of all to my endlessly supporting partner, Jodie, who wants nothing more than to see me chase my dreams. I really am the luckiest man in the world.

I'll be back with my next book, *Wolf and the Crown*, in February.

See you then,

Adam

ABOUT THE AUTHOR

Adam Lofthouse has for many years held a passion for the ancient world. As a teenager he picked up *Gates of Rome* by Conn Iggulden, and has been obsessed with all things Rome ever since. After ten years of immersing himself in stories of the Roman world, he decided to have a go at writing one for himself. He lives in Kent, UK.

Download your exclusive bonus content from Adam Lofthouse here:

Follow Adam on social media here:

 facebook.com/AdamPLofthouse
 x.com/AdamPLofthouse
instagram.com/adamplofthouse

ALSO BY ADAM LOFTHOUSE

Enemy of the Empire

Raven: Defier of Rome

Outlaw: Nemesis of Rome

War Lord: Scourge of Rome

Shadow of Rome

Eagle and the Flame

WARRIOR CHRONICLES

WELCOME TO THE CLAN ⚔

THE HOME OF
BESTSELLING HISTORICAL
ADVENTURE FICTION!

WARNING:
MAY CONTAIN VIKINGS!

SIGN UP TO OUR
NEWSLETTER

BIT.LY/WARRIORCHRONICLES

Boldwood

Boldwood Books is an award-winning fiction publishing company seeking out the best stories from around the world.

Find out more at www.boldwoodbooks.com

Join our reader community for brilliant books, competitions and offers!

Follow us
@BoldwoodBooks
@TheBoldBookClub

Sign up to our weekly deals newsletter

https://bit.ly/BoldwoodBNewsletter